Going for Two

Also by Ally Wiegand

First Base

Going for Two

Ally Wiegand

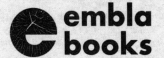

First published in Great Britain in 2024 by

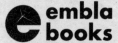

Bonnier Books UK Limited
HYLO, 5th Floor, 103-105 Bunhill Row, London, EC1Y 8LZ
Owned by Bonnier Books
Sveavägen 56, Stockholm, Sweden

A CIP catalogue record for this book is available from the British Library.

1

ISBN: 9781471416965

This book is typeset using Atomik ePublisher.

Printed and bound in Great Britain by Clays Ltd, Elcograf S.p.A.

Embla Books is an imprint of Bonnier Books UK.
www.bonnierbooks.co.uk

To everyone that worked their asses off to climb the mountain and then wondered . . . *what now*? I promise you the possibilities are endless. Just because you climbed one peak, doesn't mean it will be the only one of your life. Keep looking for the next adventure.

Lottie's Bucket List

1. Find a spark with someone by the end of the year! GET SOME ACTION!

2. Kiss someone at midnight on New Year's Eve.

3. Have a real family Thanksgiving with NO work.

4. Watch the sunrise from the best view and not from my car on the way to work.

5. Go sledding to make up for all the times I never got to as a kid.

6. Wear matching Christmas PJs with the people I love.

7. Have a day where you say yes to everything.

Chapter 1

Lottie

I was about ten seconds away from downing my third glass of champagne of the evening. The buzz from the alcohol was the only thing keeping me from wielding the salad fork in front of me against yet another man who had managed to corner me at my table. Weddings were already one of my least favorite experiences—seeing as I was one of the last of my old friend group to still be single and I was getting further from thirty with every passing day. Pair that with men seeking me out to talk about my new job as the in-house physical therapist for the Chicago Bobcats and you have a less than enjoyable experience.

The amount of mansplaining I had to endure over the past few hours should qualify me for some kind of compensation.

"Nolan Hill should have retired after last year. There's no way he will be able to lead this team with the injuries he has at the caliber the league has gotten to," the man—Todd, I think—told me, as if I hadn't pored over the medical files of every player on the team this past week and wasn't likely to be more familiar with the quarterback's ailments than him. "He's keeping the rookie they just drafted from getting some experience under his belt."

My head moved up and down involuntarily as my body slipped into cruise control. It was a habit I had to learn early on in my career whenever I found myself being talked down to by someone who had way less authority on the subject than me. The last thing I wanted to experience today was someone named Todd trying to school me on the very thing I'd spent years surrounded by, so it was better to just let him get his opinions off his chest.

"It's selfish to stick around for another year just to try and go out on a high note. The odds of him winning a third Super Bowl at the pace he went last year are slim." Todd's high school football state championship ring flashed on his finger and had me fighting the urge to roll my eyes. "He's more likely to set the record for most sacks in a season if we have another repeat of last year."

I could easily tell him how the NFL was full of the best medical professionals in the world—which now included myself—but I knew that would only open me up to more uneducated responses and skepticism. I could tell him that Nolan Hill had one of the quickest reaction times from snap of the ball to release of his throw ever recorded in league history. Or I could tell him that, of course, the Bobcats would stick with their two-time Super Bowl quarterback—even if he'd been plagued with injuries late in his career. But everyone's an expert when it comes to professional sports.

My hand inched closer to the fork on the table in front of me, but the sound of a high-pitched voice had me snatching my hand back into my lap. A sigh escaped through my lips. That voice wasn't the saving grace I had been hoping for. That voice symbolized me jumping from one boiling pot of water into another.

"Charlotte! I had no idea you'd be here." Vera Busch, who was one of the most popular girls at my high school growing up, approached me with a saccharine smile on her face. Todd took one look at the woman in the high-end red dress that looked like it had come straight from *The Stepford Wives* and bolted.

Okay, Todd. You talk a big game until the real enemy appears. Not so tough now, are you?

"Hi, Vera. You know I wouldn't miss Heather's wedding,"

I told her with my best fake smile. My jaw clenched tightly as Vera gave me air kisses on both cheeks, as if we hadn't grown up in a small farm town with one gas station and a pizza joint that was only open after Friday night football games.

"Well, it's wonderful that you still make time for all of us, seeing as you've been so busy with your work." Vera's smile was nearly sinister as she watched me eagerly for any reaction to her words. But the last thing I'd do was fold in front of Vera Busch. That would be like giving the last Infinity Stone to Thanos.

It wasn't a secret that I'd poured all of myself into my career and that level of dedication left little room for much else. Which was exactly why I was still single at the age of thirty-two and dateless at yet another one of my friend's weddings. I'd never been ashamed of the sacrifices I had to make in my life to get me to where I am. Those sacrifices landed me a job as the youngest physical therapist to join an NFL team's staff. Even having to defend myself to someone like Vera Busch wouldn't make me regret my decisions.

"Hopefully you have time for dating with the season starting," Vera added. "Our biological clocks are such an unfortunate thing."

My hand inched back toward the salad fork as I tried to keep the smile on my face.

"You know, I believe Bobby is still single. You remember Bobby, right?" It looked like Vera was clearly getting some sort of sick enjoyment from making my singleness the main topic of conversation. "He's right over at the bar. I can walk you over—"

"There you are," the voice of my true savior rang out. My baby sister, Olivia Thompson, sank down in the open chair next to me with two full glasses of champagne in her hands. I gave her a grateful look as I downed the rest of the champagne in my glass before taking the new one she offered.

"Vera, you must tell me the name of the doctor that did

the work on your face. I've been searching for someone who can accentuate a resting bitch face." Olivia's smile matched Vera's as she stared down the woman whose mouth was now hanging open in shock. "Careful, you'll catch flies."

Vera's mouth opened and closed like a fish as her face turned the same color as the red wine she was gripping tightly in her hand before she turned on her heel and left us at our designated table in the back of the room.

"Thank you," I whispered to my sister.

"Vera's always been a menace and I have very little patience for it anymore," Olivia replied, as if what she had done was just another day's work. "Don't listen to her. You're doing much better in life than she is. She's just jealous we got out of that sad little town and that's the best that she'll ever get."

"Maybe," I replied as the groom got up to give his speech to Heather.

Was I really doing much better than Vera Busch?

It wasn't the first time I had questioned where I was in life and probably wouldn't be the last. It first started when I got the call that I'd gotten the job with the Chicago Bobcats. I had been bursting with excitement. All my hard work had paid off over the past year. I had climbed the ladder and made all the right connections to land this job. Except when I hung up the phone, the excitement quickly died off when I realized I had no one to celebrate with. I had climbed the mountain and ended up with no one to share the view with once I'd reached the top.

That feeling had only intensified as I caught up with my friends during the cocktail hour before the reception. There was another engagement, a pregnancy, and the celebration of their kid's first steps. When it was my turn to share my life update, all I could give them was the news of my new job. While there was excitement, I couldn't help but notice the looks full of pity on everyone's faces. As if a single, thirty-something woman was the saddest thing they had ever seen.

I'd always been proud of my independence and success.

I was the most sought-after sports physical therapist in the Midwest because of the success of my private practice. I had some of the best athletes in the world coming to me for treatment. I had never cared about my lack of a dating life before, but recently it felt like all I could notice was how I hated going home at night to an empty apartment. Or how when I would take myself out to eat and tell the hostess I was dining for one, they gave me a look that made me want to turn around and walk right back out.

None of those things had ever bothered me before.

But as I watched Heather's new husband look at her like she hung the moon, I felt something I hadn't ever before—longing. I had never prioritized dating in my life because I hadn't exactly had the best example of a healthy relationship growing up with parents that argued with each other more than they cared about parenting their children.

A hand covered mine and gave it a small squeeze. "Are you okay?" Olivia looked at me with concern.

Neither of the Thompson sisters had been known for their romantic relationships. While I had never given dating much importance, Olivia looked at it as a source of entertainment. Romance had never been in our vocabulary after watching the destruction of our parents' relationship and how that had affected us as kids. Which was exactly why Olivia was looking at me like I potentially needed medical attention.

"Yeah," I whispered back to her. "I'm okay."

"I'm honestly disappointed I took tonight off for this stupid wedding. Let's bail after the first dance," Olivia suggested as the first chords of our friend's dance pumped through the DJ's speakers. "We can go to our favorite spot in the city and celebrate before you start tomorrow. Then there will officially be two Thompson sisters in Chicago professional sports."

That ache of longing in my chest grew as I watched the way the newlywed couple danced in a room full of people as if they were the only two there. They were so attuned to each other, they moved as one around the dance floor. The groom leaned down to whisper in Heather's ear, telling her something that had her throwing her head back with joyous laughter.

I wonder how it would feel to have someone know exactly how to make you laugh.

The closest I'd ever gotten to that kind of joy was through my job—between the relationships I built with my athletes and the joy I had when I nailed someone's recovery to give them the chance of returning to what they love to do. All of it was fulfilling, but I was certain it was nothing compared to being known completely by someone else.

Maybe now that I'd achieved my dreams there was finally time for me to focus on something besides a career. Maybe there was more out there than the next achievement I could list at the bottom of my resume. Maybe there was a different kind of achievement I could strive for—like filling my life with memories that I could look back on fondly with someone when we were old and grey.

I might have achieved things in my life that were tremendous, but there were plenty of things I had yet to do that I had never given much importance to before. I didn't want to wonder what those experiences were like anymore.

Olivia and I snuck out of the reception once we got to speak with Heather and the dance floor filled up. Neither of us really enjoyed being around the people of our past. It reminded us too much of raised voices, doors slamming, and pretending that everything was fine to all the people in that very room.

I tossed the keys to Olivia as we approached the car. Her ability to endure the people at the party without the need to drink more than one glass of champagne was far greater than mine. The two of us sang at the top of our lungs to all our favorite songs as we drove back into the city and toward our favorite place. The lights on Lake Shore Drive passed overhead as we circled around the city to the north side. The parking lot was empty when we pulled in. The sun had long set and anyone that had been enjoying the last few days of good weather in Chicago was gone.

We made our way down to the beach off 12th Street hand in hand with our heels dangling from our fingers. Before either of us could sink down onto the sand, we turned together to look at the massive stadium that sat looming over Lake Michigan—Gateway Stadium, the home of the Chicago Bobcats and the place I'd be spending many of my weekends this year. While the team's practice building was on the south side of the city, the stadium was positioned proudly as part of the skyline.

"Are you excited?" Olivia's voice brought me back from my spinning thoughts.

"I am." I gave her hand a squeeze.

"I'm not sure I can give you advice. Football's quite different from baseball." Olivia worked for the Chicago Cougars, the city's professional baseball team, and was at the end of her fourth season with the team. She had a huge hand in inserting the Cougars' marketing into pop culture moments. This season the team was positioned to make it to the playoffs and potentially make a run at the World Series.

Olivia approached her job with a more carefree attitude than I did, like going out with the team during the off-season or even helping our friend, Maggie Redford, fall in love with the team's shortstop, Tommy Mikals. All things I considered distractions.

I was sure that any advice that she could give me would be far from anything I would find useful.

"You're probably right," I agreed as the two of us devolved into a fit of laughter.

"Maybe don't fall in love with anyone. I mean, it ended up good for Maggie, but man—the drama."

"I don't think that will ever apply to me, but thanks for the sentiment. I already get enough scrutiny being a woman in this industry. There's no need to bring any more attention to myself."

"I think you're about to go on the ride of a lifetime," she told me absentmindedly as she continued to look up at the modern lines of the stadium.

"Maybe."

"You don't think so?" Olivia's brows pinched together as she looked over at me as if the four glasses of champagne I'd consumed at the wedding were affecting my head. "This is rumored to be Nolan Hill's last season. At the very least, I'm sure you'll be around a media frenzy."

"Maybe."

"Okay, what are you thinking in that big, beautiful head of yours?" Olivia leveled me with a look.

"I've just been wondering if I'm missing something lately," I admitted to her quietly once I finally tore my eyes away from the stadium and turned around to study where the lake blended in with the night sky.

"Like what?" Olivia sank down in the sand and I followed suit.

"I wonder if I've missed out on life and it's too late. Sometimes I feel like I focused too much on a career that will never matter when it comes to the end of my life, and I haven't invested any time into making moments that I'll look back on to prove that I really *lived*."

"It's never too late," my sister replied fiercely. It was easy for her to say. She had always been the more free-spirited of the two of us. "What do you want to do? Bungee jump? Go to a new country? Karaoke? Eat at a five-star restaurant?"

Leave it to Olivia to immediately dive into an idea without questioning it at all. She has always had one of the biggest hearts.

"I'm not sure. I need to think about it," I admitted. All I knew was that something was missing.

"We'll make a bucket list, and we'll make sure you check every last bit of it off." Olivia laced our hands together as the two of us watched the dark water lap against the shore. "You deserve to be happy, Lottie. And happiness is more important than a good career, no matter what Mom and Dad thought."

It was odd for the roles to be reversed, with Olivia telling me what it was that I needed and deserved. I had always played that role for her as I filled in for our parents. "Do you ever miss them?"

"Our parents?" Olivia looked at me as if I really was having a medical episode. "Our mother died five years ago, and our father has been absent from our lives since the divorce. Neither of them deserves to be missed. Those two fucked us up."

"They didn't fuck us up," I argued. "We've made it just fine on our own."

"Neither of us has ever had healthy long-term relationships and have never actually celebrated a holiday." My sister looked at me as if she were daring me to prove her otherwise.

Maybe now that I didn't have work to distract me, I realized that I just missed the idea of what my parents were supposed to be—a family.

A moment later, the lights in the stadium turned on and threw long shadows across the beach. I glanced over my shoulder and wondered who could possibly be there this late at night.

Chapter 2

Nolan

"The Chicago Bobcats could be poised to have another successful season. They have an extremely veteran staff on both sides of the football. Their defense is expected to lead the league this year again after coming off last year's season where they allowed the least number of points," the commentator, Daniel Rice, said.

"They'll need that same performance this year, Scott, if they plan to have the kind of storied performance they are hoping for with keeping Nolan Hill at the helm of their offense," the other commentator, Micky Rice, added.

"I still can't believe that their GM would go and take a first overall pick in the draft with the star rookie quarterback, Caleb Willis, and not start to build their staff around a kid like that. With the experience they have on this team, they have more of a chance of pulling that kid along rather than putting their faith in Nolan Hill for another year. He started last season fresh off rehabilitation for his ACL tear from the previous season and he just never quite looked like the Nolan Hill we all know. Then he went on to throw the most interceptions in NFL history. Who decides to give someone like that one more chance?"

"Can you turn that shit off?" I growled.

One of the new athletic trainers rushed to grab the remote from where it lay on one of the training beds and turned the channel to the Chicago Cougars baseball game. Adam Steel, the star pitcher for the team, was in the middle of delivering a fastball that tallied him another strikeout. The reporter noted it as his tenth of the game.

I made a mental note to send him a message later tonight.

When the athletic trainer turned back around and saw the hard set of my jaw, he quickly diverted his eyes and scurried back to his station.

"Can we not scare the new people already? Our first game is in just over a week," Derek Allen, one of my best friends and the best tight end to ever be in the NFL, asked me from the table next to mine.

I didn't bother giving him a response.

"Derek's right, Nolan," Hawthorn Smith, my other best friend and starting kicker for the Bobcats, added from across the room, where he was submerged in one of the hot tubs. The guy barely did anything at practice compared to the rest of us, but he made sure to always take advantage of the hot tub every day. Who could blame him?

"There's no reason for you to treat any of the staff like that, and to be honest, if you keep that up around the team, the camaraderie this year is bound to be low," Hawthorn continued.

I pressed my lips together to avoid a snide remark from escaping. This wasn't my friends' faults. It was only mine.

"Don't listen to that bullshit." Derek lowered his voice so only I could hear him. "You are going to leave this league a hall of fame guarantee."

"I can't handle a repeat of last year, Derek." I could barely get the words out. I hadn't spoken those words out loud to anyone. Instead, the fear of going from the face of the NFL to the laughingstock played out in my head nearly every day.

"Have you been meeting with the sports psychologist?" Derek asked me.

I nodded, but didn't tell him how I was beginning to realize that it was going to take more than visualization and mental exercises to fix the fucked-up landscape of my head. My injury from two seasons ago hadn't just changed me physically. It had taken every piece of confidence I had ever had and obliterated it into dust.

Last season was a perfect example.

I had never played like that before—so unsure of my skills. I had been in the league for thirteen years. I had an endless amount of experience to rely on to remind myself that I was capable. But the moment I had stepped on the field last year after trying to rehab my injury, all that previous experience felt like it belonged to a different person. My legs felt unsteady beneath me. My brain was three beats behind the pace at which I needed to be playing at. I had been too busy worrying about the strength of my knee to focus on who was open or notice when one of my guys was being covered deep on their routes. I threw the most interceptions of my career.

I hadn't felt like Nolan Hill, two-time Super Bowl champion and two-time MVP.

"We're going to make this your best year yet. I refuse to let your old sack of bones leave without a third ring to put on your fingers."

"I'm only eight years older than you, asshole." I tossed the towel I was using to cover the ice pack on my knee at Derek.

Derek caught the towel effortlessly. "Round that up and that's a decade, dearest Nolan."

"Did you guys hear about the new physical therapist we hired?" Hawthorn asked from where he was still submerged in the hot tub, his eyes now closed.

"What happened to Roger?" I asked about our old physical therapist. I was sad to hear Roger was gone, but the two of us had nothing more than a surface level relationship.

Therapy was the worst part of my day. Not because I disliked it or thought it was a waste of my time. I knew that it wasn't. Therapy reminded me of my failure. It reminded me that my body couldn't withstand the demands of this game much longer. Therapy reminded me that soon, I would be nothing more than a name and a stat line. Roger hadn't pushed me that hard with my recovery, and I could only hope that the new hire wouldn't either because I wasn't sure I could mentally take it.

"Sounds like him and his wife had to move back closer to his parents. Health scare with his dad," Hawthorn told me. "From the sounds of it, it might have happened as recently as a few weeks ago."

"I heard the new physical therapist is some kind of sports therapy guru," Derek added. "I think some of the guys on the Lynx have gone to her before. She got Nash Rausch back on the ice in record time."

Great.

"I'm sure she'll be a great addition to the staff." I slid my ice pack back into the freezer by the door before putting my sweats back on.

"Apparently she's hot, too."

I rolled my eyes at Derek's enthusiasm.

"Keep it in your pants." Hawthorn eyed him with the look of a father with three young daughters as he got out of the hot tub and toweled off.

Derek gave him an incredulous look. "I don't shit where I eat."

"And that is why you haven't had a serious girlfriend," I mumbled as I waited for my friends.

"I'm doing just fine, thank you very much." Derek crossed his arms over his chest. "You don't have much room to talk. You haven't dated anyone since Rachel."

Hawthorn winced at the mention of my ex-fiancée.

"Eventually you'll have slept through the entire city of Chicago and regret it." Hawthorn clapped Derek on the back as the three of us exited the training room. "Alright boys, I have three beautiful girls waiting for me at home. I will see you two bright and early for practice."

The sun was just starting to set as we walked out to the

parking lot. The three of us had used today as a prep day for the week to come. Preseason games had come and gone. The pressure and intensity of those games was never very high, and it had been a decent start for me to get my headspace under control. But this Sunday we were opening against the Nashville Cowboys, who were runner-up in last year's Super Bowl.

It wasn't a match-up that would ease us into the season. I had to be at the top of my game.

"Want to grab a drink?" Derek asked me as we walked up to our cars.

"Not tonight. I have some things I need to do before tomorrow," I told him. Derek nodded like he understood before he slid into his car and left me standing alone in the parking lot.

I waited until the taillights of his car disappeared before I turned and walked back into the facility. I hadn't lied to Derek that I had things to do, but I wasn't going to tell him that my plans were to rewatch my games from last year. I could hear him trying to talk me out of it, saying that the staff sports psychologist would advise against it.

He was probably right, and I was probably a glutton for punishment.

The building was nearly empty. I slipped into one of the empty film rooms and pulled up the file of videos the coaches had made me. I flipped the lights off and settled into one of the chairs in the back of the room.

The film was a mash-up of every play I was a part of last season.

The plays bled into each other as the hours ticked by.

Missed snaps.

Overthrown receivers.

Sacks.

It was hard to reconcile that the quarterback on the screen was me because I didn't recognize him.

I wanted to leave this game, which had been all I'd known

for most of my life, on my own terms. I wanted to be a three-time Super Bowl champion. Part of me knew that a win or a loss wouldn't make the transition out of the league any easier, but it would give me the chance to write over the past two seasons of mishaps. It would solidify my legacy and all my hard work.

By the time the film was over, a tightness had settled in my chest. The sky had faded into an inky black. It was well past a reasonable time to still be in the facility, but I had one more stop I wanted to make tonight to complete this twisted idea of therapy I was trying to give myself.

There weren't many cars on the roads this late at night as I drove toward the stadium. When I turned off the interstate onto Lake Shore Drive, I felt the tightness in my chest free—only a little—at the sight of the stadium butting right up to Lake Michigan. The lights were off and the parking lots around it were empty.

I found the switches for the stadium lights and threw them on before making my way out to the field. To some, seeing an NFL stadium completely empty and without life might give off an eerie feel. To me, it was *peaceful*.

I'd sacrificed so many parts of my life to achieve all I had in my career thus far, but there was a piece of me that felt like it still wasn't enough. I hadn't done *enough*.

My devotion to my craft had ended a relationship—even though that relationship was bound to crash and burn eventually. It had taken up most of my free time to enjoy much else in life besides chasing the ultimate dream I had laid out for myself from a young age.

This job was a privilege. For many people, this was more than just a sport. It was a national pastime. Families shared traditions with their favorite teams. They looked up to their favorite players as idols. Thanksgivings and Christmases were had with the games of the day playing in the background.

I didn't take any of that lightly.

I was entering a quest this season to figure out how to

fulfill my potential as a player without driving myself crazy with the standard I was asking of myself. However, I knew none of the success I wanted would be achievable if I didn't consider the person I was as well.

I understood that holding myself to such a standard could be a miserable place to live because I could be setting myself up for failure. But I wouldn't accept anything less than my best this season, and that started with getting myself in the best physical and mental shape possible to lead this team to a championship.

I couldn't allow any outside distractions—like the talk shows—to get to me this year. I had a mission to accomplish and there would be very little that would stop me.

Chapter 3

Lottie

"Your office is right in here." The owner of the Bobcats, Gary Martinez, pushed open a door in the training room and flipped the lights on.

I stared at the modern office with floor to ceiling windows for a wall and looked out onto the practice field. The cabinets along the back wall were black and the carpet had subtle hints of navy and red, the Bobcats' colors. A TV hung on the wall directly across from my desk and I even had a window to look out into the training room.

"I can't thank you enough for this opportunity." I reached out to shake Gary's hand.

"When I interviewed you for this job, I knew you were the perfect choice and not just a convenient quick fix for losing Roger." A familiar zing of pride filled my chest. "I'm sure some of the early birds will start rolling in soon, so I'll leave you to get settled in. Don't hesitate to give me a ring if you need anything. I'm real excited to have you here, Lottie."

Gary left me to a completely empty training room without a soul in sight.

This was peace.

The facility had every modality I could possibly need to help a player when they sustained an injury: infrared lights, cold and hot tubs, ultrasound, shockwave therapy, among others. I was in the middle of admiring the anti-gravity treadmill when the door opened and the first person of the

19

day walked in. He wore a Bobcats quarter zip and had a backpack slung over one shoulder.

"You must be the new physical therapist," he greeted.

"Charlotte Thompson." I walked over to shake the man's hand. I noticed his quarter zip had his name and title stitched on the left side—*Ezekiel Williams, Head Athletic Trainer*. "But you can call me Lottie. I'll answer to either."

"I'm Zeke. I run the athletic training side. Excited to work with you. I know we'll be working closely together. I went ahead and created a file of the players I think you'll be working with most of the time." Zeke unlocked the smaller office next to mine that all the athletic training staff shared. He set his bag down on one of the desks and pulled out a thick folder.

"Thank you," I told him as I took the folder and flipped it open.

A photo of Nolan Hill stared up at me with handwritten notes on his medical history next to it.

"You'll mostly be working with Nolan. He's two seasons off of a left knee reconstructive surgery on his ACL. He's the coaching staff's priority for us as last season he didn't seem comfortable yet on his knee. We believe he hasn't rehabbed that knee enough for him to feel full stability on the field. The coaches don't want to worry about that problem this year."

Deep brown eyes looked up at me from the folder. I took in his close-cropped, curly hair, clean face, and the small wrinkles by the corners of his eyes. He was handsome in the conventional sense and perfect to be considered as the face of a franchise.

"You may also work some with Derek Allen, one of our starting tight ends. He's coming off of a strained hamstring from last year due to chronic tightness in his back. There are a few others on that list that have ongoing issues, which we thought you'd be the best to serve them while we help manage the normal aches and pains that come up during the season."

"This is perfect." I gave Zeke a smile. "This is more in depth than the files that Gary gave me last week. So, I'm extremely grateful."

I turned to head back into my office but stopped short when I heard Zeke clear his throat.

"I also wanted to warn you about Nolan"—Zeke paused— "he's grown exceptionally . . . hostile these past few seasons. So don't be offended if he's not all sunshine and rainbows."

This wasn't the first time I had heard someone describe Nolan Hill like this. There were whispers among the professional sports world that Nolan had grown angry after his injury, or even bitter, but I thought differently. I had watched countless games that showcased his mishaps and his reactions full of anger afterward—the helmet throwing, the yelling, the looks of disappointment. To me, Nolan Hill wasn't angry or bitter . . . he was *desperate*.

"Thanks for the heads up." I raised the folder of information up as one last acknowledgment before I went to tuck it away in my office. As soon as I was behind my office door, I flipped the folder back open and met the pair of intense brown eyes.

I believed Nolan was desperate because he was afraid of the end. Desperate I could work with. No matter how off-putting Nolan may try to come off, desperate meant he would do anything to succeed.

I had spent part of the last week poring over the routine that Roger had for Nolan while tweaking it to incorporate some exercises I felt would benefit him on the field. I pulled that plan out of my bag and laid it on my desk next to Zeke's notes. Roger had mentioned that it was hard to get Nolan in the training room, but I figured if he wanted this bad enough, he'd show up.

A knock sounded on my door, pulling me from the rabbit hole I often went down when I think about one of my athletes' regimens. I looked up to find the same intense brown eyes I had just been staring at. Those eyes were set in a tan face that still had some color from training camp and the preseason games that made him look almost rugged. The lines of his face were pronounced—sharp cheekbones and a jawline that would have women lining up around the block for a chance to see—there wasn't an ounce of baby fat left on his face. His shoulders were broad and stretched nearly from one side of the door frame to the next. He wasn't as muscular as his running backs or his defense. He was long and sinewy with a muscular build that he had honed over the years to be a machine on the football field. But it was those brown eyes I couldn't stop looking at. They looked at me with a hardened gaze—as if he were annoyed that I was standing in front of him. The Nolan standing in front of me wasn't the guy in the picture on my desk that looked at the camera with eagerness.

Neither of us said anything at first as we sized each other up. The quiet grew heavy the longer it went on without either of us being willing to be the first to speak.

I watched in fascination as a muscle jumped in his jaw before he finally conceded whatever standoff we were in. I tried to keep the smile off my face when I realized I had made Nolan Hill uncomfortable. Which was fine in my book. I was here to break the cycle that occurred during last year's season, which included his old routine with Roger.

"I'm Nolan Hill."

Straightforward. To the point.

"I'm Dr. Charlotte Thompson." I managed to stand from my desk and walk across my office to extend my hand to him despite the pressure I felt lingering in the room. I'd never felt anything but confidence when it came to my job and one athlete that was angry at the world for something that happened to him wasn't about to stop me.

Nolan's large hand wrapped around mine, dwarfing it. His palm scraped against my palm as he squeezed my hand with what I personally thought was intentionally more force than necessary.

If he thinks he can intimidate me into whatever form of submission he has in mind, he's sorely mistaken.

"I presume Roger gave you the details of my routine?" If I knew Nolan Hill better, I may have thought I saw a flicker of fear in his eyes as he waited for my answer. His voice told a different story, however. It was one full of superiority and authority. The message was clear in that single question.

You will not change the status quo for me.

"He did." I chose my words as carefully as I could. I was already painfully aware that this working partnership was like a field full of landmines that I'd been told to walk through without a map.

Nolan sucked in a breath before letting it out slowly, his shoulders sinking down away from his ears. His eyes searched my face. His hand still gripped mine. I had this odd feeling that I was being observed by a lion that was trying to figure out if I was a gazelle. I slowly took my hand back from his without breaking eye contact.

Whatever observation Nolan had drawn from me, it must have been sufficient. He backed out of my office doorway, giving me space to walk out into the training room after him.

There was one thing that Nolan Hill needed to learn about me though: I could be just as stubborn as he was when it came to my job.

"I have some tweaks to Roger's plan," I told him as the two of us stopped at one of the training tables. Nolan didn't say anything as he slid out of his sweatpants and onto the table in a pair of shorts that landed mid-thigh. Muscular thighs flexed as he pushed himself up into a sitting position.

Defiance flashed in Nolan's eyes before he told me, "I'm not sure adding in anything new the week before a game is the smartest idea."

I had to restrain myself from putting the heat pack down on Nolan's knee with more force than necessary. One of my biggest pet peeves was people questioning my decisions. I hadn't spent an exorbitant amount of money on an education for a degree and title to prove my competence to have someone tell me that I didn't know what I was talking about.

"With that mindset, you'll never make any changes to a routine—even if it's needed." Nolan's eyes narrowed as he watched me set the electro-stimulation machine to the appropriate settings. I could tell he wasn't used to someone pushing back on his judgement.

Not so fun, is it?

"I just think a seasoned professional would understand the potential hazards of making changes to a routine so close to a game day."

Seriously? I looked up at the heavens above me. *You give me my dream job and then force me to deal with this asshole?*

"Well, since we're both seasoned professionals in our craft, I'm assuming you know that Kurt Russell with the New York Gladiators has a meeting every Monday with the Gladiator training staff to reevaluate last week's plans to make sure they will suit the upcoming week."

The silence that followed my statement was loud. I had a feeling throwing out the quarterback that he was often compared to would do the trick. Nothing worked better than using an athlete's competitive personality to your advantage.

Nolan grabbed the remote from the table next to him and turned up the volume on the television in the training room.

I bit my tongue as I formulated a plan. I'd let Nolan have this week to do whatever he thought was best for himself before I challenged him again. Nolan watched me with a scrutinizing stare as I placed the pads on the proper area to stimulate the muscles around his knee and prep them for the movement they were about to do during practice.

The doors to the training room slammed open and a tall man who was more muscle than man burst into the room, with a shorter man following closely behind him.

"What a glorious day!" The taller one, who I realized was Derek Allen, sang out. "Don't you think so, Zeke?"

Derek asked as he poked his head into Zeke's office. Zeke just blinked at him.

"Zeke." The other man behind Derek gave the athletic trainer a wave.

"Hawthorn." A smile spread across Zeke's face.

Hawthorn Smith. Kicker.

"How come you don't smile at me like that, Zeke?" Derek asked as he grabbed a heat pack for himself.

"Because you terrorize him every day of the season," Hawthorn told him as he breezed toward the hot tub.

Derek turned around and noticed me and Nolan. "You're the new physical therapist!"

"I'm Charlotte Thompson, but you can call me Lottie," I told him as I took the pads off Nolan's knee. I could feel his eyes on me as I addressed Derek.

"Well, Lottie, welcome to the Bobcats. The greatest team in the NFL—although I may be biased," Derek whispered the last part from the table next to us.

"How many shots of caffeine did you have this morning?" Nolan asked, his eyes now closed as I massaged his knee. The previous gruffness he had addressed me with gone.

"Probably one too many," Derek replied sheepishly.

"I've got five down that he's going to puke today," Hawthorn told Nolan from where he'd submerged himself in the hot tub.

"I'll put down ten." The previous tense set of his shoulders eased.

"Alright," I cut in before their bets could escalate. "Grab a band and start doing these exercises."

I tossed the list of exercises I had made down onto Nolan's chest. He cracked an eye open. I cocked a single brow at him as a challenge.

Nolan and I held eye contact, each of us daring the other to blink first.

"Are you having a staring contest?" Derek asked. Nolan blinked; our standoff was broken. Nolan sighed before he walked over to the wall of bands to grab one, paper clutched in his hand.

I grabbed a sanitizing bottle from near the hot tubs to wipe off the table we had used when I caught Hawthorn's gaze. He gave me a wink.

Nolan completed the exercises without complaint. I kept a close eye on him as I worked on Derek's lower back, all while getting peppered with questions from the tight end.

"Where are you from?" *A small town outside of Chicago.*

"Are you a football fan?" *My middle name is Madden after John Madden, if that says anything about the family I was brought up in.*

"Do you have a favorite team?" *Born and raised a Bobcats fan.*

"Are you just saying that because you're trying to get on my good side?" *No.*

I didn't have a moment to take a breath until I was walking out to practice with Zeke. I didn't mind though. I'd always enjoyed the way my body and mind went into cruise control when they were overloaded with tasks.

Luckily, once practice got into full swing, Zeke was too busy with tending to the players with his athletic trainers to talk to me. Which gave me the perfect opportunity to study Nolan as he moved through the different drills his coaches were throwing at him. Today's practice was scaled down in intensity with the coaches wanting to ease the team into the week ahead. Even still, I watched Nolan move through a few snaps. His movements were smooth from years of practice. His eyes scanned his receivers with methodical analysis as he made his decision for his open target.

However, after about an hour of watching him, I noticed a pattern. Every time he was pressured by the defense on his right side, his movements grew sloppy. He didn't move as confidently within the pocket. By the end of practice, I could confirm that Nolan Hill wasn't fully recovered from his knee injury. Unfortunately, I was going to have to figure out some way to win him over and convince him to let me do my job so I could help him.

I may have walked into a taller order than I originally realized, but I never backed down from a fight.

Chapter 4

Lottie

"He sounds like a dick," Olivia said as she shoveled another spoonful of ice cream into her mouth.

"I don't think he's a dick," I told her. "I just think he's . . . standoffish."

"That's the polite way to call someone a dick." Maggie gave me a sympathetic look. Olivia reached over to clink her spoon with Maggie's.

After first breaking down the Cougars win from earlier in the day, both Olivia and Maggie began to grill me on my first day with the Bobcats. I recounted my interaction with Nolan and how I had felt like he was testing me throughout the entire day. Even after practice, Nolan waved me off when I told him it was best if he came in for treatment. He had mumbled something about how he never came in for treatment after practices.

It took everything I had in me not to explode on him on our first day together. I had worked my tail off to be deserving of the accolades and the respect people gave me when it came to my craft, but not Nolan. It didn't matter to him that I had perfected Nate Rousch's therapy regimen to get him back on the ice three months sooner than anyone had predicted. Nolan Hill didn't care about any of that. He was only concerned with everything going according to his plan this season, and I was clearly *not* a part of his plan.

"No matter what we call him doesn't change that I think

I'm in for a long season. He's fighting me on everything and if I don't figure something out with him soon, the coaches will be breathing down my neck asking why Nolan isn't performing well."

"How are you going to handle him?" Maggie asked.

I had spent all evening trying to come up with a plan to win over Nolan Hill, but I had come up empty-handed every time until I realized I didn't need to win him over. I only needed to promise him his deepest desire—going out on top. "I'm going to exploit the one thing he wants more in this world than anything—to win. If I can figure out a way to equate what I can do for him to results on the field, I think I'm in business."

"You better not let him take up all your free time. You promised that you'd start prioritizing yourself more." Olivia leveled me with a look that could have stopped one of the Bobcats' three-hundred-pound linemen dead in their tracks.

"I know."

"Let's get some accountability for those words." Olivia jumped up from my couch and ran off toward the kitchen. I watched her rustle around in different drawers until she came running back toward the couch with a piece of paper and a pen. "We're making a bucket list."

"I didn't think you were serious about that," I told her.

Olivia ignored me and numbered the piece of paper with a one. "What's our first item?"

"I think you should put yourself out there again and try dating. You may even find your person," Maggie chimed in.

I opened my mouth to protest, but it was too late—Olivia was already writing it down.

"What did you write next to that?" I asked as I moved to get a better view. "Olivia! No!"

Olivia had written *GET SOME ACTION* in big letters next to the first item on the list. I grabbed the pen from her hand and crossed it out.

Olivia rolled her eyes. "You are no fun."

"What's next?" Maggie asked, trying to help calm the situation between the two of us.

"Well, if we're talking about my love life . . ." I trailed off for a moment as I let myself dream about something other than my career for once. "I've always watched couples in love kiss on New Year's Eve. I suppose that goes together with dating. I just hope that I am with someone at that point."

"I'm so excited." Maggie bounced up and down from her spot on the couch. "This is *so* going to be the year for love."

Maggie had always been ever the romantic since I first got to know her when she and Olivia joined the Cougars. After she started dating Tommy last year, she had become downright insufferable. I honestly wondered if those two would ever move out of the honeymoon phase. But judging by the way she sighed dreamily every time her phone chimed, I was guessing that wouldn't be happening anytime soon.

"I also want to have a real Thanksgiving this year. Without any arguments and with a homemade turkey."

Olivia's eyes softened at my next one. She understood the desire to have something as simple as every person I love sitting down at a table together full of gratitude. We grew up in a household where we were lucky if our parents withheld having a fight until after dinner. For the two of us, we just considered Thanksgiving an extra-long weekend off school. When I got older, I would spend the few dollars I earned at my job at our local grocery store on a pumpkin pie for Olivia and me to share behind our closed bedroom door.

As soon as I allowed myself to speak that kind of longing into existence, it was like the floodgates had opened and all the things I wanted to do to heal the pieces of myself that were broken at such a young age came rushing out.

"I want to wear matching pajamas on Christmas morning." Olivia groaned at that one, but she didn't hesitate to write it down.

My desire to work had started at a young age. It was never because I was ambitious to make something of myself. At least, not at first. It started as just a way to get out of the house. Then work became a way for me to try and prove to my parents that I could do something with myself in the hopes that I would then get their attention. Eventually, working just became the only thing I knew how to do.

I knew I was worthy of so much more.

I rattled off a few other things to Olivia before I came to a stalemate with all my desires written down in her neat scrawl.

"I have one more thing," Olivia told me as she started to write down the final item. "Have a day where you say yes to everything."

"A 'yes' day?" I asked.

"I think that's a fantastic idea," Maggie exclaimed. "You spend so much time saying no to things because of work. It's time you get to say yes."

The three of us admired our handiwork before Olivia took the list over to my fridge. She placed it front and center with a magnet where I would see it every day.

"If we weren't playing on Sunday, I would be begging for tickets to the Bobcats' first game," Maggie said as she finished off her pint of ice cream.

"You better be getting us some sideline passes for the first time we get to come." Olivia pointed her spoon at me as she sat back down on the couch. I was tempted to take it away before she tried to wield it like a weapon.

"Only if you get me tickets if the Cougars make it to the playoffs."

"Deal!" Maggie exclaimed. Olivia raised an eyebrow questioningly at her. "What? I like watching Derek Allen play. He's nice to look at."

"You have someone nice to look at at home every day," I reminded her.

"Doesn't mean I can't appreciate God's work on that fine specimen of a man."

Olivia burst out laughing. "You must have a thing for ladies' men. I heard Derek loves to get around."

"People can change." Maggie stared down at her phone lovingly as she read the newest text from her boyfriend. That man was wrapped so tightly around Maggie's finger that it was a miracle she didn't lose circulation.

"Derek's nice," I told them with a shrug. "A bit hyper at times, but I think he means well."

After Nolan had brushed me off for treatment after practice, Derek immediately followed me back into the training room with another endless stream of questions.

"Did you like practice?" *Yes, you guys look very solid this year.*

"I don't think I asked you. Do you have any siblings?" *A younger sister.*

"Is she in town?" *She works for the Cougars.*

"Holy shit. You two make a formidable pair. Is she single?" *Over my dead body, Allen.*

I pretended like I didn't catch the look that Hawthorn and Derek exchanged when Nolan walked right past the training room. Or the way Derek's ramblings seemed to kick into overdrive, as if he was trying to distract me from the fact that Nolan Hill was actively avoiding me. No matter the reason for it, I appreciated Derek's efforts.

"Maggie, you're a genius!" Olivia's squeal of excitement brought me back to reality.

"Wait, what?" I asked.

"We're going to set you up a dating profile," Maggie explained. "What better way to start on your first item on your bucket list?"

I was being serious when I told them that I wanted to go on dates. I had dated plenty of people through college and after, but many of them never made it to a third date. By the end of the second date, it often became painfully obvious whether we were compatible or not. I'd never particularly liked the game that was dating in your twenties, but if I wanted a shot at more than sweaty athletes and working far after the sun had set, I needed to play the game.

"What do you think about these photos?" Olivia asked as she shoved my phone back in front of my face.

As Olivia swiped through the photos, I cringed at how plain they made me look. All six photos looked like they could have been my professional headshot on the Bobcats staff page.

"I looked through everything and these are the best I could find." Olivia gave me a small shrug, as if to say *sorry, you're kind of boring and this is the best I could do*.

Those six photos were enough to prove anyone that called me a workaholic right. There were no photos from a vacation. Very few with friends out having drinks. None with family besides Olivia. But I was actively making the decision to change that for myself starting today.

"I guess it'll do." I sighed.

"We can take some new photos and wait to put up your profile, if you'd like?" That was why I loved my little sister. She was the first person to jump off the cliff, but she at least made sure I was prepared and comfortable before I jumped off the cliff with her.

"No, that's okay. Might as well not be something I'm not. There's enough catfishing on those apps already, best not add to it."

"Well, we can at least work on these questions they'll put on your profile." Maggie snuggled in closer to Olivia on the couch to peer at the phone in her hands. "Let's do this one! What's the best way to ask you out?"

Judging by the panic that entered my body at the question, I was more out of practice with dating than I thought.

Just keep it simple.

"Probably if someone asked me to dinner or drinks at least two days in advance, confirmed it the morning of, then showed up on time." The way Olivia and Maggie looked at me with wide eyes, I guessed that my response was rather clinical.

"Okay . . ." Olivia drew out as she typed my response into my profile.

"What is a simple pleasure of yours?" Olivia continued through the questions.

"Quiet Sunday mornings drinking coffee on my balcony."

"What's your love language?" Maggie asked.

"Words of affirmation."

"A praise kink," Maggie replied. "I like it."

"Do *not* put that on there!" I exclaimed.

"What would make you fall hard?"

This question made me pause. What *would* make me fall hard? It wasn't someone who checked all my boxes in the typical sense. That hadn't worked out for me thus far. I needed someone I didn't expect. Someone who pushed me and made me a better person. Someone who challenged me.

"I think I would fall the hardest for someone who just allowed me to be *me* at my very core. Which includes all my messiness, all my nerdiness, and all the pieces of myself that I must hide from the world out of fear I'd be judged. I think if you find someone like that, you've found your slice of peace in this life."

Olivia typed away madly on my phone before she showed me her final reveal. Although I may not have the most exciting life in the world, those answers were enough for me to feel like I was at least staying true to myself.

I had landed the job of my dreams. Now it was time I landed the life of my dreams.

Chapter 5

Nolan

This was not part of my plan. *She* was not part of my plan. Dr. Charlotte Thompson. She was all of five foot two inches but had the sass and stubbornness of someone twice her size. She was infuriating. She was making it harder than Roger did for me to blow her off. Especially because Derek and Hawthorn wouldn't shut up about her. All I heard all week was how great she was or how good at her job she was.

When it came to Charlotte Thompson, she was everything I normally admired. She was ambitious and smart, but that was the perfect combination for someone who would stop at nothing to try and fix me. I didn't need fixing.

What I hated even more than the way her eyes seemed to not miss a single thing at practice was the way her blonde hair bounced so perfectly in that goddamn ponytail. Or the way her blue eyes narrowed as she challenged me. Or the way she smiled whenever Derek said something utterly ridiculous as if he was *actually* funny. Or how I was acutely aware of where she was always in vicinity to me when we were at the practice facility, only because I wanted to avoid her and her prying gaze.

"It's about time you arrived," Adam Steel said as he threw open his front door. Two small children hung off him like monkeys—one of his sons clung to his left leg, while the other had him in a stranglehold as he hung off his back. If the sports world were to see the soon-to-be hall of fame baseball pitcher in his favorite place—home with his family—they wouldn't believe their eyes.

Every year, Adam hosted the three of us to celebrate the start of the NFL season in September while I had him over to celebrate the start of the MLB season in March.

"Hawthorn and Derek are already in the back."

Adam turned to walk me toward his back patio, his two sons still hanging off him. Nora, Adam's wife, and Sarah, Hawthorn's wife, were congregated in the kitchen with glasses of wine in their hands.

"Nolan!" Sarah exclaimed when she saw me. She rushed over to give me a hug, a bit of wine sloshing over the side of her glass.

"Hi, Sarah." I gave her a quick kiss on the top of her head. "It's nice to see you."

Adam walked over to Nora after he extracted himself from his sons' grip and grabbed her wine glass from her hand. With his free hand, he spun his wife in a circle before returning her wine glass back to her. Nobody had more moves than Adam Steel, which shocked nearly everybody. I was certain there wasn't a person on this world that loved his wife more than Adam.

"Excited for the game on Sunday, Nolan," Nora told me as she smoothed her hair down from Adam's spin. A brilliant red covered her cheeks as she stole a sly glance at her husband. The two had been married for nearly a decade and still acted like two kids young and in love.

"Me too." I gave her a curt nod before slipping through the doors into the backyard.

Derek and Hawthorn were lounged out in two of the Adirondack chairs that sat around the fire pit.

"Feeling good about the first game?" Adam asked me as he followed me out the back door.

"I'm hoping for better than last year." I tried to keep my voice light and not give away that doing better was quickly becoming all-consuming.

"Judging by the fact that he disappears right after practice, but his car is the last one in the parking lot after every practice . . ." Hawthorn threw me a knowing look. There was very little I could slip by him.

Adam was nearly as bad. He was looking at me with a scrutinizing gaze that felt like he was reading every desperate thought in my head—how loud the voices had gotten. Adam opened his mouth like he wanted to say something before Derek interrupted him.

"He's just trying to avoid Lottie."

"Who's Lottie?" Adam asked.

"Charlotte Thompson," Hawthorn filled him in. "She's our new physical therapist. She's fantastic. It's just this guy's got a stick up his ass about everything this season."

"Thompson? Is she related to Olivia Thompson?"

"She told me she had a sister that works for the Cougars," Derek told him.

"Olivia's one of our media people. She's great. But back to you, Nolan." All three of my friends looked back over at me. "What's going on with you?"

I let out a sigh as I thought about whether I wanted to tell them the truth or not. Which was that after every practice this week, I stayed until the late evening watching game film. My coaches thought that I was devoted to the success of this season. Which might be true, but there was more beneath the surface. I'd found myself so anxious at night with thoughts racing through my head that I wasn't able to sleep more than a few hours. Nothing was quelling that anxious feeling inside of me and I was beginning to realize that my anxiety wasn't just for ending up on top at the end of this season. It was also for what was to come *after* this season, when I finally hung up the jersey for the last time.

I had spent over two decades of my life playing this sport. It was all I'd ever known and in five short months it would all be over. I hadn't thought much about what was next after my football career was over. It had always seemed so far off in the distance that I hadn't needed to worry about it yet. Now I was rounding the corner and about to face it head on without any plans. To make matters even worse, there was a beautiful woman who was good at her job and just so happened to see right through all my bullshit.

But could I tell my friends that? What would that make me look like?

"I just want this season to go well." I decided staying vague would be the best option. "It might sound stupid, but I know this team can win a Super Bowl and all I want is to do my part well, so we have a chance at doing that."

"Man, this is a team sport. That's not all on you to worry about." Hawthorn reached over to grasp my shoulder and give it a squeeze.

"No matter what, I need to figure out what happened last year and not let it happen again."

Derek and Hawthorn went silent.

They watched me crumble last year. They watched me throw helmets on the sideline, get in arguments with coaches, and curse at myself loud enough that parents would give me the look while trying to shelter their kids. None of those things were me. Or at least not the me that I like. I let a war happen inside my head and I let that war rule me and my actions last season. I was going to try everything to make sure that didn't happen again.

"We've got your back, Nolan." Derek reached out to give my back a brotherly smack. "You're not doing this alone. So, stop trying to pretend like you aren't practically sleeping at the practice facility like a maniac."

"I haven't slept there!" I exclaimed.

"Not yet," Hawthorn mumbled into his beer.

Adam finally spoke up. He normally stayed quiet and listened to the conversations around him, and the few times he did speak was like a wise sage sharing their advice. "No matter what you're trying to do with your season this year, Nolan, you'll run yourself into the ground putting that kind of pressure on yourself. It's your last season with the jersey on. You need to focus on trying to have fun."

Adam had just announced that this season would be his last. However, the playoff prospects for the Cougars were looking far more likely with each win the team racked up. For him to think I should enjoy my last season instead of focusing on coming out on top was probably much easier from his situation. He wasn't absolutely fucked in the head from an old injury.

"Yeah, Nol," Derek added cheerfully. He was already a few beers in as he enjoyed his last Friday night before the season got into full swing. "We're going to have a blast this season. So, you need to lay off all of us and especially Lottie. She's just trying to help you. She's a lot smarter than you think and she may just have some new ideas that you find will be good for you."

"Since when did you and Lottie become besties?" Hawthorn asked.

"Since she let me ask her questions during treatment and she doesn't ever say no. She's got a good vibe to her. I think she'll make a great addition to the team."

Even if Derek may have been on to some form of truth about Charlotte Thompson, that didn't stop me from thinking about how she rubbed me the wrong way. I could already tell we were going to be like oil and water. That was the last thing I needed on top of everything else I was going to have to work through this season.

Sarah and Nora announced dinner was ready shortly after, saving me from any further questioning. We ate outside, enjoying one of the last few nice days before we would enter deep fall and it would be too cold in Chicago to be outside.

I tried to stay present through the dinner and enjoy moments like these that were all the firsts of many lasts to come this season. I knew our friend group would still hang out, have dinners, and enjoy each other's company, but after this season, Adam and I would enter a different chapter in our lives while Hawthorn and Derek continued.

It was late by the time the plates had been cleared and the conversations had begun to die off. Hawthorn and Sarah called it quits first to get home to their three girls. Derek and I stayed a few minutes longer as we talked with Adam about his thoughts on the end of the Cougars season. They had three weeks before the playoffs started, and they were only four wins away from clinching the divisional title. It was looking like the group could have a Cinderella season with Adam, Jamil, and Tommy at the wheel. Tommy Mikals had settled into his role as captain with the team and played steady so far, consistently showing up when the team needed him during key moments in games. Jamil was having a record-breaking season, and he was only eight home runs away from breaking the MLB record for most in a single season. The press and fanfare around him had brought elevated attention to the team as they drove forward toward their shared goal.

Derek and I said our goodbyes as Adam walked us toward his front door. Nora had disappeared nearly an hour before to put their two boys down for bed.

"Nolan, one second." Adam put a hand on my shoulder to stop me from following Derek out the door. Derek flashed the two of us a smile before he got in his car and drove off, leaving me and Adam standing on his front steps.

"You'll kill yourself before you even get to retirement with how much pressure you're trying to put on yourself to achieve one last great hurrah before the inevitable comes."

I should have known that Adam would see right through me down to the real problem I was facing.

"Easy for you to say." I regretted the bitterness behind my words the second they left my mouth. Adam had been one of the first friends I made in this town when I first entered the league. The two of us ended up at the same charity event, both of us just starting our careers, and became friends through our shared experiences.

"The Nolan Hill I know wouldn't let one season unravel

him. The Nolan Hill I know would come back stronger by putting his head down and doing what he knows best. He's one of the hardest-working people I know, and he would stop at nothing to get his shit together."

"I'm trying, Adam. I really am." My voice cracked as the last word left my mouth and I sighed as I realized that I had exposed just how badly I was doing.

My friend stared at me for a few long beats before he spoke again. "You need to find a way to trust yourself again. Stop obsessing over what you did wrong and start thinking of all the things you've done *right* over your career, Nolan."

Adam cleared his throat as if he was thinking over what he was going to do next before he reached out and wrapped me in a hug that I didn't know I needed in that moment.

"I know you'll figure it out. Don't forget who you are and what you've sacrificed to get here."

Adam stepped back so he could look me in the eyes.

"And don't be scared about retirement. We've spent our whole lives always dedicating and sacrificing for our sports. Now it's time to just enjoy slowing down for a bit. It won't be easy. Trust me, I'm sure I'll drive Nora crazy by the end of the first week—but hell, maybe the two of us will be commentators or something. The opportunities will come."

The opportunities will come. That sentence bounced around in my head all the way home.

Chapter 6

Nolan

Don't forget who you are.

The dull roar of the crowd rumbled on just down the tunnel that opened onto the field. I could see the flash of the cheerleaders' pom poms as they waited for us to run out. My teammates bounced around next to me, trying to contain the adrenaline rush.

I repeated Adam's words again like a mantra as I waited for our signal to start toward the field.

Don't forget who you are.

I spent all day yesterday rewatching game film after my conversation with Adam Friday night. Except this time, I didn't bother watching any of the film from last season. Instead, I watched film of myself throughout my career. It was a reel of highlights that I hoped would bring back a sliver of the confidence I used to have. By the end of the day, that old excitement that I used to get before the first game of the season had started to come back. It was a completely different experience waking up early for today's game. It felt like Christmas morning, and I was too excited to sleep in. It gave me hope that maybe I was on the right path to the season that I'd been dreaming about.

I had continued to avoid Lottie at yesterday's practice. Which I'd come to realize would be much harder than I thought it would be because she seemed to arrive at the practice facility earlier than anyone else—even me. By the end of the week, the two of us had fallen into some sort of understanding. She would leave a list of exercises for me to do after the initial heat prep and electro-stimulation and I would do them without arguing. Other than that, our interactions had been minimal.

One of the Bobcats' staff members gave us the green light. In a flash, Derek took off down the tunnel as he led the rest of the team out onto the field. The roar of the crowd grew louder to an almost deafening decibel as soon as we emerged. The first time seeing a full stadium with excited fans would never get old. There were fans that had tickets for generations, super fans that would dress to the nines in full team regalia, and little kids watching their very first NFL games. Those were the people that we played for—Bobcat nation—and their energy was contagious.

Media waited around the edge of the field to catch the first photos of the season that would be posted on social media apps within minutes. The average person probably wondered what it would be like to stand in our shoes—the pressure that came from the fans, the attention from the media, the theatrics that the NFL layered on top of anything, and then the fact that this was our job and if we didn't perform, we were reprimanded just like a normal nine-to-five.

As a rookie, it had almost been too much between the pressure and the expectations. Sometimes it still was. But over a decade in and the noise from the crowd faded away, the cameras with long lenses to capture each moment of the game disappeared, and only the field, my team, and the football remained. This was the sport that I fell in love with at ten years old. It was the game that I learned from my father, and he had learned from his. It had taught me life lessons that had made me into the man I am today, even if it had hardened me within these last few years.

The national anthem and coin toss passed in a blur of anticipation as my fingers itched for the first snap and throw of the game. We won the coin toss and decided to receive the kick. After our kick returner got us good positioning on the field near the thirty-yard line, I was running onto the field with the offense.

Coach Randolph, my head coach, called the play, which came in over a headset in my helmet. The cheers from the fans around the stadium were so loud that I could barely hear him. I had to cover the ear holes in my helmet to try and muffle the noise. This wasn't something new when playing at Gateway Stadium. The energy inside was a part of the home field advantage that we had as a team. We'd grown accustomed to the noise the stadium held on game day. We knew how to respond. It was the other team that had to adjust and figure out how to play in these conditions.

After I relayed the play call to the team, we lined up in formation. It felt like slipping back on a pair of well-worn shoes, perfectly molded to my feet. Or getting back on a bike that I hadn't ridden in some time—muscle memory took over.

Scan the defense.

Do I see anything I need to tell my team about?

Should the play still be on?

Set. Hike.

In the moment, it felt as though time had slowed down and minutes had passed between lining up on the line of scrimmage and when the ball was snapped, but in reality, it was only a few seconds.

When I finally felt the leather of the football in my finger-tips, I went into autopilot. My eyes scanned for my first intended receiver for this play to see that he was covered before shifting to the next receiver. The second I saw an opportunity, I let the ball fly right into the hands of my target.

First down.

For the first time in months, when I thought about football, I didn't feel the overwhelming need to succeed hanging over me. Instead, I found myself smiling as we executed play after play.

That was until the second quarter.

The first quarter had gone off without a hitch. We'd managed to score a touchdown—a long route for Derek that he'd managed to stretch out for a score—and also get within kicking distance for Hawthorn to get a field goal on a stretch where none of our plays were breaking through for another score. We were winning going into the second quarter ten to nothing, but the momentum changed quickly.

With a few adjustments between quarters, San Diego's offense had managed to break through our defense to make it a three-point game. With only two minutes left until the half, there was an expectation to get another to keep the lead.

But it seemed that San Diego's defense had also made an adjustment.

A moment after the ball was snapped into my hands to start the first play of our possession, I realized I was being rushed. There is nothing more terrifying in this world than a three-hundred-pound lineman running full speed at you with the intent of putting you on your back. Panic seized my body immediately. In the matter of a second, all the memories of being sacked from last season flashed through my mind—freezing, panicking, and being unable to think about anything else for the rest of the game.

It's happening again.

My body slammed violently into the ground with the force of the lineman landing on top of me and smothering me for a few seconds before the pressure disappeared. I was left staring up at the sky above me, the ball still miraculously clutched in my hands. Derek came into my view and extended a hand down toward me.

"Maguire was out of position and missed his block. That's not on you, bud." Derek slapped my shoulder pads before looking at me expectantly for the next play with the rest of my team. But there was a ringing in my head that was disorienting me, and I could barely make out what my coach was calling in my helmet.

The clock was running down, and I had no idea what

Coach Randolph had called. Before my team could figure out that I was out of sorts, I called a passing play to Derek with the hope that I wasn't making a mistake. If this didn't work, my coach wouldn't be happy that I'd gone rogue.

As soon as I called for the ball, I found Derek on his route. Luckily, muscle memory took over and my body managed to drop a ball into his arms despite the mess in my head. Derek broke the tackle the guy on him was trying to make and ran the ball in for a touchdown.

Cheers erupted around the stadium. Coach Randolph clapped me on the back and told me that was a much better call than what he had on when I ran back to the sideline. Derek and Hawthorn cheered and said things like "the old Nolan is back."

None of that was true. All I cared about was getting into the locker room before I let my vicious thoughts take over in front of everyone.

The energy in the locker room was high as the coaches tried to calm us down to talk about next half's game plan, but I could barely focus on the white board in the middle of the room to see what the plan was.

A body stepped in front of me and blocked my view of the locker room. "Come with me," Lottie told me with her arms crossed over her chest. The look on her face told me that I wasn't going to avoid her this time.

No one blinked an eye at us as she led me back into the training room off the locker room. The second the two of us entered the room, she turned to look at me.

"What happened out there?"

I blinked. Had she seen me nearly lose it?

"What are you talking about?" I asked. It was better to play it safe and let her reveal her cards first.

"You played the entire first quarter and most of the second quarter like you were back five seasons ago. You looked great." I didn't bother with reveling in her compliment. I *had* felt great that first quarter and a half, but I knew something else was coming. "Then on that last drive, it was like you froze. It reminded me of some of the film I watched from last year. Any pressure on your right side and it's like you collapse."

Had that lineman come from my right side? How the hell did she connect all of that?

"Here, let me look at your knee." Lottie motioned for me to get onto the training table before she pushed up the leg of my pants. She rubbed her hands together and breathed into them first. "Sorry, my hands are always cold."

My eyes snagged on the way her lips puckered as she blew out hot air. I nearly had to physically shake my head to snap out of the trance the dark red of her lips had caught me in.

"How'd you notice that I panic with pressure on the right side?" I asked as she pressed on my knee.

"I watched film." Her answer was short, which was probably deserved after I had dodged all her attempts to try and help me this week.

"I spent this last week reading all of Roger's notes on your recovery after surgery. You barely completed half of the evaluations you needed to before the team threw you back in last season. Your knee hasn't quite recovered, and I think you know it. You're painfully aware of it on the field. Any pressure from that side has you reeling."

I wanted to glare at her and tell her that she was wrong. I wanted to laugh at her and say that maybe she wasn't as good at her job as she thinks she is, but then . . . I'd be lying.

When Lottie looked up at me, I realized I had never told *anyone* what exactly went on in my head during games post-surgery. The war I started with myself once I realized my body would never be the same felt like a slow poison that would kill me before my knee would. If I wanted a shot at winning the Super Bowl during my last year, I was going to have to clue someone in. I wasn't going to last the full season unless I figured out some way to address this.

"The injury happened when I was rushed on the right

side two seasons ago." Lottie nodded her head. She must have watched the film from that game. Part of me hated knowing that she had seen me on the ground, helpless. "I did the normal therapy post-surgery. Brace, crutches, the whole nine yards. The coaches had been anxious to have me back on the field when last season rolled around, but I knew I was going to be short of getting my knee back to where it needed to be. I tried to compensate for it, but all I could think about was my knee during the game, which made my reaction times slower. I was more at risk for a sack."

"I can help you, if you'd let me." Lottie's face was set with determination, as if she was expecting a fight.

"I have one season left." It was meant to be a brush off, much like what she had expected from me, but there wasn't much fight to my words.

"Here's the deal, Hill." Lottie faced me as if she were a soldier preparing to head into battle. "You want to win a Super Bowl. That's every quarterback's goal heading into the season. You want it more than anything else you've ever wanted in life—especially this season. You want to leave this game the hero you've painted yourself to be your entire career. But you will only get sacked enough times that you get replaced by the rookie you glared at this entire week during practice if you don't let me help you."

"I didn't glare at Caleb all week," I managed to mumble through the partial shock of her words.

"I'm not going to even argue with you on that, because you and I both know you were." Lottie pulled tape from her bag and started adding extra support to my knee. When she was done, she pulled my pant leg back down and gave me a look that I knew she'd used many times throughout her career whenever she faced opposition.

"Let me do my job, Nolan."

Lottie had called me out on what I wanted most—to win. If I wanted to do that, the two of us were going to have to work together.

"Fine."

"Great, we'll start tomorrow at six in the morning."

Six in the morning? Was she crazy?

I opened my mouth to protest, but she silenced me with another scathing look.

"Now, you still need to win *this* game. So, here's what we're going to do. This should provide you with enough support that when you do get pressed from the right side, it over-compensates for you. But we're going to try and keep that from happening. Work out of the left side of the pocket, no matter what side the defense is pushing from. And trust yourself, for fuck's sake—you're Nolan *fucking* Hill. You're a two-time Super Bowl champion and you own about ten different records in the NFL. Now go win the damn ball game. I hate losing."

I had to stop my jaw from hitting the floor as I watched Lottie leave the room. Her thick blonde hair was in a braid that swished from side to side in time with her hips as she walked away. I had to give it to the woman, she had teeth, and she knew how to use them.

Chapter 7

Lottie

Nolan listened to my advice during the second half and played to the strength of his left side, rather than trying to make something happen with his right that would only put him at risk. After he threw his second touchdown of the third quarter and came off the field celebrating with Derek, he paused long enough to catch my eye from where I stood behind the team. If I hadn't been watching closely, I would have missed the almost imperceptible nod of his head.

Our defense managed to hold off San Diego's attempt at tying the game up at the end of the fourth quarter, clinching the first win of the season. The team celebrated on the field as reporters flooded around them to grab a photo of the players. An ESPN reporter stopped Nolan a few feet away from me.

"Nolan, that was an impressive game you had today. You threw for five total touchdowns at nearly three hundred yards passing. You must be happy with the strong start of this performance for the season."

The reporter, I recognized, was Harper Nelson. She was up-and-coming on the scene. Players loved her because she often asked knowledgeable questions during her interviews. Fans loved her because she was beautiful, with tan skin that balanced her chocolate-brown hair and hazel eyes. I had to admit that she was striking, but my heart still ached for the girl that had to combat being relevant for her looks rather than how good she was at her craft. I remembered seeing an article where she talked about being a female reporter in the sports industry and how she worked hard to remain knowledgeable about the game, so she was known for more than being a woman.

"It's the kind of start we wanted to have as a team. But this season is a marathon, not a sprint. There's a lot of games ahead of us that we'll have to chip away at." I watched Nolan morph into the player that was the nation's beloved quarterback. Gone was the hardened gaze and the pessimism I had witnessed this past week. He was the All-American guy as he talked with Harper.

"You battled through some adversity with your linemen not quite getting into position at times. What do you think you need to do moving forward as an offense?"

"I think it's just practice and getting more looks together. The offense will gel. We have some new blood on the line, and I think with more practice and a few more games, we'll be running on all cylinders."

"Thanks, Nolan." Harper flashed him a quick smile before she backed away with her cameraman.

Nolan noticed me waiting for him in the tunnel when he approached. He slowed from his previous jog to a walk as he got closer. His gaze held none of the disdain he usually looked at me with.

Progress.

"Thanks," Nolan told me. I had to bite back a laugh at how hard it seemed it was for him to say that word. "For the advice you gave me at halftime."

"I wasn't the one that just went out there and threw for nearly two hundred yards in the second half. You just needed a little reminder about who you are." I gave a small shrug of my shoulders. Nolan's eyes bounced around my face as if he were looking for something. I almost missed the ever-present annoyance that was on Nolan's face and the absence of it had me searching for something to fill the silence that was starting to grow between us.

"I think maybe a truce is on the table. No more avoiding me at the practice facility?" I asked cautiously. A sheepish smile crossed Nolan's face like he'd been caught red-handed. I noted the way that smile softened his facial features and showed me a different version of him.

"I'm a man of my word. I'll see you tomorrow at six."

Nolan Hill was indeed a man of his word. The next morning, his black Range Rover pulled up next to my car at ten minutes until six while the sky was still dark. I had been leaning against the hood of my car waiting when he pulled up.

I watched Nolan take in my leggings, running shoes, and long-sleeved workout shirt. He was dressed in a pair of shorts and a well-worn Bobcats crewneck; a Cougars baseball cap covered his normally tousled brown hair.

"You are not dressed in your usual attire," he said, speaking the obvious.

"Well, that's because we aren't doing the usual routine." I pushed off the hood of my car and started off toward the trail head that wove its way through the woods of the residential area that surrounded the Bobcats' practice facility.

"Where are we going?" Nolan asked, his long strides keeping easily up with my short ones.

"For a run. I want to switch things up and see how you do before we get into the training room."

I took off into a light jog the moment my feet hit the pavement of the trail head. Nolan and I fell into a steady rhythm with each other, the first few minutes of the run passing with comfortable silence. I appreciated Nolan's sudden willingness to listen to me and not fight over his treatment.

"So, you want to tell me about why you avoided me all last week?" I asked as we passed the first house in the surrounding neighborhood.

Birds chirping in the morning air and the pounding of

our shoes on the pavement were the only sounds filling the space between us before Nolan finally answered me. "I don't particularly like therapy."

He gave me an embarrassed look, much like the one he gave me at the game the day before.

"It reminds me of the reason why I got hurt in the first place." I could tell that whatever Nolan was thinking about, it often weighed heavily on his mind. "I had missed those defensive players rushing me on the right side because I'd been lost the whole game. I hadn't had time to read the playbook that week as thoroughly as I should have . . . I had other things going on that drew my attention elsewhere. So, I wasn't as quick at finding my receivers that game and it eventually caught up with me. I let other things distract me and it cost me nearly everything."

"What was on your mind that week?" The professional side of me wanted to know what I was up against with trying to mend him, but I was also curious to know what could have shaken Nolan so much that it would affect his game like that.

"Now, I don't think it's fair that I'm the one answering all the questions here."

I noted Nolan's evasion, but I appreciated that he was at least trying today—even if it was difficult for him. It was only fair that I met him halfway. "What questions do you have?"

I could feel Nolan's gaze heavy on me. "You seem to know a lot about football."

"That's not a question," I replied.

The scowl I was used to seeing Nolan wear passed over his face again. "Why do you know so much about football?"

"My father coached high school football. I grew up with a game on all fall and winter. He liked to joke that it was in my blood."

What I hesitated to share was how football was the only thing that my father had ever really cared about. He thought coaching high school football was more important than even his family. Games became more important than holidays, birthdays, and eventually his marriage.

"He seems like a dedicated father," Nolan commented, oblivious to my pained expression.

I remembered a time when I desperately wanted my father to come home, only to be told that he had game film to watch—for a high school football game. He acted as if he were on the verge of winning the Super Bowl with the level of importance he thought it deserved.

Eventually, my mother pulled away from Olivia and me, as well. Too wrapped up in grief for a dying marriage to focus on the two children that were still there, that still needed her. She left me to raise Olivia on my own. They both did.

"He was dedicated to something. That's for sure," I mumbled.

Nolan's steps slowed for only a moment as he finally picked up on the bitterness lacing my voice. To his credit, he managed to navigate the conversation away from my father without knowing why he needed to.

"I don't think I've ever had a medical professional in my corner that speaks about football the way you did to me during halftime yesterday."

Nolan's comment nearly made me stumble to a stop. He hadn't added anything about never having had a female medical professional in his corner that could speak on football like that. He'd simply stated he'd never had *anyone* speak about football like that with him—my opinion wasn't questioned because I was a female. That simple distinction meant more to me than he probably realized.

"I have a feeling most people were probably just too scared to cross that line with you."

Nolan chuckled at my observation. That sound actually did send me stumbling this time.

Nolan reached out an arm to steady me. "Careful. You're the one supposed to be keeping me from injuring myself, not the other way around."

That melodic laugh rang in my head as I righted myself and continued down the trail. It was rich and showed a completely different side from the standoffish Nolan Hill I'd grown used to over the past week.

"How come you act so gruff with everyone in the facility?"

My question must have struck some kind of a nerve with Nolan because I watched that muscle jump in his jaw as he thought about how to answer.

"I'm not sure I have a valid reason. But I'm trying to get better."

Nolan pushed himself a few strides ahead of me and I noted the tension in his back. Maybe this season was about more than just winning a Super Bowl for Nolan. Maybe it was about righting some wrongs he'd done to his teammates these past few years and making some new memories to leave them with.

Slowly, the tension eased in Nolan's back and he fell back into stride with me. "How has someone so young managed to become a physical therapist for an NFL team so quickly?"

By giving up everything I should have been doing.

"I sacrificed a lot." It was Nolan's turn to side-eye my simple response. I sighed before expanding. "I stopped hanging out with my friends from college to the point I eventually stopped being invited to things. I went on dates with people, but it never went anywhere because nobody wanted to date a workaholic. I missed out on a lot of life."

Nolan was quiet for a few more minutes as we reached the turning point on our jog to start heading back toward the practice facility.

"You aren't a workaholic. You just have ambition." His voice was strong as he corrected me. It almost caught me more off guard than his laugh. I had never expected him to say anything so nice to me.

"Maybe so. I did end up here, after all." The repetition of running had my mind wandering off toward the bucket list stuck to my fridge at home. "But hopefully I can make up for lost time."

"How so?"

"It's silly," I told him. It was my turn to evade a question. I had already said too much. There was no reason to give him the full truth of my pathetic life. He had everything he ever wanted, and if he found out all I wanted for New Year's was to be kissed, I was sure he'd laugh at me. Not to mention he was a player. Admitting that I was venturing off on a quest I'd been convinced to go on full of experiences I felt I missed out on felt too personal. Something I shouldn't disclose.

The practice facility finally came back into view. But before we got any closer to it, Nolan reached out a hand and wrapped it around my wrist to pull me to a stop.

"I'd like to know what you think is silly about making up for lost time." I noticed how serious he was, and I realized that this was his olive branch to me. This was his way of trying to form some semblance of a relationship between us so he could meet me halfway. The hesitation still stopped me for only a moment. But now I wondered how unprofessional it really was to tell him that I was just trying to live life now instead of existing only to work.

Maybe he'd understand, a voice whispered in my head.

I wasn't sure if it was the nice gesture from him, but I found myself opening my mouth and letting some of the truth spill out. "My little sister came up with a bucket list for me. It's got stupid stuff on it. Like going out on dates, since I haven't really done that seriously in years, and watching the sunrise from the best view. Like I said, it's silly."

Nolan removed his hand from my wrist. "It's not silly," he replied fiercely. I shifted uncomfortably, unsure if I'd rather have Nolan's gruffness than this sincerity.

"Come on. Let's get going on the rest of what I have planned today so we can get out of here. I don't want to take up all of your day off." I started back up at a jog. A few seconds passed before I heard Nolan begin to follow me.

The two of us walked into the empty practice facility together and made our way toward the training room. I had stayed up all last night after the game coming up with the perfect routine that would not only help strengthen his knee in a way that would allow him to have a successful season, but also give him back some confidence in his body. Nolan's body was never going to be like it was when he was younger, but that didn't mean he couldn't invent a new version of himself.

"Here's what we're going to do." I started grabbing tape and wrap for Nolan's knee. "I'm going to do the same tape job I did at the half yesterday. Then we are going to go out onto the practice field."

Today I had more access to Nolan's entire leg without him in his football pants. I warmed my hands again before pushing up the hem of his shorts a little further to expose more skin. Nolan tensed on the table, and I pulled my hands back as quickly as I could.

"Are my hands still too cold?" I asked. Nolan kept his eyes on his feet as he shook his head no.

"Just took me by surprise." Nolan's voice sounded strained as he shifted on the table.

"Is anything sore?"

Another head shake.

I remembered what he told me earlier on our run, *I don't particularly like therapy*.

It wasn't the first time I'd ever had an athlete tell me something along those same lines. Everyone had a different reason for why, but I was going to make it my mission to change Nolan's mind.

I stared at him for a second longer before I put my hands back on his thigh and began to work the muscle. This time his muscles stayed relaxed. Once I finished the short massage, I made quick work of the tape support and wrap cover.

"Let's go to the field."

Nolan remained quiet the entire walk to the field and I tried to stir some conversation to keep him in the good mood he was in.

"You've been used to playing a specific way your entire career. But your body has changed. That doesn't mean you still can't compete at the highest caliber or at your highest potential." I walked the two of us over to the basket of footballs that was sitting on the sidelines. "However, if you dissect your stats, you play off your left side better than your right with or without an injury. There're a couple solutions to help you while we work on strengthening your knee—you let your linemen know to protect your right side more than before and we work on evasive maneuvers when you get pressured from that direction. That way, when it does happen, you don't lock up on the field."

I didn't catch Nolan off guard this time with the in-depth football analysis. Instead, I watched him slip into the legendary quarterback that he was known for being. For the next hour, we walked through different drills that would give Nolan ideas during the game.

We worked together like two like-minds as we bounced ideas off each other. Gone was the apprehension Nolan had for me and gone was my need to prove myself to him. We were on the same page for that hour, with both of our areas of expertise bringing a new perspective.

"How do you feel?" I asked him after his hundredth run through the drills.

Sweat glistened down Nolan's face and he sucked a few deep breaths in to calm his heart rate. There was something new in his eyes that I hadn't seen before—a sparkle.

"Fucking fantastic." That same melodic laugh filled the space around us, and I couldn't stop the smile that broke across my face at the sound. "Thanks to you."

I was used to getting recognition from my athletes in their recovery process. Normally, all I felt was proud of another job well done. This time, I felt something new as Nolan looked at me with that unfiltered smile—a small fluttering in my chest.

He tossed the football back in the cart as he walked past

me. He reached out and gave my upper arm a squeeze before he disappeared toward the locker room.

"Same time tomorrow?"

"I'll be here," I told him.

Right before Nolan crossed the threshold back into the practice facility, he paused and turned back around. "Hey, Lottie?"

"Yeah?"

"Your bucket list isn't stupid. So don't let anyone make you think that."

I felt my cheeks heat at his words. For some odd reason, I was relieved that he didn't think I was a loser for dedicating so much of my life to my work that now I felt the need to make up for it.

"Can I tell you something, too?" I asked him before he walked away.

He nodded.

"Your teammates deserve this version of you."

Chapter 8

Nolan

Charlotte Thompson was infuriating.

I had promised myself that there would be no distractions this season. I would give every last piece of myself to this game before it was all over. How was I supposed to avoid what I was beginning to realize was the biggest distraction of all when her entire job was trying to help me win a Super Bowl?

She saw things about the way I was playing this season within a single drill that I had spent months trying to figure out through game film. She was smart, hardworking, and managed to know exactly how to push all my buttons while we worked together. She outsmarted me on every turn.

Worst of all was how I couldn't stop thinking about how beautiful she was.

But somehow, I still woke up every morning excited to go to the practice facility to work with Lottie. After the run, she would put me through different exercises to strengthen the muscles around my knee. She actively tried to frame the treatment like a workout in an effort to switch my way of thinking about therapy.

By the end of the first week of working together I was beginning to realize that maybe Charlotte Thompson wasn't all that bad, which made trying to dislike her all the more difficult.

The first day that Derek and Hawthorn walked into the

training room to see me working with—and not avoiding—Lottie drew shocked looks. By the fourth day, I noticed them becoming looser around me. I was clearly a hard friend to have over the past two seasons.

By the time Friday rolled around, I had concluded that I needed to get my head out of my ass and start acting like the leader this team deserved. Lottie was right. This team deserved the version of myself that wasn't weighed down by negative thoughts and heavy expectations.

Which was exactly why I was trying to balance a dozen boxes of donuts to bring into the practice facility for everyone. It would take more than a box of donuts to make up for some of my selfish behavior these past two seasons, but it was a start.

"Do you need help?" Lottie's voice rang out from next to me. I risked a look in her direction and nearly lost all the boxes.

It was mid-afternoon and I hadn't seen her yet today. She had given me the day off before we traveled to New York tonight for the game on Sunday against the Gladiators.

Today Lottie was wearing a tight white tank top that showed off toned, muscular arms and a black silk skirt that hugged the curve of her hips. A slit ran up the side of the skirt that revealed equally toned legs. Her hair was slicked back into a bun, and she had on more makeup than she normally wore to the facility. My eyes raked over her. My breathing grew shallow and my chest tightened.

What the hell is this woman doing to me?

I must have been staring because I watched a brilliant red spread up Lottie's neck and into her cheeks. "I had a date today for lunch. You know, the whole bucket list thing? I came straight here and was going to change inside."

"How'd it go?" I pushed the words out through a clenched jaw.

Lottie sighed as she took a few of the donut boxes from me. "No spark. I should have known better than to get my hopes up about men on a dating app."

I grabbed the door for Lottie and tried to keep my eyes trained on her face.

"Maybe the next one?"

"Maybe." Lottie shrugged her shoulders absently. "I'm not betting on it, but I did want to put myself back out there again. You've got to play the game, as they say these days."

I didn't think anyone like Charlotte Thompson should have to "play the game". Men should be dying to get a chance to take her on a date.

"Anyone would be lucky to take you on a date," I told her. I sucked my lips into my mouth, shocked I let something like that slip.

"Can you tell them that?" she asked me as she helped me drop the donuts off in the cafeteria for everyone to snack on. "I didn't ask you, what's up with these donuts?"

"I thought it would be nice for everyone to celebrate the first travel day."

Lottie opened her mouth like she wanted to say something before she thought better of it. A small voice in my head wanted me to tell her the idea came to me because of her but I ignored it.

"I should go change. I'll see you at practice." She gave me a small smile before she gingerly grabbed a donut and disappeared toward her office. This time, I admired the long line of her legs as she walked away.

"Did you bring these in?" I heard Derek exclaim from behind me. I turned away from where Lottie had just been to see him holding a donut in each hand.

"Thought I'd start a tradition for travel days this year," I told him.

"Did you fall and hit your head on the way here today?" Derek asked me between bites. "Because judging by these donuts and the way you just unabashedly checked Lottie out, I would say you did."

"I was not checking her out!" The way my voice cracked may have said otherwise.

"And you told *me* to keep it in my pants." Derek wielded a donut at me.

"Everything is staying firmly in my pants." I scowled at my best friend. "Matter of fact let's not talk about anything in my pants when it comes to Lottie. We have a professional relationship."

"For now . . ." Derek cocked an eyebrow at me before he headed back toward the locker room with his second donut.

"Absolutely not." I grabbed a donut for myself and chased after my friend. "Don't you dare tell Hawthorn I was checking Lottie out. You're worse than a goddamn tabloid."

Derek took off running toward the locker room with both donuts clutched in his hands, maniacal laughter bouncing off the walls after him.

That night we loaded onto the plane that would be taking us to New York. Tomorrow we would have a walk-through practice before our game on Sunday. We didn't normally travel a day early, but New York was already significantly colder than Chicago and our coach wanted us to get acclimated.

Derek, Hawthorn, and I chose seats at the front of the plane and started to dig into the food that the team catered for us on flights. Lottie was one of the last to climb on and I watched her take in the plane as she tried to figure out where she was going to sit.

"I have an open seat next to me," I told her before she could walk by us. I heard Derek snicker from across the aisle. I almost threw my dinner roll at his head.

"Thanks," she whispered as she put her carry-on luggage in the compartment above us. I stood up and backed into the aisle to give her enough room to slide into the window seat.

One of the flight attendants handed her a bag of food once she sat down. She took the bag and stared at it for a moment.

"Not used to being wined and dined?" I teased. She looked at me with wide eyes.

"Not particularly."

"Welcome to the NFL."

The two of us sat in silence while we took off. I watched as Lottie logged onto the plane WIFI only to immediately get a notification from the dating app that she was on. I reminded myself why she started this whole thing in the first place. She felt like she was missing out on life. After becoming one of the youngest medical professionals in the NFL, Lottie hadn't looked around like she had finally gotten everything she wanted. Instead, she realized she didn't have everything she wanted. It was admirable.

Here I was, with two Super Bowls already under my belt. I had everything I wanted, but I was still being greedy to not let that be enough. I wanted more from the only thing I knew.

The two of us were almost complete opposites. We wanted two different things. Yet she was still doing everything in her power to help me achieve my dreams. It felt only right if I tried to help her achieve all the things she wanted because she was doing the same for me.

"I think I have a way to knock one of those things off your bucket list," I told her once we reached cruising altitude.

Lottie looked at me with those wide blue eyes again. "Really?"

"I need to make a call when we land, but meet me in the lobby at five tomorrow morning."

Understanding dawned across Lottie's face when she realized what item on her bucket list I was going for. After a moment of consideration, she nodded in agreement.

I didn't want to think about the way my chest released the anticipation I hadn't realized had gathered there while I waited for her answer.

Lottie closed her eyes and leaned her head against the window as she tried to catch a few hours of sleep before we landed.

"Psst."

I groaned when I heard Derek trying to grab my attention from two feet to my left.

"What?" I hissed, hoping Lottie could fall asleep quickly.

"You always take the window seat," Derek reminded me.

I just gave him a shrug. I hadn't even hesitated to give Lottie the window seat. Everyone loved the window seat and I thought it'd be rude to take that from her simply because that was the easiest way for me to sleep on flights.

I was thankful Hawthorn was already passed out with his headphones on next to Derek so he didn't join in with this line of questioning.

"Is your cold heart melting, Hill?" Derek's eyes gleamed with delight.

I subtly flipped him off before I tried to settle into my seat and get comfortable enough that I could fall asleep. Lottie stirred next to me and I prayed Derek hadn't woken her up or I'd throttle him when we landed.

The following morning, I waited in the lobby of our hotel. Only the early risers either going to the gym or getting a head start on the day were milling about. Even though we were in the city that never sleeps, the only noise outside now was the late fall chirp of birds before they headed south for the winter.

The ding of the elevators grabbed my attention. Every time I heard that sound, my head snapped over to see if it was her. I felt like a puppy waiting for their owner to get home. This time, Lottie walked out of the doors of one of the elevators dressed in a light brown sweater that was tucked into a pair of black jeans that tapered at her ankles, showcasing a pair of brown leather booties. Her blonde hair was bouncy and curled at the ends, and the pieces fell perfectly to frame her face.

"How do you look so put together this early in the morning?" I asked her once she got close enough.

"I think by now you would realize I'm a morning person."

The soft smile she gave me brought out one of my own. I watched her eyes drop down to my lips for only a split second before she peered behind me.

"Where are we going?"

"You're just going to have to wait and see," I told her as the two of us emerged into the crisp, fall air of a New York City morning. The car I'd ordered the night before was waiting for us on the curb. Our driver opened the door and I motioned for Lottie to slide in first.

"This feels fancy," she whispered once we were both inside. "Please tell me you didn't spend a bunch of money on this."

"What's the point of having money if you can't spend it on the things that you want to?" I watched her study me carefully as if she were trying to figure out a way to make up for something that she didn't need to make up for. "You wanted to experience life outside of your job, so what better way to start than being driven to the Empire State Building to watch the sunrise."

Those blue eyes widened at the same time her mouth dropped open in shock. I found myself smiling that I'd managed to surprise Charlotte Thompson.

"This is the most I think I've ever seen you smile," she said before she went back to watching the skyline out the window. I should have been annoyed that she pointed out something like that. I hadn't cared these past two years whether people disliked my attitude or not. But for some reason, I found my mouth screwing into a frown at her words because I felt ashamed she even had to tell me that. I wanted to look at the world again with excitement, like Lottie was in that moment.

We left early enough to beat most of the traffic heading into downtown. One of the attendants of the Empire State Building was waiting for us when we pulled up. I watched as Lottie's head tilted back so she could look all the way up to the top of the building that was still lit up from the night before.

"The sunrise should start in about ten minutes," the attendant told us as they ushered us toward the elevator. We climbed a few flights of stairs after we got off the elevator before finally coming to our destination.

Lottie gasped when the attendant stepped out onto the small landing with a railing that circled the top spire. We could see for miles—nearly all the island. Lottie's eyes drank everything in as if she were trying to commit the view to memory. I couldn't blame her, this felt like a once in a lifetime kind of opportunity. The wind was fiercer up here and picked her hair up, sending it flying around her face. She laughed as she grabbed a piece that had fallen over her mouth and tucked it behind her ears.

"Look," I told her when I noticed the first splashes of color breaking across the horizon. I could hear her suck in a breath next to me as a splash of pink threw itself across the sky.

The two of us sat in silence as we watched the sun begin to enter a new day. It was one of those moments where you knew you were witnessing something that would become a lifelong memory in your mental scrapbook, and I was doing it with the perfect person. Neither of us felt the urge to fill the silence as we took in the beauty before us from our perch. It might not have been the place she had originally imagined when she made that bucket list item, but judging from the smile on her face, I wasn't sure she cared.

Chapter 9

Nolan

It was the perfect fall day for a football game. The slight breeze that swirled around inside the stadium smelled like buttered popcorn and hot dogs. Mixed in with those nostalgic fall scents was the smell of sweaty men as both teams crouched down on the line, waiting for me to call for the snap of the ball.

It was the beginning of the fourth quarter, and we were leading comfortably, by two touchdowns. From even before the game started, I was already feeling different about this game than the first week. That familiar flutter of excitement had still filled the bottom of my stomach when I waited in the tunnel to run onto the field with Hawthorn and Derek. But instead of feeling overwhelmed with nerves, I had the smallest amount of confidence from the previous week with Lottie. The time the two of us had spent together putting me through different exercises and drills wouldn't have improved the strength of my knee by much, but it had given me the start of some ideas on how to use my body in ways that I hadn't done before to compensate for the mobility loss my knee injury had caused.

Lottie always came every morning with a new idea. She could have given some NFL coaches a run for their money with how intelligent she was when it came to the game of football. It was clear I may have misjudged her from the jump. By this morning before the game, any doubts I had about the reputation she had earned herself within the industry had faded away. She was ambitious, intelligent, and we shared mutual goals for this season—do whatever it takes to keep me healthy so I can be successful on the field. Lottie let me lead our sessions and was respectful of my reservations toward therapy, even if that went against her way of thinking. She reframed drills for me to understand the practical, real-game application they had. She listened and adjusted plans when I had objections to certain treatments. It was like watching someone who had mastered their craft operating at the highest level.

And by the second touchdown I had thrown before halftime of today's game, I was beginning to think that maybe Charlotte Thompson was magic.

"Set. Hike!" The ball snapped into my hands, and I dropped back three steps into the pocket that my linemen made for me as they blocked the Gladiators' defense. My eyes locked on to Derek, who was open down the field. I started to pull my arm back to throw when I felt a blow to my side. It felt like getting hit by a car as you were standing still. A crack sounded in my ears, and I felt my neck snap back before my body made impact with the ground.

A groan passed my lips as I screwed my eyes shut and tried to will the ringing in my ears to stop. I could feel hands on me as people rolled me onto my back. Voices sounded like they were shouting at me, but they were so far away. Finally, after I willed a few small breaths in through my nose, I cracked my eyes open only to see a pair of vibrant blue eyes staring back at me. They were the same pair of eyes that I was beginning to find myself getting lost in for brief moments whenever I looked into them—similar to what was happening now.

"Nolan, I need you to tell me what hurts." The noise from the stadium began to filter back in as the ringing in my ears faded. My vision widened to take in more than just those blue eyes that reminded me of a beautiful summer sky on a cloudless day. Lottie's face was etched with concern as her eyes scanned my face, waiting for a reaction from me.

"Just got my bell rung," I managed to tell her. My voice was strained with pain that I hadn't yet registered.

"Can you move your arms and legs?" Her hands were on either side of my helmet as she tried to stabilize my head.

"Yes," I told her. I wanted to ease the worry I saw in her eyes as she continued her assessment. "I'm fine, Lottie."

I saw the relief I was looking for pass over her face before the mask of professionalism she was so good at wearing slammed back down.

"We'll need to take you back into the locker room for concussion protocol."

I groaned, but this time not because I was in pain.

"There's four minutes left in the game." My argument was weak. I knew the rules of the NFL. Anytime you were hit in the head, you had to be assessed for a head injury.

"Caleb can handle it. You're up by two scores." I didn't miss the way her voice softened as she mentioned the rookie quarterback. She knew I was having a hard time with realizing that my time in the league was coming to an end quickly and someone would soon take my place.

"Let's get you up," Lottie said. Her face pulled away and I realized just how close she had been leaning over me. Her hand extended toward me, and I reached up to grab it. A feeling of contentment washed over me as I wrapped my hand around hers. Her smaller one fit into mine like a matching puzzle piece. She pulled backwards to give me enough leverage to push myself up onto my feet.

As we began to walk off the field, I realized that both she and Zeke had a protective arm around me as they made sure I didn't fall over on our way to the locker room. Once I was secure on one of the beds in the training room, Lottie told Zeke that she could handle the testing so one of them could still be on the sidelines for the rest of the team.

"I'm beginning to wonder if the football gods have it in for me," I told Lottie once the two of us were alone.

I watched as she started the concussion protocol testing. Her cheeks were flushed a beautiful shade of red. I wasn't sure if she was flushed from the chill in the air today or from the adrenaline of having to run onto the field to reach me.

"This will be good for Caleb to get a few minutes of game time experience," she replied. Spoken like a true sports expert. "You know, you're missing out on helping him out."

"I don't really find pleasure in helping out my replacement," I told her.

"Everyone gets replaced eventually, Nolan. We're all just renting our spots in the jobs we occupy. Someone will replace us on our way out. That's how the world works." I watched the red in her cheeks deepen as she grew more passionate. "You love this organization more than anybody else. You've done your entire career with this team. That's a rare feat. If you took the time to help Caleb prepare for next season, you'd be helping this team."

When she put it in perspective like that, it made me sound like a real asshole.

Lottie turned the computer she was working on toward me so I could test myself against my baseline. She sat across from me with her arms crossed over her chest and a look that would turn anything to ash if it were possible.

"What?" I asked her, as I clicked through the test.

"You need to work with your linemen. That's two weeks in a row you've taken bad hits because of missed blocks." A small smile spread across my lips as I saw the furrow of her brow, the downward skew of her mouth, and the way she stewed in her seat.

"Are you worried about me, Lottie?" I teased her. The small smile broke into a full-blown grin when she scowled even more at my question.

"It's my job to be worried about my athletes," she grumbled back to me.

"You know, it's nice to have someone worry about me," I continued. "It's been a while."

"If you're comparing me to Roger, I'm offended," she told me. "It doesn't sound like he was very good at his job."

"He definitely was not you, Lottie." She blushed again. "But I wasn't comparing you to Roger, I was thinking about the last time someone cared about me protecting myself on the field, which was my ex."

Lottie's eyebrows shot up. "If you're saying your ex cared about you in a clinical way for the success of the team, then she wasn't a very good girlfriend."

"She was my fiancée," I corrected her. "And she's an ex for a reason."

Lottie's mouth snapped shut at my confession out of what I was sure was shock. I hadn't given up much of my personal life to her this past week despite her subtle attempts at trying to learn more about me.

"Let's get you back out there. You passed. You're all clear." Lottie stood up, ending the conversation.

The cheers of the Bobcat fans grew louder when the two of us exited the tunnel back onto the field. There were two minutes left in the game and Caleb was still on the field leading the team in a drive down the field. He had eaten up a lot of the clock and all he needed to do was take a knee and the game would be ours, but it appeared our coach was giving him a chance at scoring his first NFL touchdown.

When coach noticed me standing back on the sidelines, he pushed the microphone attached to his headset away from his mouth.

"He's all clear," Lottie told him.

"Do you want to finish the game?" The question left me at a crossroads. I wanted to play in every minute of this season that I possibly could because with every minute that passed, I was approaching the end. But I knew it would be selfish to take this moment away from Caleb just because I could.

Lottie's words from earlier rang through my head. If you

took the time to help Caleb prepare for next season, you'd be helping the team.

"No, let Caleb finish this drive out." Coach's eyebrows shot up. Last year I wouldn't have even let a thought like that cross my mind. I could also feel Lottie's eyes on me, and I stole a glance in her direction to see what she was thinking.

Her eyes shined bright as a small smile pulled the corners of her mouth upwards. My chest grew warm at the sight and as I turned my attention back to the rookie who was in the middle of passing to an open receiver in the end zone, I knew I had made the right decision. The joy that surged through me as my teammates went wild for the rookie was the first time I felt proud of someone else's accomplishments. I joined in with Derek and Hawthorn as they tried to lift Caleb up onto their shoulders.

Lottie was right, working with Caleb wouldn't take away from my goals and successes this year. It wouldn't take away from the legacy I was trying to leave behind—it would only add to it.

I fought my way through the crowd of my teammates to finally make it to where Caleb had been placed back on his feet. The rookie had taken off his helmet and I could see the way he was eagerly trying to take everything in around him as if he wanted to imprint this moment on his brain forever. I remembered that very feeling after the first game I got to play in the league over a decade ago now. I knew, like many had already said, that Caleb had a long career in front of him and this was only the first of many more moments to come for him.

Once I was close enough, I reached out to pull on his shoulder pad to grab his attention. Caleb's smile changed into a look of concern when he saw me.

"Are you alright, man?"

You are definitely an asshole for ever viewing this kid as some form of competition or reminder of your career ending.

"I'm all good," I told him. "Doc cleared me. I came out just in time to watch you on that last drive. You looked confident as hell."

Caleb's smile returned to his face, now magnified from my compliment. It made me remember how badly I wanted those little scraps of kudos from the people I looked up to when I was in his position, and I was surprised to find myself enjoying giving him a little bit of joy from simply reassuring him that he would be just fine in this league.

I glanced over toward the sideline to see if I could spot Lottie hanging around the corners of the stadium. I caught a glimpse of her blonde ponytail and the navy and red jacket she was wearing today. Her eyes were locked on to me and I knew she must have watched me fight my way through the crowd to get to Caleb.

When she noticed that I was looking at her, she gave me a small nod before disappearing down the tunnel toward the locker room. Charlotte Thompson was helping me with more than just the recovery from a knee injury. She was transforming me into someone who could look back on how he left his career with a smile, no matter the outcome.

Chapter 10

Lottie

After Nolan's near miss of being out for a few weeks due to a concussion, he buckled down on working with his new linemen. He was a man on a mission. Every morning after the win during the second week of the season he would show up for our daily run, go through the exercises and drills I threw at him without any arguments, and then work with his linemen all the way up until it was the scheduled practice time. He was spending almost every waking hour at the practice facility between working on getting himself better prepared, getting his teammates better prepared, and fulfilling his media obligations.

Going into the third game of the season, the attitude among the team was at an all-time high. I noticed fewer people were treading carefully around Nolan during the week. The offense was even starting to come together and work like a single unit. Which was all due to Nolan utilizing the respect he'd garnered from his career for the good of his team.

The team carried that progress into the third game and walked right by the Nashville Smokies in a shutout win. Nolan took a few sacks still during the game, but I watched him get back up without any hesitation before getting back in the huddle with his team and proving to them why he was their leader.

After I had finished all my treatment duties for both Nolan and Derek after the game, I excused myself to get ready for a date that I had agreed to earlier that day. I hadn't given up on the dating app that Maggie and Olivia had set me up on just yet, but all the dates I'd been on thus far had been more disappointing than anything.

I could hear the music kick on in the locker room as I finished applying my makeup, which meant the media were long gone and it was just the team.

My date was in downtown Chicago at an Italian restaurant I hadn't been to yet. My date—Henry, a tech engineer—had suggested it. I had told him that I may be a little late getting there depending on how quickly I could get out of the stadium after the game and the traffic that would allow me to get across town to the restaurant. Henry had gotten at least one point in my book for not asking any questions about how someone like me got a job in the NFL—I'd gotten five of them just this week in my dating app instant messages—and instead told me to take my time.

Maybe chivalry wasn't dead.

The hallway was almost empty with only a few players trickling toward the player parking lot after their postgame showers. The music that had been coming from the locker room turned off as soon as I stepped out into the hallway dressed and ready for what I hoped would be a romantic Italian dinner with Henry.

As I turned to walk to the parking lot where my car was parked, the door to the locker room burst open. Derek, Hawthorn, and Nolan were too busy laughing at whatever they had been talking about before to notice me standing there at first until Derek almost knocked me over.

"Lottie!" Derek exclaimed. "I didn't see you standing there. I'm so sorry."

Derek reached out to steady me before I ended up on the ground.

"You look nice, Lottie." Hawthorn gave me a small nod of approval at the outfit I had planned for tonight's date.

I had picked my favorite black dress and paired it with

my knee-high black boots before topping the outfit off with my double-breasted brown wool coat. My hair was still up in the ponytail I had worn for the game, but I had slicked back any stray hairs that had pulled loose.

"Thanks, Hawthorn. Great game, guys," I told them before trying to excuse myself from the conversation to get to my date on time.

"You have plans tonight?"

I glanced back over my shoulder to see Nolan's eyes roaming over me from my hair to my boots.

"A date actually." I gave Nolan a smile that I hoped relayed that I was still working hard on my goals just like he had been. But instead of him giving me a smile back at the bucket list item I was trying to cross off, he gave me a frown. I could see Derek glancing between me and Nolan as we stared at each other in a familiar standoff.

"Where's your date?" Derek's overly excited question managed to break the tension building between me and Nolan.

"Formento's, over in West Loop. I heard they have one of the best meatballs in town."

"My wife, Sarah, loves that place. We've celebrated every pregnancy there," Hawthorn told me.

Who would have thought Hawthorn was a hopeless romantic?

"I need to get going though so I'm not later than I already am. Henry was nice enough to understand that I was coming from the game."

I heard Nolan scoff from behind me as I turned to walk away. "Henry?"

I didn't bother giving him a response. He knew that the only date I'd had so far had been a dud and this one could very well be more of the same, but who was he to judge? I had withheld my judgement when it came to his actions so far this season. I had stood by and proudly watched him try to change himself for the better.

Couldn't he do the same for me?

"Have fun!" Derek called after me, in a suspiciously happy tone.

Henry had already ordered one of the more expensive bottles of wine by the time that I arrived. But by the end of the salad appetizer, there was still no spark between the two of us.

He was the perfect picture of charming, with blonde hair and blue eyes, a button-down shirt that was tucked into a pair of khakis, and a blindingly white smile. But when the conversation mostly centered around the finance app that he was currently building for his new company, I realized that I would need more than one bottle of wine to get through this dinner.

Only during the main course did Henry finally decide he would ask me about my own life after he'd told me nearly every detail of his own.

"So, you work for the Chicago Bobcats?"

"I'm their in-house physical therapist," I told him.

"Do you think you'll always stay in sports? Or do you think you'll go into private practice in the future?" I watched Henry twirl his spaghetti around his fork using a spoon and knew the two of us had grown up in very different households. "I think you could get a lot more money in private practice and potentially have some well-connected clients. It's who you know in the business world."

"I think I'll stay in professional sports for as long as I can. It's where my heart is."

Henry's eyes were more focused on his spaghetti than on me. "Football is a dying sport, Charlotte. All the aftereffects that are starting to become known from head injuries are bound to run that sport into the ground."

I cringed at the use of my full name. Nobody used my full name other than my father, and that wasn't exactly the reminder I wanted during a date. I had even asked Henry to call me Lottie at the beginning of the date, but it seemed he insisted on using Charlotte instead.

Any response I had died on my lips as I stared at him with my mouth slightly agape. I'd never had a problem standing up for myself about how I'd earned the right to be in the profession I was, but that had always been with people who weren't a part of my life. They weren't supposed to champion me and my life the way a true partner or my family were supposed to. I had never had to defend myself with anyone that was supposed to care about me.

Suddenly I recognized the feeling churning in my stomach. It was the same way I had felt when my father had called me by my full name and laughed when I told him that I wanted to play football—only because I wanted to spend more time with him. If I showed interest in what he loved, maybe he'd love me too. My father had always looked down on any interest of mine that I tried to share with him, and the way Henry wrote off the profession I had worked so hard on my entire life had me feeling like I was a little kid again looking for recognition.

"Excuse me," the waiter interrupted, which I couldn't have been more grateful for in the moment, "but this bottle of whiskey was sent from the table over there in the back. They mentioned that you may enjoy your dinner with something a little stronger than wine."

I followed the waiter's hand motion to see three men that I thought I had left at Gateway Stadium. Derek had on a pair of sunglasses and a wide smile, while Hawthorn and Nolan both looked like children who had been caught red-handed. My eyes narrowed as Derek waved at me.

"Excuse me," I told Henry. I ignored his protests and questions of where I was going as I stalked across the dining room toward the table in the corner.

Hawthorn looked like he was trying to somehow pass through the wall he was sitting against while Nolan avoided making eye contact. Derek lowered his sunglasses once I was right on top of them.

"What the *hell* are you guys doing?"

"Did you like the whiskey?" Derek asked.

"Why are you guys here?" I asked again.

"I thought the whiskey was a nice thought," Hawthorn added casually, as if the three of them hadn't just been spying on my date. "That man looked like he wouldn't let you get a word in and in my experience, whiskey is a much better drink for situations like that."

I pinched the skin between my eyebrows and let my eyes drift closed as I took in a deep breath. When I opened them again, I met a pair of rich brown ones that looked at me with an emotion I hadn't seen from them before—concern.

But why would Nolan Hill be concerned about me? Why would he care?

"I am currently on a date with a man who is a tech engineer that I'm trying to figure out if I want to go on a second date with and you *three*"—I pointed at each in turn—"will not ruin this for me. Don't you have somewhere else you could be to celebrate your win?"

"I don't think there is anywhere else we'd rather be."

I wanted to rip the cheeky grin on Derek's face right off. "You are unbelievable!" A few dinner patrons gave us curious glances as my voice began to rise to what my mother would have told me was not an "inside voice."

"And you—" I turned to glare accusingly at Nolan. "You of all people know what doing this means to me, even if Henry isn't going to be the person I end up marrying."

Nolan's eyes bored into mine as the table fell silent. Finally, he cleared his throat—his eyes never leaving mine. "You deserve to be going out on dates with someone who's interested in *you*, Lottie. Someone who's interested in what you have to say and knows exactly who they're on a date with. Someone who would never take that for granted. That's who you deserve to go on a date with. Not someone like Henry."

I saw Hawthorn's eyebrows shoot up at Nolan's comments and Derek's lips twitched upwards, as if he was fighting to keep a smile off his face.

You deserve to be going out on dates with someone who's interested in you, Lottie.

I wasn't sure why my heart was racing at such a simple endearing sentence, but it took nearly an entire minute before I was able to trust myself to speak again.

"Thank you for the sentiment, but I'm going to go back to my date now and for my sake, please don't remind me that you're here if you stay."

Nolan's jaw clenched and that same muscle jumped in his jaw from whenever I did something that annoyed him. Everyone had to kiss a few frogs to find their prince. Who was Nolan to judge me for that?

When I returned to Henry with an apology ready, he waved me off and told me that my absence gave him time to order us dessert. The waiter set down a tiramisu that looked delicious, but I couldn't focus on the decadent flavors that exploded in my mouth while I ate it because all I could feel were a pair of eyes on my back for the rest of my date.

Chapter 11

Nolan

"So, are we still not going to talk about how you had to death-grip the table on Sunday night at dinner when Henry and Lottie left?" Derek asked me as the two of us walked toward the practice facility to get some extra work in with Hawthorn the following Wednesday.

I knew he was only asking to get on my nerves and, well, it worked.

"I was not death-gripping the table when they left," I growled at him.

Derek's smile grew wider. "And you also didn't tell Lottie that Henry wasn't good enough for her because you care even the smallest bit about who she's on dates with?"

"Also no." I could feel heat spread across my chest, up my neck, and into my face as I tried to convince myself of something that I had come to realize this week might not be true.

"You're the one that even suggested we go to Formento's, remember?" I tried to remind Derek.

When I had first met Lottie, I didn't have anything against her personally. Her position was simply a reminder of the worst parts of myself that I didn't know how to fix. Now that she and I were beginning to work through the mess that I was, I was beginning to realize that maybe she wasn't as bad as I originally thought. That's all.

She was simply becoming someone I cared about like a

friend, which was why I hated watching her leave with that tech idiot who didn't even hold the door open for her when they left.

"And you haven't gone from Nolan the Grinch to Nolan the Elf these last few weeks because of her?" Derek continued to press as we walked toward the locker room.

"It's only September. Why are you comparing me to Christmas characters?"

Luckily, Derek's line of questioning was silenced for the time being when we walked into the locker room to find Hawthorn talking with Caleb Willis.

"Hey, guys," I slipped back into my approachable team captain hat now that Caleb was present. "What's going on?"

"I just wanted to come in to get some extra work," Caleb told me as he laced up his cleats. "I've realized the size of the shoes I'm going to have to fill next year, and I think I'm going to need more practice than just what I'm doing during the week with the coaches."

The look that Hawthorn was giving me behind Caleb's back pushed a sigh out of me. My distaste toward the kid might have been a little unnecessary.

"We're getting in extra work today too," I told him. "You can join us. Derek can run a few routes for you."

Caleb's face lit up at the invite and I ignored the small part of me that felt guilty. I could have been lifting him up from the beginning of the season if I had just gotten out from behind myself.

"We'll meet you out there," Hawthorn told Caleb as he slapped the rookie on the shoulder.

As soon as the locker room door shut behind us, Hawthorn gave me the kind of smile that I wanted to wipe right off his face. "What's gotten into you these past few weeks? First you want to throttle Lottie's date for treating her poorly, then you extend an olive branch to Caleb after avoiding him like the plague all season."

"You and I both know it's not a *what* but a *who*." Derek

shared a smile with Hawthorn. Now I wanted to throttle both of them.

"For the last time," I ground out. "None of this has anything to do with Lottie. She's a great person and she's gone out of her way to help me figure my shit out. The least I can do is help her with hers."

Hawthorn and Derek exchanged a knowing look but were smart enough this time to keep their mouths shut.

"Lottie and I are like oil and water." I'm not sure why I felt the need to try to convince my two friends how Lottie and I would be the worst possible idea ever, but here I was. "She may be one of the most intelligent people I know, but she drives me crazy whenever she manages to outsmart me on something. Then she gives me this smirk like she knows she's beat me that makes me want to rip my hair out. We argue constantly. It would be a nightmare."

"Whatever you need to say to make yourself believe it." Derek gave me a sympathetic pat on the back before he went to jog down the field for his warmup.

"You get it, right?" I asked Hawthorn. "You and Sarah are like the perfect complements for each other. Lottie and I are most definitely not. I'm not sure why Derek won't let it go."

Hawthorn studied me for a few beats, as if he were debating on how he wanted to break something to me. "Let's not forget those few months when Sarah and I fought all the time because we were trying to get comfortable with each other. And let's also not forget that I would die for that woman if I had to. There's not a single other soul on this planet that understands me down to my very core. Blending two lives together can be difficult. You must learn how to mold some of the worst parts of yourself to be better suited for the person you're with. Because sometimes the perfect person for you is the person who will call you on all your bullshit."

My friend jogged away from me, leaving me standing there dumbfounded at his words. I had been counting on Hawthorn to call Derek crazy. Instead, Hawthorn had only caused me more confusion. This past month with Lottie had challenged me. She'd called me out on how I was trying to operate this season. She had forced me to be honest with myself and question if I was going to look back on this season with pride or regret. I didn't even want to try and unpack why I'd found myself caring about those stupid dates she'd been taking herself on. If I looked too closely, I was scared I'd have to put a name to what was happening.

"Thanks again for doing this." Caleb's voice pulled me away from the thoughts of a blonde-haired girl.

"I had plenty of people take the time to mentor me when I first joined the league," I told him. "It's only right if I pay it back."

For the rest of the morning, Caleb and I ran through different plays to help him get better acquainted with the offense that our coach ran. I was impressed with how eager he was to learn. His intuitive questions and ability to pick up on different things quickly reminded me a little bit of myself when I first entered the league. We both had a tenacious need to learn as much as possible with a ridiculous athletic ability that I knew would take Caleb as far as mine took me.

Derek and I walked him through different scenarios, and I was impressed by how smart he was when it came to football. The hours flew by as I coached Caleb on everything from his form to his timing. I felt more energized by the time we decided to call it quits than after returning from a bye week, and as the four of us walked out of the practice facility together, I wondered how I could ever leave football behind after this season.

It was what made up the very essence of myself. It was what I was *good* at. How was I supposed to find something else that made me feel the way sharing my knowledge of the game with someone else did?

Chapter 12

Lottie

The first week in October was like a religion when it comes to baseball. Fall was not only in full swing, but for sports fans, it was the start of playoffs. Lucky for Chicago, the Cougars managed to come away with the divisional win and had positioned themselves well in the postseason.

Maggie and Olivia had stayed true to their word and gotten me tickets to the Cougars' first postseason game. However, they did more than just snag me tickets. Olivia, being the marketing mastermind that she was, convinced her boss to give an entire box to anyone from the Bobcats that wanted to come and support the Cougars the Monday night after the team won their fourth game of the season. The coach had given everyone the day off after the win and nearly everyone had been excited to spend their time cheering on their fellow Chicago sports team.

But of course, Olivia had to take a potentially fun day for me and make it a point of her enjoyment when she insisted I bring a date to the game. So instead of enjoying a beer and a hot dog while cheering on people that I considered my friends, I was listening to Cole talk about how he'd been a lifelong Cougars fan after his grandfather took him to his first game as a kid. Surprisingly, it was the first date I'd been on that I was enjoying, even with Derek, Hawthorn, and Nolan eyeing me the entire time from the other side of the box.

"Is that your sister?" Cole asked me as he spotted Olivia taking pictures from the visitor's dugout.

"That's her!" I waved like a maniac until Olivia noticed me and waved back.

"You two seem like you really love each other," he noted. "I've always wanted a sibling, being an only child and all."

"She can be a pain in my ass sometimes, but I love her."

The roar of the crowd stopped me from saying anything else as Tommy Mikals sent a ball flying over the outfield fence, giving the Cougars the lead. Popcorn went flying as the guys around me cheered louder than the fans in front of us. Their enthusiasm was enough for the Cougars' media team to put our box on the Jumbotron, earning an even bigger cheer from the crowd when they realized the Bobcats were here.

Cole tried to speak over the noise. "This might be the most epic first date ever."

I admired Cole's hazel eyes and dark brown hair that was cut close to his head. He was one of the more attractive men I'd gone on a date with. But there still weren't any butterflies in my stomach when I looked at him.

"You think so?" I gave him what I hoped was a flirtatious smile. Cole returned a smile of his own that gave me enough confidence to believe that he was interested in me too. Maybe he'd be the first date so far on this escapade that would make it to a second one.

"How often did you say you get tickets to these games?" Cole's eyes were locked on Jamil Edman as he stepped into the box. Jamil was having the best season he'd ever had in his career. He'd broken multiple MLB records so far and was on target to break a few more. He had skyrocketed into stardom over the last few months and had become a fan favorite player.

"I'm not sure. Olivia didn't mention. I had a deal with her for these tickets," I told him.

"Well, maybe you can make another deal with your sister

for more." Cole leaned toward me with a twinkle in his eye. "Then maybe we can do this again for a second date."

My hopes blossomed when I realized that I hadn't been imagining it when I thought Cole was interested in me. I ignored the fact that he hadn't asked me many questions about myself; maybe he was too distracted by the game or the fact that it seemed like Nolan always had one eye on the two of us as if he were waiting to intervene again.

At least this time he and his friends didn't try to do any reconnaissance.

After the game, Cole and I walked toward his car. The anticipation was building quickly inside of me the closer we got. The back of Cole's hand brushed mine and for the first time that day I felt a tingle race up my arm at his touch.

Would he kiss me?

Do I want him to?

"I had a great time today," Cole told me once we stopped in front of a modest blue sedan that looked like it had been driven for many miles.

"Me too." Which wasn't exactly a lie. I did have fun watching the Cougars win the first game of their three-game series to move on to the next round of the playoffs.

Cole stepped forward and I knew instantly that he was going to kiss me. I held my breath and watched as he got closer and closer until I let my eyes flutter shut. His lips pressed awkwardly against mine at first but after we relaxed, I realized he was quite a good kisser.

When the two of us pulled away, I watched his eyes lock on to something over my shoulder.

"Hi, man. I was hoping I could meet you before the day was over." I turned around to see Nolan coolly assessing Cole. "The season has been going great this year."

"Thanks," Nolan replied curtly as he stared directly at Cole.

When Cole realized that Nolan wasn't going to elaborate any further, he gave me an awkward wave before jumping in his car. I watched him roll the window down with a manual lever once he was inside.

"I'll message you," he called after me as he started to drive away.

"And you should ignore it," I heard Nolan tell me from behind.

I turned around to face him. "What the fuck is that supposed to mean?" I asked him.

Nolan looked at me like the answer to my question was obvious. "He's using you."

I clenched my fists to try and reel in the irritation building inside of me. First, he showed up with Hawthorn and Derek to my date at Formento's. Then he had the audacity to tell me that this date was using me and wasn't worth my time. I took a couple of breaths to try and control what came out of my mouth next.

"No, he's not," I argued with him. "I think he was really interested in me. I wouldn't mind going on another date with him. He might need one more to really warm up."

"That man had more of a hard-on for Jamil Edman than he ever will for you."

My mouth dropped open. "He kissed me, Nolan! And he leaned toward me practically the entire date. He was interested in me." I was beginning to wonder if I was losing my sanity when it came to Nolan Hill, because why did I feel the need to justify *my* date with him?

"That was not leaning, Lottie."

I watched a complicated mix of emotions cross Nolan's face as his eyes looked off into the distance. His eyebrows pulled together as if he were debating what he wanted to say next. The moment seemed to stretch on forever until his eyes drifted down to meet mine. His nostrils flared and I swore I could see his brown eyes turn nearly black.

Nolan closed the distance between the two of us until his large body took up every square inch of my vision. He was close enough that I could smell hints of cashmere and vanilla, close enough that I could see gold flecks in his brown eyes, and the wrinkles around them that he'd gotten from the way they crinkled when he smiled.

"This is leaning." His breath came out on a whisper as his head bowed down toward mine. His lips were a breath's width away from mine and I could feel the weight of his words as he spoke.

The air whooshed out of my lungs and my body froze in place as I was stuck in the center of Nolan's gaze. My heart beat so wildly I was afraid I was about to go into cardiac arrest.

Did Nolan know CPR?

"You're not just entering someone's space, Lottie." The only sign that Nolan was anywhere near as affected as I was in this moment was the rise and fall of his chest. His chest barely brushed against mine with each inhale, but every minuscule amount of contact set my chest on fire. "You're taking the first move and initiating that first display of affection. It's about the other person accepting that person's invitation, just like you are now. It's about being vulnerable."

My eyes widened when I realized that I had drawn closer to him and that was why there were only centimeters between us. The second Nolan had entered my personal bubble, he'd become my sun and I'd been brought closer into his gravitational pull. Suddenly I was keenly aware of how attractive Nolan Hill was—the sharp jawline, the way he smiled with his entire face, and those long lashes that framed his dark brown eyes.

As quickly as Nolan first stepped toward me, he was gone in a flash, suddenly five steps away from me. I was left flushed and disoriented as I tried to pull myself together. Tried to tell myself that I needed to put even more space between us. Tried to tell myself this wasn't professional. What if someone saw us? What would they say? I could get be fired.

My brain was spinning out of control, unable to keep my eyes off Nolan's tongue as it slipped out of his mouth and wet his lips, while every warning bell was going off inside of my head.

This was never supposed to happen. I was better than this—lusting after a player. But that still didn't stop the thundering of my heart as Nolan clenched his fists together like he was trying to keep himself from reaching out for me one more time.

"He wasn't giving you that, Lottie." Nolan's voice came out gruff and I noticed just how flushed he was as well.

Before I could get a word out, Nolan turned on his heel and left me standing there with the mess of thoughts bouncing around inside my head. I watched him weave between the cars still in the parking lot before disappearing long before I finally felt like I could move.

My fireplace crackled in the background as it tried to take the slight chill out of the air that had crept into Chicago with the beginning days of fall. The leaves outside of my apartment window had even started to show hints of oranges and reds. Olivia and Maggie had covered themselves with blankets as they lounged around my living room.

"So, you're telling us that Nolan Hill looked like he wanted to devour you?" Olivia asked from where she sat on my couch with a bowl of popcorn.

"I never said that," I sighed, as I continued to stare at the ceiling of my living room from where I lay in the middle of the floor.

Maggie reminded me of how I had recounted the turn of events after the game. "You said he was staring at you intensely and then basically tried to sweep you off your feet."

Once I finally snapped myself out of whatever trance Nolan had put me in, I had immediately called Olivia to see if she was still at the stadium. Maggie overheard me telling her what happened and declared that to unpack the events that had unfolded we needed popcorn and wine.

"He *was* staring at me intensely. I've never seen Nolan

look at anything like that before. Not even during a game," I told them.

"Do you think he likes you?" Olivia tossed a piece of popcorn up into the air and caught it in her mouth.

"I thought he hated me when we first started working together. Recently, I thought that we were moving past tolerant to amicable. I never, in a million years, would have told you I thought Nolan Hill found me attractive. I just thought . . ." I trailed off when I remembered how Nolan had looked at me on the date that they crashed. He'd looked almost territorial as he watched me from across the room. Then again when he saw me still dressed from my previous date before New York—he'd looked like he was seeing me in a new light.

"He did take you to the top of the Empire State Building." Maggie was taking this all entirely too seriously. "That had to be the most intimate moment ever. I could just imagine the scene playing out in a romance movie."

"I wouldn't call it intimate. It felt more like a peace offering for our relationship, like he was acknowledging that I was helping him with his goals, so he wanted to do the same for me."

"I wish I could have been there to see the unflappable Nolan Hill get flustered by my older sister." Olivia had a cheeky smile as she tried to picture what I had just lived through.

"What are you going to do about it?" Maggie asked me.

"Nothing. There's nothing I can do about it," I told her. "That would be messy."

"Maybe you need a little messy in your life, sis." Olivia cocked an eyebrow at me in challenge.

"I said I needed to live life a bit more, not turn my entire life into a giant clusterfuck."

Olivia only shrugged her shoulders before she tossed another piece of popcorn into her mouth. "It would only be a clusterfuck if people found out. Look at Maggie, she and Tommy hid the truth of their very fake relationship to the entire world."

"Not very well," I reminded her.

"Hey!" Maggie exclaimed. I raised an eyebrow at her, daring her to tell me otherwise. "That's fair," she sighed, and sank back into the couch cushions.

I wasn't about to take my turn at hiding a relationship with a professional athlete. That was the last thing I needed to spice up my life. All I had in mind was seeing more of the world, not risking everything I'd spent so long building.

But I knew that I feared more than just that. The way my entire body had wanted to turn into putty at Nolan's feet the moment he entered my personal space or the way I immediately wondered what it would be like if he had just kissed me had me panicking.

When I first started this dating journey for the bucket list, I hadn't fully realized the fear I had around it. The thought of falling in love with someone only to grow bitter and hateful like my parents lived in the back of my mind like a parasite. It wasn't until Nolan approached me in the parking lot that I recognized those feelings in myself. Maybe there was a good reason I hadn't dated anyone all these years. Maybe subconsciously I knew that was what would bring me the least potential of pain.

"How am I supposed to face him after this?" I whispered to Maggie and Olivia. Their faces softened as they looked at me.

Olivia reached out and squeezed my hand to reassure me in the same way I had done to her all those years when she was a kid. "Just act like nothing happened."

"We made so much progress on our relationship. What if he goes back to trying to avoid me? What if he thinks it will be awkward?" The question had been bouncing around in my head from the moment he had turned away from me in that parking lot. I was worried I'd be starting all over with him. I'd grown up to be skeptical of relationships after watching each of my parents fail the other. One day they'd both woken up and decided to stop choosing the other. They viewed their relationship as a mistake. I'd promised myself at a young age that I would never find myself in a similar situation. If I found the person who would stand next to me, no matter what, I was going to choose them every day.

"Then he's a complete idiot." Maggie moved to lie on the ground next to me and shortly after Olivia followed suit. The two wrapped their arms around me and I finally let the worries I'd been carrying with me slip away.

Chapter 13

Nolan

I was back to avoiding Lottie in the practice facility all because of my stupid impulses and embarrassment. I'd managed to slip around her schedule by coming to the facility a little later for my run and going through all the exercises that she normally ran me through by myself. I cornered Zeke into giving me treatment while Lottie was busy with Derek or another player. All while I found myself missing our weekly routine and her easy banter that always put me at ease during practices.

During the game the following Sunday, Lottie had picked up on me avoiding her and simply left me alone. I'd felt unsteady the entire game from being out of the routine that Lottie and I had been using. Somehow, we'd still managed to pull out a win, moving us to five wins and no losses so far in the season.

The following week heading into Monday night's game for week six was much of the same, except this time Lottie seemed to make herself scarce when it came to my schedule.

I thought the space would bring me some clarity and help both of us forget about the line that I had almost crossed. Instead, it only seemed to make everything worse. I became acutely aware of her absence while I tried to avoid her. Then I became so painfully aware of when she was near me that I couldn't focus on much of anything else. At practice my eyes would drift to where she stood on the sidelines instead of to my receivers. I watched the leaves turn from green to vibrant shades of reds and oranges as I went on our daily run by myself through the neighborhood by the practice facility as I continued to give the two of us space. I felt like I was back to square one with all the progress I had made slipping away from me.

Unfortunately, I hadn't managed to get my focus under control for our sixth game. I'd thrown two interceptions by halftime and when I sat in the locker room listening to our coach grill us on what changes we needed to make for the rest of the game, all I could think about was how desperately I wanted one of Lottie's pep talks right now. But once again, she was nowhere to be found.

The second half of the game didn't go any different than the first. The Orlando Dream handed us our first loss of the season. The silence in the locker room was deafening. It was always the hardest to deal with the first loss of the season and it was both a wonderful and terrible thing that it was happening so far in. Slowly, the team trickled out of the locker room toward the team bus that would take us back to the airport and home.

Eventually it was only Derek and me left.

"Do you want to talk about it?" Derek was sitting in the cubby of the locker he was using, fully dressed for the plane. It looked like he had been waiting for me this entire time.

"Not really," I told him. I let my eyes drift closed for a second to try and will away the itch in my head that was Charlotte Thompson. It was an itch I couldn't quite seem to scratch.

"Well, too fucking bad, because I'm going to make you talk about it anyways."

Derek raised both eyebrows as an invitation for me to start talking and explain why I'd been so out of sorts this past week. I let out a sigh as I took off the remainder of my clothes from the game. I knew I was stalling because I was afraid the moment I admitted to Derek that I was pretty sure all of this centered around Lottie, he'd grow excited and I didn't need that version of him right now.

Surprisingly, Derek waited patiently for me to speak instead of trying to pester the truth out of me. My chest felt tight as I tried to figure out how to get the words out. I'd never been vulnerable with my friends when it came to my personal life. I'd only ever spoken with them about our jobs and nothing more.

"This all feels ridiculous and I'm honestly ashamed I let this all affect our jobs," I started as I tried to navigate the conversation.

"But you like Lottie and don't know what to do about it?" Derek filled in for me once he saw how hard it was for me to admit any of this.

"I may have crossed the line with her after the Cougars game," I told him. "I don't know when it started, but I think I like her, Derek."

Derek gave me a small smile; it was one of the sincerest smiles he'd ever given me. "I was wondering when you'd finally admit it. I thought it would have been sooner than this."

"None of that matters right now," I waved him off. "Right now, I need to figure out how to fix things with Lottie. I made her uncomfortable at the game. Now I'm too much of a coward to face her and it's impacting the team."

"How do you know you made her uncomfortable?" Derek asked me.

My brows pulled together as I looked at him like he'd lost his mind. "I invaded her space without asking her and I probably put her in an uncomfortable position when she realized a player had feelings for her."

"How do you know that she cares about that? How do you know she doesn't feel the same way?" Derek pressed on. "You chose to avoid her this past week instead of just asking her. You're retiring after this season, Nolan. You're not going to be a player in four months, but you will have the rest of your life ahead of you."

Derek stood up from his locker. "Go take a quick shower. We've got a plane to catch." He paused in the doorway to the locker room. "Maybe you should think about what it is you want from life once this season is done outside of a career, Nolan. Then maybe you should give your window seat away again tonight."

The door to the locker room swung closed and left me standing alone in the Orlando Dream's visitor's locker room.

Even though I was the last player out of the locker room, I wasn't the last person on the plane. That title was still held by Lottie once she finished getting all the team's medical supplies loaded. She scanned the plane like our first flight to New York and it felt like déjà vu when our eyes locked and the window seat next to me was open.

I watched her glance around the plane as she tried to spy another open seat before she realized she was out of luck. She sucked in a breath and let it out with a sigh before she started to heft her carry-on luggage into the storage compartment above us. I quickly reached out for her bag as she struggled to get it to slide into the open spot.

"Here, let me."

Red flushed Lottie's cheeks as she watched me pluck her bag from her hands and easily slide it into the overhead compartment. Her mouth screwed together as she eyed the window seat before she pulled her shoulders back like she was walking to her death instead of sliding into a seat next to me.

"Hi," I told her once I was buckled back in.

"Hi." Her voice was barely more than a whisper and her eyes were glued on the tarmac.

"It's nice to see you." I felt like I was walking on eggshells after not having spoken to her in so long.

Lottie scoffed next to me before slowly turning to spear me with a gaze that could have melted the faux leather of the chair I was sitting on. "Oh yes, Nolan. It's so nice *finally* seeing you after you've avoided me. You act as if we're just two ships passing in the night after you expertly took every possible avenue to not see me at all!"

Quiet rage was coming off Lottie in waves and heat simmered in her eyes. Any sane person would have feared whatever she was about to do, but I found myself trapped in her gaze as if it were a trance.

"I'm sorry for that," I told her, somehow finding a way to get the words out.

"Sorry for what exactly, Nolan?" Now that Lottie had gotten started, it was clear she wasn't stopping. "What happened for you to ignore me? I thought you cared more about your season than that. But here we are with a loss that was totally preventable. You looked lost out there today!"

Leave it to Lottie to not only be hurt by my actions but still not be afraid to call me out on it.

"I don't know how to really say this," I started as I tried to find the right path forward. The last thing I wanted to do was make Lottie even more uncomfortable if I had been right and Derek had been wrong. "I'm sorry for what I said and did after the Cougars game. That was crossing a line. We were just starting to get to a good place as working partners and I would like to get back to that. I was afraid I'd made you uncomfortable, so I just wanted to give you space."

"Oh," Lottie replied quietly.

Oh?

Was she not uncomfortable?

Did she not think anything of it and I just brought it up as if it had been some big deal?

Was I overanalyzing everything right now?

Before Lottie could say anything else to send me spiraling even further, I filled the silence that was stretching out between us.

"Like I said, I'm sorry. So can we just get back to how things were before?"

Lottie stayed silent for so long after my question that I began to panic. My eyes darted from her face to where Derek was trying to watch us inconspicuously. He flashed me a thumbs up when he noticed me looking, oblivious to the distress on my face.

"Just friends?" Lottie finally replied.

I sat there for a moment before I said anything back because I was beginning to realize that the last thing I wanted to be with Lottie was "just friends". I couldn't deny any longer that I was attracted to her—from the way her blonde hair looked gold when the sun hit it just right, or the way her blue eyes looked like the sky on a perfect summer day, or the way her pink lips seemed to hypnotize me whenever they spread open into a smile or screwed together when she was thinking hard about something. Not to mention that she was the smartest person I knew, and I could sit and listen to her talk for hours.

I wasn't sure what it was exactly I wanted to be with Lottie, but I knew being friends wasn't it—but judging by the relief I saw on her face, it was the right thing to do.

"Friends." I gave her a quick nod of agreement and waited for what she would say. Even if I knew trying to be just friends with Lottie might be harder for me than the inevitable end of my football career.

"Then I'll see you tomorrow for our run?" The soft smile she gave me would have sent me to my knees out of gratitude if I wasn't already sitting.

"I'll be there."

If today's game was any proof, having Lottie in my life as a friend was better than not having her in it at all.

Chapter 14

Lottie

Everything seemed to have gone back to the way it was during those early weeks between me and Nolan. After Nolan had apologized to me on the plane back from Orlando, he faithfully showed up every morning for our run and stayed for treatment afterward. Even after the team's first loss, Nolan didn't miss a beat with coaching his team on how to move forward from it. He was the most outspoken during film, pointing out the team's mistakes—and most importantly his own—while offering how they could make the proper changes or implement strategies to stop the train wreck that happened against the Orlando Dream from happening again.

He was a true leader.

While I couldn't help but be happy for him and the progress he'd made, my mind hadn't moved on from our conversation on the flight home. Even two weeks later, my mind was still playing through our conversation and if I had done the right thing.

When Nolan had first brought up the conversation, I had been furious. I had left the Cougars game wondering if he was interested in me, but then was nearly devastated when he avoided me. I had grown certain that he'd regretted whatever had transpired between us in that parking lot. I had even started to wonder if I had imagined the tension that had built up between us when there had been less than an inch between our bodies. I would have thought that he'd confirmed my theory for me with his apology if it hadn't been for the way his eyes had kept darting down to my lips.

I had to agree with Nolan's suggestion. We could be colleagues and nothing more. But that didn't stop me from staring a few seconds too long at him after our run this morning when he'd lifted his shirt to swipe at the sweat on his forehead once we'd gotten back to the facility.

I had even stopped responding to any messages I got on my dating app over the past week. None of them seemed of any interest to me after I had started to realize that I had feelings for Nolan Hill, even if they couldn't be acted upon.

Olivia and Maggie had both noticed my lack of suitors, but I had written it off on the season getting busier, which seemed to tide them over for now. That still didn't stop them from forcing me out of my apartment on a Friday night the following week to celebrate the Cougars going to the World Series. I would have blown them off if it hadn't been for them inviting nearly all the Bobcats as well.

Derek had cornered me in the training room and begged me to go after I had told him I had plans to curl up with a cup of tea and book tonight after practice. He ended up being quite convincing and that night I found myself in a bar in downtown Chicago that the Cougars had bought out instead of curled up with a good book at home. It had been decorated to celebrate Halloween, even though it was a few days after Halloween and no one was wearing costumes.

"I'm so glad that you came!" Olivia exclaimed.

We were sitting in a large circular booth with Maggie, Tommy, Adam, Jamil, Nolan, Derek, and Hawthorn. Both the Cougars and Bobcats were slowly trickling into the bar as the night started to get underway.

It wasn't that I didn't like going out. Olivia had invited me out with the Cougars before and I genuinely enjoyed all the guys. Tommy was always sober nowadays and was fun to have a conversation with about sports. Jamil was a lot like Derek—outgoing and typically turned into the life of the party whenever he started drinking. I had never been around Adam Steel before because he never usually went out with his team. Tonight seemed to be an exception of his normal rule.

I was surrounded by great company, but it wasn't the sum of the party I had wanted to avoid tonight. It was one person in particular—Nolan Hill. I was afraid that if I consumed any alcohol, I would do something that would jeopardize all the work he and I had done to get back on good terms with our working relationship. The last thing we needed was for me to put him in an uncomfortable position by drunkenly telling him I thought the white t-shirt and Bobcats letterman jacket he was wearing might have been the hottest combination I'd ever seen.

Olivia and I had been among the first to arrive after the two of us got ready at my apartment. The moment I saw Nolan Hill walk in, my entire body lit up like that navy and red letterman jacket had been a Molotov cocktail thrown directly at me. I somehow managed to suppress the groan that wanted to escape from my lips at the sight of him tonight, so I didn't draw any suspicion from my sister.

That was also on the list of last things I needed.

I wasn't sure when it happened. It must have been somewhere between Nolan Hill cornering me in the parking lot outside of the Cougars' game and him telling me he just wanted to be friends, but there was a heightened awareness of how attractive Nolan was and how I couldn't do anything about it.

This was not a situation I thought I'd ever find myself in—attracted to one of my players, to one of my *clients*—and I was suddenly on uncharted grounds. I had been trying to dodge Nolan's eye contact from the second he walked in, because I was afraid that if he looked at me, he'd realize that I very much did not want to be "just friends" with him.

Avoiding eye contact became even harder when I started to feel the weight of his gaze on my face. Suddenly, it was far too warm in the bar for my leather jacket and tank top.

"Can we get a round of tequila shots?" Olivia asked the waiter when he stopped by to replace the bottle of champagne on the table, compliments of the Cougars c-suite.

When the tray of shots was dispersed among the table, I tried to wave mine off, but my sister was even more intimidating than Nolan Hill was on my first day with the Bobcats.

"You are having *fun* tonight." Olivia emphasized the word fun by aggressively placing the shot of tequila in front of me.

I slowly glanced up to find Nolan watching me, his eyes narrowed as if he were trying to figure something out. The second our eyes met, the entire table melted away and for just a moment it was only the two of us. I was grateful he was all the way across the table from me because I wasn't sure I would keep my hands to myself.

My hand wrapped around the shot glass and brought it up to my lips, our eye contact only breaking when I tipped my head back to let the sharp liquor slide down the back of my throat. I could vaguely hear Olivia cheer next to me as she watched me down the shot, but I could only focus on a pair of intense brown eyes as they stared back at me.

"I'll take one more of these," I told the waiter as I lifted the shot glass up.

Once the second shot of tequila was gone, I pulled Olivia out of the booth and motioned for Maggie to detach herself from her boyfriend to come up with us. There were a few of the players' wives on the dance floor, but for the most part there wasn't much dancing happening tonight—just a large amount of alcohol being consumed as the celebration continued.

The only solution to quell the pressure building in my chest with being near Nolan tonight was to put some physical distance between the two of us. Olivia and Maggie must not have noticed anything unusual because the two threw their hands up in the air as they began to dance to the song that was pumping through the bar's speakers.

I let myself get lost in the thumps of the bass notes as I laughed at Maggie's poor attempt at twerking. Tommy was probably losing his mind trying not to walk over and throw her over his shoulder to haul her off the dance floor. My hands ran through my hair to lift it off my neck to cool myself off as I swayed my hips to the beat of the song. My eyes drifted closed as the pressure in my chest from Nolan finally eased enough for me to enjoy myself.

Three songs passed by before Olivia and Maggie left the dance floor to get another drink at the bar, leaving me alone. I didn't mind though, because for the first time in months, I felt exhilarated by the energy around me. Just for tonight, I wanted to live in the moment. For once in my life, I didn't even mind any of the eyes that I felt watching me as I enjoyed the warmth of the tequila buzzing through my body and a good song.

The next song was a slow jam with a deep bass and just as I began to twirl in a circle, a pair of hands slipped onto the curves of my hips with a strong assured grip, but light enough that I knew I could slip out of it if I wanted to.

I glanced over my shoulder to see brown wavy hair that was styled to perfection and a pair of intense brown eyes that held a fire in them that I had only ever seen once before, in the parking lot after the Cougars game.

There was a question in them as well, as if he were giving me the out to call him on the fact that this wasn't very "friendly" of him. But instead of taking the obvious safe option—the *appropriate* option—I only turned back around and let my body move to the sound of the music. Nolan's fingertips dug into me the moment he realized I wasn't going to kick his ass and I felt more secure than a football in a receiver's arms.

I could feel the heat radiating from Nolan's body as he pulled me flush to him. After the two of us settled into each other's space his hands slipped around my hips and his fingers dipped under the hem of my tank top as they rested on the inch of exposed skin there from where it had ridden up while I danced. Before I could fully register what was happening, I felt his nose trail a path through my hair and toward the side of my jaw. Only the second it felt like Nolan had completely invaded all my space did I finally come to my senses to remember where we were and what we were doing in front of both the Cougars and the Bobcats.

The song came to an end, and I pulled myself out of his grip, ignoring the way my body noticed the absence of his warmth.

"I—" I turned to tell him that this was a mistake until I saw the look on his face. He looked drunk—and judging by the flush in his cheeks, his enlarged pupils, and the way his tongue darted out of his mouth to wet his lips when we made eye contact, it wasn't from alcohol.

"I'm going to—" My brain was five steps behind my mouth as I tried to form a full sentence. Once I realized that wasn't going to be possible while I was this close to him, I turned on my heel and darted off the dance floor toward the back hallway where the bathrooms were.

I let out a small breath when I realized most of the people that would have noticed us were too engrossed in their own conversations or celebrations. But that didn't mean we had gotten off scot-free. Just as I was about to slip into the hallway, I caught my sister's eye from where she stood at the bar with Maggie and Derek. The twinkle in it told me I was going to be hearing about this later.

The women's bathroom was completely empty when I walked inside, and I let out a sigh as I stood in front of one of the mirrors. I took in the natural red in my cheeks that made my eyes look even more clear blue and the flush that had also spread across my chest. My hair had gotten a little frizzy from all the dancing I had done. I should have recognized the girl in the mirror, but the girl I knew wouldn't have done something as unprofessional as what had just happened on the dance floor between me and Nolan.

A knock on the door interrupted my mental breakdown. I assumed it was Olivia coming to corner me and I threw the door open, prepared to defend myself, only to have the words die on my lips.

Nolan pushed the door open wider and slipped around me. His movements were quick and sure as he turned the lock on the door. I suddenly felt like I was the prey that had been cornered by a predator.

In a flash his hands were back around my hips and before I could blink, I was sitting on the lip of the sink, and he was standing between my legs. He braced his hands on either side of the sink as he leaned in until our lips were nearly touching.

"I thought we were supposed to be just friends," I heard myself tell him.

Nolan rested his forehead on my shoulder. "I don't want to be friends, Lottie."

I tried to ignore the way my heart dropped at his words.

"I tried keeping my distance from you and we both know that didn't work," Nolan continued. "I tried going back to the way things were, but that's not working either. You are all I can think about. At practice, I'm keenly aware of where you are all the time. I go home after practice to my empty goddamn penthouse and wonder if you're out on another date with some idiot that you could run circles around. I can't take it, Lottie. I can't just be your friend."

The air felt like it had been sucked right out of my lungs as Nolan finally confirmed my suspicions that he was just as interested in me as I was in him.

Before I could say anything, Nolan pulled his head off my shoulder and looked at me with such torture in his eyes.

"You can tell me to stop," he continued. "You can tell me to stop, and I'll figure my shit out. We'll go back to normal if that's what you want."

I realized that he was holding himself back from me. His knuckles were white from how hard he was gripping the sink next to me to try and stop himself from touching me. The two of us were well aware of what it meant if he did—a line of professionalism forever crossed. We'd be passing the point of no return.

But is that what you really want?

You're chasing after living after devoting yourself to working all your life. Does he not make you feel alive?

My eyes flickered toward the door, wondering if I should walk out of it and never look back. I knew Nolan would keep his word. We'd go back to being partners in his therapy plan. My job would be safe. But the hesitation I had was from a question echoing inside my brain. One that I knew would remain even if I walked away right now.

What if?

I was tired of vicariously living through everyone else I encountered. It was time I stopped watching through the windows of everyone else's lives and became the driver of my own. Because even if Nolan could walk away from this and let everything go back to normal, I wasn't sure I could.

"I'm not sure I want to be friends either."

Relief washed over Nolan's face before he wasted no time in closing the distance between us.

Chapter 15

Nolan

The moment my hands touched Lottie's face, my body released stress that I hadn't realized I'd been holding. Relief flooded through me the second I registered her words.

I'm not sure I want to be friends either.

I hadn't realized how much I liked Lottie until, for only a moment on a dance floor in a poorly lit bar surrounded by my teammates, I let myself pretend she was mine. I let myself imagine a world in which I could walk out on a dance floor and wrap my hands around her, just like I had, and send a message to every guy in that room that was looking at her with interest that she wasn't available.

I had to remind myself that it wasn't a dream the way that she had pressed her body back into mine once she realized who was behind her. Or that it wasn't a dream the way the skin of her stomach had felt so soft beneath my fingertips.

I'd watched her eyes cloud with conflict when she realized what we'd been doing in a very public scenario as she pulled away from me. The sudden emptiness that she had just occupied was enough to finally clear the fog that had lain over my mind and allow me to realize what I had done.

My eyes had followed Lottie once she had left the table with her sister and Maggie Redford. Derek and Jamil were in the middle of a lively conversation next to me about Jamil being suddenly thrust into the upper echelons of stardom this season, but I wasn't listening to what they were saying.

I could only watch the blonde-haired woman on the dance floor as she swayed to the sound of the music, looking much freer than I'd ever seen her before. For once, she didn't look like the woman who was always put together or always trying to make sure she was doing the right thing—even if it may not be the best thing for her.

The table had started to disperse. Derek had wandered off to the bar where he stopped to talk with Tommy, Maggie, and Olivia. Jamil had gone to take shots with his team and had managed to drag along a disgruntled Adam with him. Hawthorn was preoccupied on a phone call with his wife, which left no one to see me staring Charlotte Thompson down on the dance floor like a man half-crazed.

Even from the moment I walked in tonight, my eyes gravitated toward her. She nearly knocked the breath right out of my lungs with her tight black leather pants that left none of her curves to the imagination and a white top that was low-cut but still tasteful for an event like this. Lottie was slowly filling every one of my waking thoughts—what workouts or drills she'd have me do that day, what her game plan ideas would be if my knee tested well, or even how she was doing with her bucket list and if she was checking any more of those items off.

"I need you to kiss me, Nolan." Lottie's voice brought me back to the present where she was looking at me with eyes filled with need. "*Please.*"

I wasn't going to let her ask me twice.

I closed the distance between us and invaded her space. My heart beat wildly in my chest and just before my lips touched hers, my eyes drifted closed and peace filled my body. Lottie melted into my arms as her chin tilted up, mouth searching for mine.

Every inch of my body felt more alive than I'd ever felt the moment our lips touched. Both of us were slow and curious as we explored each other's bodies for the first time. My fingers traced the edge of her jaw and the soft skin below her ear—sending a shiver through her—before burying themselves in the hair at the nape of her neck.

I pulled downwards, ripping our mouths apart and exposing her throat to me. A gasp escaped her lips as I trailed kisses from her collarbone back up to the soft skin below her ear.

My senses were in overdrive trying to register everything that was *Lottie*. The way she smelled so intoxicating that I wanted to bury my nose in her neck. The little gasps of breath that escaped from her lips when I kissed a sensitive area on her neck. The way her eyelashes fanned across her cheeks and made her look almost ethereal.

Part of me thought that I only needed to get Lottie out of my system—that once I kissed her, I could move on and return my focus to things that mattered. But now I realized that Lottie was never going to be someone I could have just once. Every touch, every sound, every pass of our lips together was pulling me in past the point of no return.

When I finally managed to pull away from her, I took in the flush of her cheeks that brought out the blue in her eyes. She studied me as if she was trying to find some hint of regret there—as if she was already preparing herself for a letdown.

"Do you want to get out of—"

Banging on the door cut me off.

"Lottie? Are you in there?" Olivia's voice was muffled through the door. The doorknob jiggled.

"Just a minute!" Lottie winced when her voice came out with a squeak.

"Are you okay?" Olivia's voice was full of concern.

Lottie cleared her throat. "Yes! Just freshening up."

She lowered her voice when she looked back up at me. "I'll sneak out first and then you can leave next."

My brain felt like it was moving through molasses after having a kiss that just set my world on a completely different axis. Lottie slipped past me before walking toward the door. She ran a quick finger around her lips to check for any smudges, smoothed her hair down, and then threw the lock back on the door. Those blue eyes caught mine for a split second before she disappeared, and I heard her sister telling her that Derek was doing karaoke with Jamil.

I gave myself five minutes before I left the bathroom and was thankful when none of my friends questioned me when I told them I was heading home. They were all too distracted by Jamil's and Derek's rendition of "Take a Chance on Me" by ABBA.

Lottie and Olivia had rejoined Maggie on the dance floor and the three of them were acting like groupies at the edge of the stage, cheering their heads off for Jamil and Derek. I paused for only a second to have one last glimpse of the unfiltered smile on Lottie's face before heading out into the chilly Chicago night.

I had paced my penthouse this morning wondering if I should call Lottie before our run. I'd even opened and closed our text conversation at least a dozen times, always closing out of it before I could hit send on anything.

Did she think we crossed a line last night? *We crossed a million of them, but I knew I didn't care.*

Did she want to run this morning, or did she need space? *I was dying to see her.*

Relief coursed through me the minute I spotted Lottie's car in the parking lot when I pulled into the practice facility. I had run through a million different scenarios on my drive here—what I would do if she wasn't here, what I would do if she was here, but she wasn't happy to see me, what I would do if she was here, and she *was* happy to see me.

I was hoping for the third option when I stepped out of my car and walked over to where she was leaning against the hood of her car, bundled up against the late October early morning chill.

"Good morning!"

I kept any hint of a smile off my face at her greeting before

I figured out if all my hopes were about to be crushed. "How are you today?" I cautiously asked.

"Hungover as hell, but I'm hoping this run will help clear some of it out." Lottie bent down to stretch her legs out and my eyes shamelessly raked over them. "How are you feeling?"

I was thrown off by how normal of a conversation we were having and how obviously we were ignoring the elephant in the room. Lottie took off down our usual trail before I could reply.

"I'm fine. I didn't drink much last night," I told her. Panic rose within me when my mind began to wonder if she was about to say that she was drunk and that was why she let herself be in a position like she was with me last night— between my legs behind a locked door, moaning into my mouth.

"So how is this going to work?" Lottie asked me after the first few minutes into our run.

I nearly stumbled when I realized what she was asking me.

"Are we going to go back to like it was before like the last time? Are we going to pretend nothing happened last night? Or are you going to take me on a date?"

That familiar look of determination filled Lottie's eyes. It was like the first day we met when she held my gaze, never backed down and never flinched. Confidence poured off her and I let the smile I'd been fighting to keep off my face—out of fear that I'd be putting myself in a vulnerable position—tug my lips upwards.

"Do you want to go on a date?" I'd be more than happy to follow her lead on this.

"Well, I'm not really a one-night stand kind of gal," Lottie told me as she kept her head forward, as if she might have been too nervous to see my response.

"What about after practice today?" I asked her, watching her eyebrows shoot up. It was the Saturday before our ninth game of the season and today's practice would be the lightest one of the week.

"Okay," Lottie replied, and this time she finally gave me a smile that melted my insides. "You'll pick me up, though."

A chuckle rumbled through my chest. I had never been so happy to deal with Lottie ordering me around. I would have agreed to nearly anything if it made her smile at me the way she was right then.

"Six o'clock," I told her.

She pressed her lips together as if she were thinking if that time would work for her before agreeing. "Fine."

There was an energy buzzing around us. There wasn't the normal feeling of a challenge bouncing between us, but rather a shy anticipation for this new territory that we were entering.

And for the first time in years, I was excited to not have dinner alone in an empty apartment tonight.

Chapter 16

Nolan

Lottie's apartment was on the north side of Chicago in Evanston, which I was thankful for because the drive from my penthouse in downtown Chicago to hers was long enough for me to try to calm my nerves. I had to wipe my palms on my jeans at least a dozen times by the time I pulled up in front of her place.

The apartment was older with much more character than the modern high-rise I lived in. A warm golden light spilled out from the upper right window of the building, and I could make out the shape of a woman standing on the other side of the gauzy curtains. Leaves drifted toward the sidewalk from the trees that lined the front of the building.

I parked in one of the free spots along the sidewalk out front and took the steps slowly as I tried to settle the churning in my stomach as I rang her apartment.

Lottie's melodic voice crackled over the speaker. "I'll be right down!"

I quickly checked my reflection in the glass of the main door to the building before I saw Lottie's figure coming down the stairs. Her blonde hair was down and loose around her shoulders. She had opted for red lipstick tonight and my heart pounded against my chest at the sight. She looked almost sinful. I had told her tonight would be casual, so she had decided on a pair of jeans that hugged her legs and a loose black sweater that drew my attention back to her red lips.

115

Would I care if that stained my lips tonight? Absolutely not.

"Hi." She greeted me with one of her stunning smiles that made me a little unsteady on my feet.

"You look beautiful," I told her. It was one of the first times I'd openly commented on my physical attraction to her and judging by the way her eyes flickered to the ground and a smile spread across her face, she appreciated it.

"Where to?" Another pleasantly surprised look crossed her face when I opened her door for her and offered her my hand to help her inside.

"The best restaurant in this entire town." I didn't want to give away too much of my plans. I had thought hard all day about how I wanted tonight's date to go. Did I want to take her out to the most expensive place in Chicago? Or did I want to take her to my favorite dive that she'd probably never been to?

Ultimately, I decided that I wanted tonight to be low pressure. Neither of us was sure about anything going on other than the electric chemistry that we were slowly discovering, and I wanted us to get to know each other better without any extra expectations on the night.

When I pulled into the parking garage of my building, I could tell that Lottie was trying to remember if this high-rise had a restaurant that she didn't know about in it, and only once the elevator doors opened onto my floor did she realize what I had done.

I had transformed my dining room table into something that closely resembled an upscale restaurant with candlesticks and a flower bouquet that I had spent way too much time deciding if it said too much or too little. I'd even called Hawthorn's wife, Sarah, to see if she had any extra dinner plates that were nicer than the ones that I used. I'd ignored all lines of questioning from Hawthorn when I had gone to pick them up, but I knew that he'd probably already texted Derek about it and I was sure to face a full trial of my peers at the game tomorrow. My mom's homemade spaghetti and meatballs was staying warm in my stove.

"I figured since we ruined your date at Formento's that I could try to remedy that. It's my mom's recipe," I told her as I ushered her inside of my place.

I hadn't had anyone besides my friends over in years and suddenly I was self-conscious of everything I owned as I tried to look at it through a pair of fresh eyes. I realized the plain white walls with grey furniture with barely any art or greenery probably looked like a complete bachelor pad for a mid-thirties man, and, well . . . I suppose that was the truth.

"This was very thoughtful," she replied as she walked over to the table to take everything in.

I'd never been so nervous to make sure I got something right before. Not even with my ex, Rachel. My relationship with Rachel had always felt like a box I needed to check, which in hindsight was never fair to her. But I was pretty sure she cared more about being a part of the group of wives and girlfriends of the players than being in a relationship with me. With Lottie, it was as if her fire was trying to consume me whole and I was a willing victim to walk into the blaze.

"Let me just grab dinner. I have a few bottles of wine you can pick from, if you'd like." I motioned over to my wine cabinet where I kept a small collection of wine I liked to drink on rare occasions or with certain meals like this one.

Lottie took her time looking over each label before she gingerly slid one from the shelf. "I never pictured you as a wine guy."

"My mom is like a third-generation Italian, and wine was always a part of every meal." The two of us slid into our seats once the bottle had been poured and the spaghetti had been dished onto our plates.

"You haven't mentioned your parents before," she noted.

"They come to every game they can, but they usually try to leave to beat the traffic out of the stadiums. They stopped waiting for me to come out of the locker room after my tenth season. They've been waiting on me my entire life; it was only a matter of time before they got over it."

Lottie snorted. Her hand flew up to cover her face, her eyes going wide. I let out a soft chuckle at her obvious embarrassment. She slowly lowered her hand from her face once she'd recovered. "Well, it seems like they raised a great son. I'm sure they're wonderful people."

"They'd love you," I told her. "Especially my mom. She'd love the fire you have. You remind me a lot of her."

"I hope that's a compliment," she hedged.

"My mom is one of the best women I know, so I'd think so."

Lottie's mouth screwed to the side to try and hide a smile. "Well, her pasta might just be the best I've ever eaten," she added around a mouth full of meatball.

"She'd probably tell you that it better be seeing as she perfected that recipe over forty years."

I watched Lottie's smile slowly fade as she pushed the remainder of her pasta around on her plate. "It must be nice having parents that still support you like that."

With the way Lottie was still looking down at her food and not up at me, I knew there was something heavy on her mind. "What about your parents? Are they around?"

"They're not around." Her words came out stilted and I knew I was suddenly treading though potentially unsafe territory.

"So, it's just you and your sister?"

"It's been that way for most of our lives." Lottie gently set her fork down on her plate and lifted her eyes to mine. "My parents got a divorce after I had gone away for college, but during my sister's senior year of high school. For most of our lives our home was not a safe place. We had to live in a constant war zone, never knowing when the next fight would be, and I took on the responsibility of protecting Olivia through as much of it as I could. I hated that I couldn't be there all the time while I was at college, but I'd purposefully picked one of the schools here in Chicago so I wouldn't ever be far away if she needed me."

Suddenly everything about Charlotte Thompson made perfect sense—from how hard she'd worked for everything she had, to her no-nonsense personality, to the way she'd felt like most of her life had passed before her eyes. She'd had to raise herself and her sister practically on her own and work hard for everything that she had because she didn't have the support of a family unit the way I had.

I had grown up with parents that had sacrificed a lot to help me get a football scholarship to one of the best colleges in the nation and all to see my dreams become a reality when I was drafted into the NFL. The entire time, my parents had been there every step of the way. Lottie and Olivia had to graduate high school and then college with no one in the crowd but each other. Lottie's brusque exterior now only looked like armor rather than a know-it-all personality.

"What about the bucket list?" I asked, hoping to transition away from a heavy topic to give her a moment.

That beautiful smile that was beginning to feel like the sun itself finally reappeared. "That was all Olivia's idea after I told her I'd felt like I'd missed out on too much of my life."

"What's on it?"

"Well, you know about the whole date thing and the sunrise." Lottie paused as if she were debating saying something else, before she thought better of it. "Then there's just some things on there that I feel like both Olivia and I missed out on as kids—wear PJs on Christmas morning, have a real Thanksgiving, go sledding, kiss someone on New Year's Eve, and then Olivia and Maggie made me put down having a day where I say yes to everything."

My heart broke for the girl that never got to experience any of the things that Lottie listed off. This beautiful girl sitting across the table from me deserved all those experiences and more.

"Seeing as we haven't made it to the holidays yet, what have you marked off besides the sunrise in New York?"

Warmth blossomed in my chest that I got to be a small part of this adventure for her.

"Well, as you know I'm actively trying to cross off the dating one."

I nodded my head and tried to ignore the way my jaw clenched at the thought of any other guy taking her out on a date, especially on the shitty ones she'd been on. "What does it take to cross that one off?"

Lottie paused again and I watched a red the color of the wine in our glasses spread across her cheeks. "I want to feel the spark with someone."

"A spark?" I asked.

"You know," she mumbled as she waved her hands around like that would help me get the point easier. "Like in the movies. I don't want to settle for cohabitation with someone. I want to feel that spark. The kind of love you see in an old couple that still dances on the dance floor of weddings and smile at each other like they're still that young couple in love."

"And you thought Henry and Cole were going to give you that spark?" I teased.

"Hey!" But that infectious smile came back out for just a moment.

Silence stretched between us as it became obvious we were both thinking about the fact that we were on a *date*, and that I could either join the list with Henry and Cole or this could morph into something else entirely.

The memory of her legs on either side of my waist as we devoured each other in the bathroom at the club flashed through my mind. Electricity had raced through every inch of my body as soon as my hands touched her skin. Something had been set off inside of me that night, no longer willing to be ignored. And again tonight, that same feeling came roaring back up to the front. I *liked* Lottie and I wanted to be the person who made her feel alive, that gave her exactly what she was looking for. I could only hope that she'd eventually feel the same way.

"Well, I hope you find the right person. I think you deserve that," I told her, because I truly meant it. I was on a quest to achieve one last moment at the top of the mountain while Lottie was in search of a different kind of view than what she'd already managed to accomplish seeing. I found it inspiring that she had identified what she wanted next in her life and was doing what she could to achieve those things. I only hoped that I managed to do the same for myself.

Lottie's eyes softened as she looked at me over the candlelight flickering in the middle of the table. Those beautiful red lips pulled upwards to form the hint of a smile.

"Maybe I will," she replied with a small shrug of her shoulders. The temperature in the room felt like it rose about ten degrees as Lottie gave me a sultry look before she stood up from the table, wine glass in hand, and started to walk around my apartment.

I quickly grabbed my own glass of wine and moved to follow her. Lottie walked the wall of windows that made up one side of my apartment. I looked out over downtown Chicago and had the perfect view of Lake Michigan with Gateway Stadium off in the distance.

"I'm not sure I pictured you as a penthouse kind of guy," Lottie told me as she took in the view while sipping on her wine.

"It was one of the first purchases I made off my first contract after being drafted besides paying off my parents' mortgage."

Lottie's eyes flashed with surprise as if she hadn't pictured me doing anything nice.

I wish she could have seen me when I first entered the league—excited, happy, and not yet jaded by life.

"My mom wanted me to get a nice house in one of the suburbs, but as a twenty-two-year-old, that didn't sound as exciting as a penthouse in downtown Chicago."

"Would you ever live in the suburbs?" Lottie asked after she turned away from the view and started looking at my very minimal decor.

"I think after I retire, I'll look at selling this place. It's never felt like home. It's only ever felt like a place to sleep and eat."

"I get that," Lottie told me as she looked at the MVP trophies I had displayed in my living room next to the only picture I had in the entire apartment—a picture of me with my parents right after my first Super Bowl win. "I'm not sure I've ever had a place that really felt like a home."

Lottie's fingers reached out to barely touch the glass of the picture frame.

My heart ached and pulled me toward her until my chest was pressed into her back, much like we were on the dance floor just the night before. Everything in me wanted to kiss Lottie from the moment I watched her bound down the stairs of her apartment building. That infectious smile that warmed the fractures in my heart. Lottie had gone through so much in her life, yet she never let any of that slow her down. She dealt with parents that didn't give their children the love they deserved. She dealt with people doubting her or talking down on her worth just because she dared to be a woman taking up space in a man's world.

All I wanted to do was kiss the hurt away inside of her and try my best to make her feel even a little bit better. So I wrapped my arm around her waist and spun her so her chest was pressed against mine before lowering my mouth to hers. Touching her was like an addiction and one that I never wanted to have to give up.

It took her only a second before she matched my tempo, her arms moving to rest against my shoulders with her glass of wine still clutched in her hand. Her teeth nipped at my bottom lip and I played back by capturing hers between my teeth for a few seconds before letting it snap back.

Kissing Lottie felt like the same battle the two of us played with each other—all about who would get the upper hand once it was all over. It was a mess of teeth and tongues, hands grasping for purchase, and bodies trying to gain leverage. It was all consuming. *She* was all consuming.

I hadn't wanted anything new thrown at me this season out of fear that it would be the very reason I wouldn't reach my goals. But it had become clear that Lottie wasn't something that would pull me further from what I wanted, but rather was exactly what I needed to achieve everything I'd *ever* wanted.

Lottie surprised me by her free hand drifting down to the top of my pants where her fingers dipped inside and teased the skin there. All the blood rushed to meet her touch.

The moment a groan escaped my mouth, everything became a frenzy. Her wine glass was discarded on the mantel. Clothes were thrown in various places I was sure we wouldn't find later. But the only thing I could truly focus on was the woman in my arms as I lifted her up and her legs wrapped around my body.

I walked Lottie back toward my bedroom. For the first time, this penthouse finally felt a little bit like home.

Chapter 17

Lottie

Soft light filtered in from behind the blinds that were pulled. As I slowly woke up from the deepest sleep I'd ever had, my eyes searched my surroundings. Black bedding, grey walls, modern furniture, minimal decor.

Then last night came back to me in flashes.

Nolan hovering over me as he gently laid me down on his bed.

A trail of kisses that left my body in a heap, unable to move.

A manic tempo that had Nolan collapsing on top of me with his head fitting perfectly into the crook of my neck.

Names whispered into the dark room, just between the two of us.

The soft moments afterwards where it was just the two of us enjoying lying in each other's arms.

Then waking up in the middle of the night to do it all over again.

My eyes slowly drifted toward the other side of the bed where I found it empty. The sheets were rumpled, and the covers had been pulled back as if someone had been there, as if I hadn't just dreamed up the most intense night of sex I'd ever had in my life.

Then I noticed the sound of whistling and food cooking once I fully adjusted to being awake. Then the smell hit me, and it was *heavenly*.

It took everything in me to roll out of the softest bed I'd ever lain in. Sweatshirt and sweatpants had been laid out on the dresser across the room. They were three sizes too big. But after rolling the sweatpants and pulling the drawstring tight enough that I knew they wouldn't fall off me, I emerged into the kitchen to a shirtless Nolan with wet hair wearing only a pair of shorts as he flipped pancakes onto an empty plate. The whistle I heard was to the tune of jazz music that he had filtering through the apartment.

Everything felt rather domestic as I stood there and watched a man who faced down a stadium full of crazed fans and large men that wanted to kill him every week cook pancakes for the two of us. It was almost jarring to feel the peacefulness that something as simple as your significant other making breakfast for the both of you could bring.

I stood there in the hallway, unsure if I should enter this moment or not—it was unfamiliar territory for me—but before I could decide one way or the other, Nolan turned and noticed me.

"Good morning!" There was more energy and pep in his voice than any other morning we'd spent together so far this season, and I noticed how the way his eyes lit up brightened his whole face. Even the lazy smile he wore seemed to suit him. "I normally make myself pancakes before home games. I went ahead and made some for you, if that's alright?"

"That sounds fantastic. If your pancakes are as good as the spaghetti and meatballs last night, I know these are about to be the best damn pancakes I've ever had."

"Grab a seat at the island, I'll whip you up a plate." Nolan turned back around to the stove and gave me the perfect opportunity to study the expanse of muscles that rippled across his back. Without Nolan's gaze on me, I could remember the situation I'd found myself in.

In two months, the two of us had gone from what first

appeared to be sworn enemies for the season to realizing that the chemistry between us wasn't hatred, but something else entirely.

I still hadn't let my brain travel down the path of whether what we'd done these past two days was right or not. I wanted to live in this moment outside the realm of reality for just a little bit longer.

My phone buzzed on the counter where Nolan must have plugged it in after last night. The second I saw the name on the screen I let out a soft sigh—Olivia Thompson.

"Who is it?" Nolan asked me after he watched me hit ignore.

"Just my sister."

Nolan turned and set a plate of pancakes in front of me before placing his in front of the seat next to mine. "You're ignoring her?"

The ding of my phone rang through the air before I could reply.

Olivia: Now that I've recovered from that party two nights ago . . . were you dancing with Nolan Hill?

"I'm most definitely ignoring her," I told him after I slid my phone away and picked up the fork that Nolan had given me. There was no way I was going to give her all the details while I was sitting at Nolan Hill's kitchen island and eating his pancakes.

My phone buzzed again, and I let out another sigh before I grabbed my phone and shot off a text to her.

Lottie: Don't you have a World Series game today?

Olivia: Maggie and I were just killing time and talking about the party Friday night. It happened, didn't it?!

I flipped my phone over before turning my attention back to Nolan. "Talk to me about the game."

"I'd rather talk about when I get to see you next," Nolan told me with that same lazy smile.

I placed the first piece of pancake in my mouth before I could formulate a response. It wasn't that I didn't want to see Nolan again—I would love to. But that would require the two of us discussing what was happening between us and I was worried it would burst this perfect little bubble we were in.

"Is that something you'd like to do? Because if you haven't realized it yet, this could get complicated." I kept my gaze on my plate of pancakes to try and avoid seeing Nolan's answer on his face. "And just so you know I'm an overthinker, so if you don't give me an answer, I'll just come up with one of my own."

"Lottie." I felt Nolan gently place his hand on my thigh to try and draw my attention to his. After finally getting the courage to look at him, the look he was giving me nearly stole my breath away. "I don't care how complicated this could get. If you think I haven't already thought through every possible outcome, you'd be wrong. I have, and no matter all the different ways this could go, I want to see you again."

I did my best to hide exactly how Nolan's words made me feel. It had never occurred to me that I yearned so much for someone to actually *want* me after never being someone's priority or first choice my entire life. But I was afraid that once I showed my cards to him, I'd lose the upper hand—if that even mattered in a situation like this.

"Maybe we can discuss that after the game," I offered—if only to give myself more time to figure out if this was seriously something I wanted to pursue, despite everything inside of me screaming that I should ignore all the reasons why I shouldn't.

I disregarded the way Nolan deflated at my dismissal and focused instead on the last few bites of pancake on my plate. "I should probably head back to my apartment so I can get ready for the game on time."

"I'll take you." Nolan stood quickly and cleared our plates from the island.

"I can call for a ride," I told him. "I know you like to get to the stadium early for home games."

Nolan dropped both plates into the sink before turning to skewer me with a look. I recognized that determination. I'd seen it plenty of times on the football field. I wasn't going to win any argument with him this morning.

"Lottie, I can give you some space and time when it comes to going on another date. But I am not going to let you avoid me now simply because we slept together."

My mouth fell open. "That wasn't—I wasn't—"

"You're right though, we should probably get going so I have time to get you to your apartment and get back." With that, Nolan disappeared into his bedroom to change, that same guarded, hard exterior he gave me during those first few weeks suddenly making an appearance again.

He recognized that I was trying to protect myself and it seemed he was going to do the same.

Today's game was set to be the coldest yet of the season. There were a few warnings of a snowstorm that the weather channels promised would come next week bringing nearly a foot of snow.

After Nolan dropped me back off at my apartment, I managed to beat him to the stadium to get the training room ready for everyone to show up. Surprisingly, Nolan wasn't the first player through the doors, it was Derek.

"Morning, Lottie!"

"You're rather chirpy this morning," I noted as I grabbed a heat pack for him.

"We're seven-and-one. What's not to be happy about?" The Bobcats were playing the Detroit Mustangs today, who had a losing record so far this season. We were poised to move to eight wins and have the best record in our conference.

"How are you feeling today?" I asked him as I warmed my hands before putting some massage oil on them to work on Derek's lower back.

"I'm feeling pretty good. I think the better question is, how do *you* feel?"

My hands froze mid massage as I tried to figure out what he was asking. "What is that supposed to mean?"

Derek's soft chuckle vibrated under my hands and only grew when Nolan walked through the training room doors.

"What are you trying to say, Derek?" I asked with more ferocity.

"Only that I've never seen two more uptight people be so carefree." Derek slid off the table once my massage was done and gave me a wink before he left the room, leaving Nolan and me alone.

The silence between the two of us only hung heavy for a few moments before Nolan broke it. "What was that idiot going on about?"

"I'm not entirely sure, but I think he was trying to say he saw the two of us Friday night."

Nolan groaned and I knew exactly why. If Derek Allen saw the two of us do anything compromising Friday night, it was equivalent to the town gossip knowing the biggest secret the town had ever had.

"I'm sure it'll be fine," I told Nolan as I began our pregame treatment routine we'd been doing so far this season.

"If you think Derek Allen isn't going to act like Paul Revere and tell the entire locker room the moment he sees it with his own eyes, you're mistaken."

My head snapped up to meet Nolan's gaze once I'd secured the electro-stimulation pads around his knee. "Should we be worried?"

"With the guys on the team?" Nolan clarified. "No. Everyone loves you and there are other things to be concerned about than the two of us dancing at a party. Derek doesn't know anything else; I haven't spoken with him about it."

Relief washed over me. The two of us sat in the training room in silence as a few of the linemen filtered in and out to get their ankles taped.

"Can we talk after the game?" Nolan asked, breaking

up the silence. He didn't say that he wanted to talk about going on another date. Gone was the tough exterior he had given me this morning.

"Yes, we can," I told him. "But you've got a game to win first."

Shortly after Nolan left the training room, I bundled up against the cold for the game and headed out to the field. Everything started normal this game. Nolan threw a touchdown pass to Derek. Hawthorn kicked the extra point. It was starting off exactly how everyone thought this game would go—a sure win.

That was until just before the second half.

Nolan had taken the snap and dropped back into the pocket only to have to scramble to his left when pressure came from the right side. He tried to give himself more time as his eyes stayed down field, hoping for an open receiver before he'd get sacked. But he couldn't get the ball out before he was brought to the ground with his legs tangled up underneath one of the defenders that had brought him down.

The entire stadium gasped when they saw it because everybody knew there was no way Nolan was going to get up from that hit completely unharmed. I took off running onto the field as soon as the referee blew his whistle. It took only a few seconds to get to him with my heart beating wildly the whole way.

Nolan had rolled over onto his back by the time I got there and was groaning in pain as I kneeled next to him.

"What is it?" I asked, trying to assess where the injury occurred.

"My knee," Nolan groaned as his hands went to grab at his injured knee.

"Can you bend it at all?" I asked as I noticed swelling already.

"Not well," he told me. Pain marred his face as I prodded the injury.

This was my job. I was used to dealing with my athletes getting injured. I was always a sturdy pillar for them during moments like this, never showing them any panic. So, the worry deep in my stomach as I tried to get Nolan to sit up was a new discovery.

Zeke and another trainer helped me get him to his feet and support his body weight as we walked to the training room. I heard the crowd cheer behind us as Caleb took the field in place of Nolan.

"Goddamnit!" Nolan yelled as soon as we were the only ones in the training room. "This can't be happening. Not now. *Why* now?"

Nolan was falling apart in front of me, with the threat of an injury pushing him off his equilibrium and toward an unknown outcome.

I stayed quiet as I helped Nolan slide onto one of the beds. I needed to assess the knee first to see if he needed an MRI or if the team doctor needed to be called in, but I also wanted to give him a few moments to work through what was currently happening. Injuries could be devastating for athletes, and even more so for an athlete in Nolan's position in the middle of his last season. If this was serious, there was a good chance he had just played the last snap of his career.

"Nothing feels torn," I told him after I did my initial assessment. Nolan had covered his eyes with his arm and still hadn't looked at me yet. "But I still want you to have an MRI done."

"If you think it's fine, then it's fine," Nolan replied with an edge to his voice.

"I also think you should get an MRI," I fought back. It had been over a month since the last time that Nolan had second-guessed my professional judgement.

"I'm not getting the MRI."

"This isn't up for discussion."

Nolan finally dropped the arm covering his eyes and looked

at me, where I was sure he saw a steely gaze that was seconds away from turning into a blazing fury.

"Lottie, if that MRI comes back with bad news, that's the end of my career." The desperation that I normally saw in Nolan's eyes when it came to his hopes for this season was nearly pure anguish now.

Understanding dawned on me. Nolan was like a wounded animal backed into a corner, lashing out at anyone—even someone trying to help him. I had to remind myself that this wasn't personal. When this was all said and done, he didn't mean what he was saying. He wasn't mad at me. He was mad at the game.

"You still have your entire life after this year, Nolan. This is for your lifelong health, not just to throw a ball down a field," I told him, trying to reach him in his moment of hurt.

Cold silence filled the room after I finished.

"I'm not sure I want anything other than your medical opinion right now," Nolan finally replied.

"Well, it doesn't seem like you want that either," I told him as I called for the MRI specialist to come to the training room.

Nolan's gaze drifted away from my face and back up toward the ceiling. I slipped out of the room as soon as he was in someone else's hands. It was clear I wasn't going to get through to him right now. I forced myself to let all his comments roll off my shoulders as I walked away, but I knew I'd still be thinking about them later tonight simply because I cared about him and I hated seeing him feel like everything was out of his control.

When I got back out to the field, it looked like Caleb had managed to score another touchdown to keep the Bobcats ahead. I noticed the way Caleb moved on the field and realized there was something familiar about it.

He looked like a younger version of Nolan Hill.

But the real version of Nolan was being a complete asshole with only a narrowed focus on himself. I understood the pain an athlete went through during an injury—both mentally and physically—but having to take the brunt of Nolan's felt different after last night.

Suddenly I was grateful it had been only one night between us—if only to spare my heart from the pain of realizing Nolan only had the space in his to care for one thing this season, himself.

Chapter 18

Nolan

The MRI on Sunday came back negative, confirming Lottie's assessment that nothing was torn. But by the time the results came back, Caleb had led the team to another win and Lottie was busy helping Derek after he took a hard hit in the fourth quarter. That win helped solidify our position as first in our conference heading into next week's bye week. I heard the cheers all the way from the locker room as the team celebrated Caleb's performance. Some athletes in the same situation might have been jealous over their backup's success, but I was surprised to find myself only happy that Caleb was given a chance like that.

Before the doctor left me, he suggested that I had aggravated my previous injury and that it might take a few weeks for me to get back out on the field. The news had sent me reeling.

A few weeks?

A few weeks meant I would miss an entire game of my last season, maybe more. I felt the potential loss like a gaping wound. I had gone most of my career thus far without having to miss very many games, but even the games I had missed weren't anywhere near to being some of the last I would play.

I had hovered outside of the training room in hopes that I would be able to catch Lottie and apologize to her, but she was gone before I had the chance. Only Derek was still in the locker room when I finally walked in to change out of my uniform.

"What's the news?" Derek asked once he saw me.

"Nothing's torn. I just strained the old injury." I let out a sigh the second I sat down in my cubby.

"Lottie seemed rather upset after the game," Derek told me. He was trying to be subtle, but I could sense the underlying accusation in his tone.

"I was upset that I got injured." Even I knew my defense had fallen flat as soon as it left my mouth.

Derek stood with his back to me as he finished packing the bag he brought to the stadium, and I watched his shoulders slump when he heard my excuse. Slowly, he turned back around to look at me.

"Nolan, you know I love you, but sometimes you are a complete asshole."

Immediately I felt the urge to defend myself. "You know how it is when you get an injury and the fear of being out the rest of the season."

The laugh that erupted from Derek was not one of actual enjoyment but rather disbelief. As if he couldn't believe I was being serious.

"Nolan, have you ever looked at your life and wondered if you're happy?"

My brows pulled together in confusion. "What does that have to do with anything?"

"Just answer the question," Derek replied. "Are you happy with your life right now?"

"Well, we're first in the conference after today's win," I started.

Derek cleared his throat, interrupting me. "I want you to consider if you have anything outside of this job that makes you happy."

Silence filled the locker room as I tried to think of something other than football that made me happy. However, the only thing that kept coming to the forefront was the past day spent with Lottie.

"Have you thought that maybe your career shouldn't be the only thing you have in life that makes you happy?

Especially when it will eventually end. Because when it's all said and done, you'll be left with a bunch of trophies that brought you happiness in the moment it happened but then collect dust for the years to come. Maybe it's time to find other things that make you happy to prevent you from feeling so devastated when things like this happen. New hobbies? Maybe a new *person* in your life?"

Derek asked the last question as if he had been there this morning as Lottie and I ate pancakes at my island.

"I have plenty of people in my life."

This time Derek looked at me as if he were truly disappointed in me. "Nolan, every career comes to an end. Whether you retire, get fired, or make the decision to change careers. In all those scenarios, there is another chapter. I would hate to see you living in the previous chapter rather than enjoying what's to come for you. Very few of us have the chance to be remembered after we die by many, but we are all remembered by few and it's those few that matter most."

"What does this have to do with Lottie?" I asked, exasperated by Derek's strangely coded lecture.

"Everything, Nolan. It has everything to do with Lottie." Derek threw his bag over his shoulder then and walked out of the locker room, leaving me to wonder if my friend was more perceptive than I originally made him out to be.

Monday morning, I showed up to the practice facility for treatment with Lottie fully prepared for her to hand me off to Zeke after how I treated her yesterday at the game, but I was surprised to find her sipping on a mug of coffee in her office. My MRI was up on one of her TVs and exercises were taped to her walls with sticky notes attached to them.

"Good morning," I greeted her cautiously.

"Morning," Lottie chirped, no sign of the previous hurt on her face from when she'd left the training room at the stadium yesterday. "How is your knee feeling today? Good news that it's not torn."

Lottie brushed past me to head out into the main room, leaving me feeling unsteady on my feet, and not because of my knee.

"It's sore," I told her as I followed her toward a training bed. "I made sure to ice it and elevate it last night. I think some of the swelling went down."

"Let me take a look." Lottie warmed her hands up before reaching down to gently assess my knee. The moment her hands were on my skin it was like a visceral reaction—my heart rate sped up and my entire body felt like it wanted to lift off the table to be closer to her touch.

All last night I replayed how rude I had been to her with Derek's lecture in the background as if it were a movie with a voice-over. My focus had been only on myself, and I neglected to think about anybody else. My only fear was that I had ruined something before it even got started.

"I have a new treatment plan for this next week in hopes that we get you back on the field before the next game," Lottie told me, bringing my attention back to her.

"You really think you could get me back before our next game?" I asked, hope blossoming inside of me. After I got out of the shower last night, I'd stared at the ugly swelling like it was a bad omen for my season.

"If not, it seems like Caleb can hold the fort down for one more game."

I tried to smile in agreement with her, but just the thought of missing out on one of my games soured my stomach.

Lottie must have noticed the scowl on my face because she stopped her massage and stepped away from the table with her arms crossed over her chest.

"What?" I asked.

"You may not have seen Caleb yesterday, but he really did hold his own. I know he'll have your back." Lottie's face turned into a scowl that matched my own and a sigh pushed out from between her lips.

"It's not about Caleb," I told her. I left out how I felt it was about losing out on *my* season, but Lottie seemed to fill in the blank for me.

She took her time before responding to me, as if she were heavily weighing if she wanted to say what was on her mind. "Have you ever heard of *mudita*?"

I shook my head.

"It describes the joy one has toward another's good fortune or success."

It had been years since I'd ever felt like I was being scolded, but I suddenly remembered what it was like.

"I think the best leaders have that quality. Maybe you should read up on it."

Words had never pierced me harder. It was one thing for Derek to comment on how I wasn't living the best life outside of work, but to have Lottie tell me that I wasn't being the best in the one thing I cared about stung.

"Thank you for your observation," I told her after a moment, my words stilted.

Silence sat heavy between us as Lottie moved to restart my knee massage. There was a part of me that felt desperate to fill it, to go back to the easiness that was between us during our dinner date. I didn't like the rift that was growing between us because of my actions.

"Can we talk about yesterday?" I asked her.

"I'm not sure there's anything to talk about."

I shook my head, needing to get some of this guilt off my chest. "I need to tell you I'm sorry."

Lottie didn't look up from her ministrations. "I appreciate that."

"Can we go back to how we were yesterday morning?" I asked.

This time Lottie walked away from the table to grab a tool that would help her push some of the swelling out of my knee.

"I'm not sure about that," she said. "I don't want to date someone who prioritizes their work over the people in their life. I lived that as a child, and I don't intend to do the same as an adult."

"This season is just important to me." I felt like I was a broken record, constantly reminding everyone around me of it.

"That may be so, but is it so important that you neglect the people in your life for it?" Lottie gave me a sad smile as if she understood the predicament I was in, but still took pity on me.

"I know I need to do better," I told her. "Just don't give up on me?"

"I couldn't possibly, Nolan. I'm one of your medical professionals. This is my job." Lottie strapped a light ankle weight to me before instructing me to do the first exercise on her list.

"I wasn't talking about as my physical therapist, Lottie. I was talking about not giving up on us. I know I need to work on myself, and I intend to."

I watched Lottie wring one of the towels through her hands before she gave me a short nod and walked out of the training room.

After I finished therapy, I went to search for Hawthorn or Derek to talk about the conversation I'd just had with Lottie. But before I could get there, I stumbled across Caleb working through different routes out on the practice field by himself.

Lottie's words rang through my head.

Have you ever heard of mudita? *It describes the joy one has toward another's good fortunes or success.*

And then Derek's.

I would hate to see you living in the chapter before rather than enjoying what's to come for you. Very few of us have the chance to be remembered after we die by many, but we are all remembered by few and it's those few that matter most.

Before I could change my mind, I pushed out onto the practice field and walked out to Caleb.

"Hey!" The rookie flashed me a smile I felt like I didn't deserve. "How are you feeling? I heard the good news that nothing's torn. I wasn't sure if you'd be ready for the next game, so I wanted to make sure I was . . . just in case."

I saw a younger version of myself in his eager face and I hated that I was so self-absorbed that I hadn't paused to remember that a team was only as good as its weakest link. Caleb wanted the success of the *team*, and it was time I started wanting the same thing.

"Can I walk you through some of the routes for the game?"

A smile spread across Caleb's face before he gave me an eager nod.

"I'd appreciate that, Nolan. Thanks."

I wanted to rewrite the public perception of me with my last season, but I didn't want to do it if it meant ostracizing those around me. I could at least start with Caleb. Next, I would have to figure out how to fix things with Lottie.

Chapter 19

Lottie

"The first snow accumulation of the season is happening today with this massive snowstorm that's barreling across the Midwest. Parts of Chicago could see upwards of twelve inches after it's all said and done. Kids, you may just have yourself a snow day tomorrow if this accumulation manages to stick around. Be careful out there, folks! A snowstorm this early in the season can often bring a lot of panic for those that don't feel prepared. Just remember, this snow will probably melt by mid-week, there's no need to stockpile water or toilet paper."

The snow was coming down in sheets outside. It was a ghost town. Snow days in the city were some of the most magical moments during the holidays. The fireplace in my apartment—one of the reasons I fell in love with the place—was roaring trying to keep everything warm.

A few children squealed with joy down on the street outside where their father pulled them on a sled down the middle of the unplowed road. As I watched them over the rim of the hot chocolate I held in my hands, a sense of longing panged inside of my chest.

The buzzer went off in my apartment, pulling my mind away from how I had never had a parent be the one to spread the magic of the holidays for me and Olivia.

"Who is it?" I asked into the buzzer.

"It's me," my sister's voice crackled back. "Open the damn door. I think I may lose a toe to frostbite."

I hit the buzzer for her to get inside and waited the few seconds it took for her to get to my door. My sister barreled in wearing all Cougars gear from head to toe. The team had won the World Series this past week and the city was still riding the winner's high after celebrating like it was the last day on earth during the parade a few days ago.

"Did you drive here?" I asked her, ready to unleash one of my many lectures about being more careful.

"No, I took the train." Olivia shook the snow off her before she noticed that I was still in my pajamas. "What are you wearing?"

Confused, I replied, "My pajamas? It's the Bobcats' bye week. We don't have a game today."

"Did Nolan not call you?" Olivia asked.

Nolan.

I hadn't heard from him all week and I felt his absence every morning as I went on a run by myself.

"Nolan? Why would he call me? I haven't talked to him in days."

"Jamil told me that we were all going sledding and that it was Nolan's idea." Olivia held up her phone to show me her text conversation with the outfielder.

Before I could tell her—again—that Nolan hadn't told me anything of the sort, the buzzer to my apartment went off.

"Who else is here? Isn't the city shut down?" I asked as I went to answer it. "Who is it?"

"It's Nolan."

I glanced back at my sister to see her raise an eyebrow at me. "He knows where you live?"

I waved her off and ignored the pleased smile that spread across her face. Nolan's large frame appeared on the other side of my door. His face was guarded, like he was fully expecting me to throw him back out on the street—which

I can't say I didn't debate, if only for a split second before I opened my door to allow him inside.

"Did you drive here?"

Nolan nodded. "I was careful, I promise." One of his small, rare smiles showed for only a couple of seconds before he returned to being guarded once again.

"Hi, Nolan!" My sister was perched on the arm of my couch, watching our interaction as if it were more interesting than the final inning of the World Series earlier this week.

"Hi, Olivia." Nolan gave my sister a quick nod before he looked back over at me. "Can we talk?"

"About the impromptu sledding you told everyone but me about?"

He winced when he saw how irritated I was but continued to stand his ground. "Among other things."

I took in the steely, determined look in Nolan's eyes and knew that he was going to figure out a way for this conversation to happen, even if I turned him away now.

"I'll just be . . . in your room," Olivia announced loudly before she scurried toward my bedroom in her attempt to give us some privacy. Although I watched her leave the door cracked, presumably to spy on whatever conversation was about to transpire.

That sneaky little bitch.

"I have a lot of things I need to say and I'm not sure any of it is going to make sense," Nolan started. He wrung his hands together as he began pacing in the middle of my living room. "I know that I haven't been the best version of myself this season, and I'm not even talking about my performance. I've been a shitty friend to everyone, and I pushed you away when that's the last thing I want to do."

"Nolan." I gently said his name to stop him in the middle of his rambling speech. "I know this season means a lot to you and that's okay. You don't have to explain yourself."

His face crumbled with anguish. "But that's just it, Lottie.

143

I do have to explain myself, because even if this season does mean a lot to me, I don't want to let it ruin the relationships I have with the people that are most important in my life."

I heard an intake of breath from my bedroom and had to fight the urge not to yell at my little sister to close the door the rest of the way.

"I never got to tell you this last Sunday—but I like you, Lottie. I didn't expect this to happen when I first met you. I wanted to avoid you at all costs and not because I found you utterly distracting by how beautiful you are, but because I was scared that someone as smart as you would see just how pathetic I am. A grown man who can't just fucking move on. What I didn't expect was for you to still see through all my different pretenses and accept me for it all while working with me to figure out how you could best help me achieve everything I want."

Nolan's words stripped me bare. I had never expected him to be so vulnerable with me, especially after his injury during the last game. I was certain he was the exact kind of man I needed to avoid—someone who put their career and interests over the people in their life. I had watched my father constantly choose football over my mother and then Olivia and me.

I deserved more than to be an afterthought.

"I don't expect you to forgive me right now. I'm not sure I deserve that," Nolan continued. "But I wanted to extend an act of good faith or an olive branch. I know you wanted to go sledding for part of your bucket list and I called in the troops to make that happen."

A voice in my head told me I needed to trust easier and not expect every man in my life to abandon me, but that was a trauma that still had years of healing. I hated my father for how badly he'd managed to stain every aspect of my life without even caring enough to do so intentionally.

"I only want you to know that I care about you, Lottie. I didn't want to admit out loud that I'm scared of what's next for me after this season is over, but I must if I want to do better. I'm not perfect, I know that. I'm just asking for you to take a chance on a guy that's in the process of trying to figure out who he is now."

It would be hypocritical of me to not forgive Nolan because I understood what it meant to reinvent yourself. I remembered an eighteen-year-old Lottie promising that someday she'd be somebody people wanted instead of being discarded and she worked every day of her adult life to achieve that when it came to her work. Maybe Nolan and I weren't that different—he wanted to be loved and remembered, just like I did when I first stepped out on my own.

"I'll go change," I told him. I wasn't ready to tell him that I forgave him yet and especially that I hadn't stopped thinking about him all week, even after he tossed me to the side so easily. Instead, I could at least meet him in the middle on this. I didn't miss the relief that filled Nolan's brown eyes before I disappeared into my bedroom.

"You didn't tell me about you and *Nolan Hill*!" my sister whisper-shouted at me the moment I closed the door behind me.

"That's because I wasn't sure there was anything to tell," I told her as I dug around in my closet for clothes warm enough to go sledding in.

"What happened?" Olivia asked as she threw herself onto my bed.

"The best way to describe Nolan is he's a man who's afraid of the unknown, and for a moment on Sunday, he let that get in the way of our relationship—both professional and whatever else is happening between us." My voice came out muffled as I pulled my thickest sweatshirt over my head.

"We're all afraid of something, Lottie," Olivia said, with a look on her face that suggested she was familiar with the feeling.

"Is everything okay?" I asked her.

Olivia waved me off and flashed me one of her carefree

smiles. "Oh, I'm fine. Now tell me, big sister, did you sleep with Nolan Hill?"

There wasn't any chance that I was going to be able to hide the truth from her. She knew me better than anyone else and the flush creeping up my neck was bound to be a dead giveaway.

"Oh my gosh!"

I tried to hush her because the man we were speaking about was only on the other side of my door.

"Was it good? Damnit, why is everyone getting some action around here except for me?"

I cringed because although Olivia and I were best friends, I still didn't want to hear about my little sister's sexual escapades.

"Who knew my perfect older sister would be the one to do something so scandalous."

"It's not scandalous," I argued, growing hot for something other than the many layers of clothes I had on.

Olivia rubbed her hands together like an evil villain. "Oh, today is going to be so fun."

"No, no, no." I pointed a finger. "You are not going to mess with Nolan. Absolutely not."

My sister just gave me one of the smiles that I knew meant trouble before throwing my bedroom door open and walking back out into the living room. Nolan was now waiting for us on my couch and avoiding eye contact.

Damnit, Olivia. Could you have spoken any louder?

"We're ready," I told him. Nolan jumped up like he was thankful for something to do to avoid the awkward tension that Olivia was eating up like popcorn.

"Everyone should be waiting for us over by the stadium."

"The stadium?" I asked.

Nolan opened the front door and gestured for us to go first. "There's a great sledding hill right between Gateway Stadium and Lake Michigan."

Olivia bounded out to Nolan's black Range Rover that

was parked on the curb next to all the other cars that were covered in inches of snow. "I call the backseat!"

"Nobody calls the backseat, Olivia."

"They do if they want a front row seat to her sister and the guy that's clearly smitten with her," Olivia stage-whispered loud enough I was afraid Nolan would have heard her yet again.

"Get in the car," I sighed.

The roads and nearly every parking lot we passed were completely empty the entire way to the sledding hill next to the stadium. The view was like something out of a movie with everything around Gateway covered in a blanket of snow. Lake Michigan was grey and angry as the wind from the snowstorm raged on. A group of kids were packing snow together to make snowballs and throwing them at each other while squealing with joy. A group of adults stood off to the side watching them, and once we were close enough, I realized it was Adam and his wife, Hawthorn and his wife, Maggie and Tommy, Jamil and Derek.

I knew that Nolan probably invited everyone with the intention of making this as comfortable for me as possible. I had to admit it was nice having all the people I considered my friends—and was beginning to think of as family—so willing to do something like this with me.

Nolan parked his car and went to pull three sleds out of the back.

"Here, let me help," I told him as I took one.

"Finally!" Nolan and I turned to see Derek looking at us as if he'd been waiting for hours instead of minutes. "I've been waiting for you three to get here so I can be the first one down the hill."

"Not if I have anything to say about that," Olivia called out to him as she grabbed the other sled from Nolan and took off running toward the top of the hill.

"Wait a minute!" Derek shouted as he held his sled over his head and took off after her. "How are you so fast?"

"Be careful! If anyone gets hurt, the coaches are bound to be upset and so will I." I tried to suppress a smile as I watched my little sister let out a joyous laugh at the top of her lungs as she enjoyed doing something that we'd never got to experience in our lives.

"Ready?" Nolan asked me as he motioned up the hill where Olivia was sticking her tongue out at Derek after she reached the top first.

Nolan's shy smile made him look like a little kid again flirting with the girl he liked. This was the Nolan Hill that I'd come to like—the one that showed up with donuts for his teammates, gave up his favorite seat on the airplane to make me comfortable, watched the sunrise with me to thank me for my help, and took the time to see *me*. He wasn't perfect, but neither was I.

So, I found myself extending my hand to his as my own peace offering. Nolan studied it for a few seconds before he reached out to take my gloved hand in his. As the two of us climbed up to the top of the hill together, Derek and Olivia went speeding past us—both shouting at the top of their lungs about who was in the lead.

Adam Steel was at the top once we finally made it, helping his kids get onto their sleds and giving them a big push.

"It's nice to see you again, Lottie," he told me.

I smiled at him. "Congratulations on the World Series win. It must be nice retiring on something like that."

"It was. Now it's Nolan's turn." Adam slapped Nolan on the shoulder with affection before he pushed his youngest down the hill with enough force to make his wife yell at him to be careful. "Now I get to make different memories with the people I love."

"Happy for you, Adam," Nolan told him. "Truly."

"You're next," Adam told us. "Do you guys want a push?"

I followed Adam's gaze down to the sled in Nolan's hands. "Oh, we weren't going to go down together."

"Oh, come on. Nolan will get you more momentum going

148

down. It'll be fun, I promise." I noticed the twinkle in Adam's eye and concluded that he was either the most oblivious person ever to the lingering tension between me and Nolan or he was the world's best mastermind.

Adam took the sled out of Nolan's hands and positioned it on the ground before motioning for me to take a seat first. My heart began to race inside of my chest at the thought of being close enough again to Nolan to feel him. I heard snow crunch under Nolan's boots as he positioned himself behind me. Slowly, I felt his weight come down on the sled as his chest pressed into my back.

"Is this alright?" His breath tickled my ear as he leaned close enough so only I could hear him. He threaded his arms around my waist so he could be the one to hold the reins of the sled.

It took me a few moments to get my breathing under control before I squeaked out, "Yes, that's alright."

That same feeling of peace filled every inch of me once his arms tightened around me. It was the same feeling I had a hard time identifying in Nolan's penthouse because I'd never truly experienced it before.

"Ready?" Adam called out from behind us. Before either of us could say anything, there was a sharp push that sent us careening down the hill.

Wind rushed around my face as we rocketed down the steep incline. Laughter bubbled out of me as we picked up speed. Nolan pulled me tighter into his chest, tight enough that I could feel his chest rumble first before I heard his laughter over the wind roaring in my ears.

The sound melted away any lingering hurt I had from the moment between us in the locker room. By the time we slowed down at the bottom of the hill, I'd realized that Nolan and I were just two people broken inside trying to figure out a way to make themselves whole again.

We were one and the same.

Chapter 20

Lottie

"So, you're saying that I won't be able to play tomorrow?" Nolan asked me from where he lay on one of the training tables at the practice facility the day before the Bobcats' tenth game of the season.

I watched Nolan war with his emotions as he tried his best to not let the desperation clawing inside of him win. He was trying to stick to his word when it came to how he treated people when things didn't quite go his way this season. But the sadness in his eyes told anyone who looked closely enough how he really felt about sitting out another game.

"You worked with Caleb this week. You made sure he'd be ready for something like this," I reminded him. "You really have a knack for coaching."

Nolan sighed, but his eyes softened when I reached out to squeeze his hand to give him whatever reassurance I could.

The spark between us hadn't quite returned to the blaze that it once was, but it was still there simmering beneath the surface as the two of us tried to start fresh over this past week. It slowly grew with passing glances, innocent touches, and the wonder of what it would feel like to kiss him again.

But any chances of stealing a few moments to ourselves were squandered with our focus being solely on trying to get Nolan well enough to play in tomorrow's game. The two of us spent hours in the training room trying everything we could to minimize his pain and swelling. When we weren't working together, Nolan had taken the time to help Caleb in the off chance that he wouldn't be able to take the field, while I researched every treatment I could get my hands on that could potentially help Nolan's injury.

"You've helped Caleb get this far. I know how important this win would be for the team. So, coach him through it."

"How do you do that?" Nolan asked me as he slid off the table. He'd plastered a small smile on his face but the droop in his shoulders caught my eye.

"Do what?"

"Know exactly what to do next?" Nolan's hand reached out to brush against mine. "Every time something doesn't go to plan, it's like you've got the next six options ready."

I stretched my fingers out, so my pinky curled around his. "Well, that isn't true. I never know what to do next. I can just see what you're good at, Nolan. The only question is if you enjoy it enough to feel the same."

It was just the two of us in the training room, nearly the entire place had been emptied after practice had ended. Nolan laced our fingers together and a genuine smile pulled at the corner of his lips as he looked down at our joined hands.

"I have this sense of fulfillment whenever I watch Caleb get something that we've been working on." I stayed quiet as Nolan worked through his thoughts.

Having to pivot and to find something else to do with your life after you'd figured out what you were truly good at had to be difficult. It probably came across as rich coming from me—someone who had spent much of her life putting her worth into her work—but I wanted to share my recent revelations with him. The only thing that really mattered was making ourselves happy, even if that was sometimes the hardest choice.

"I can see myself being good at coaching. It keeps me around football and lets me use my knowledge and skills to better others," Nolan concluded.

"Isn't the quarterbacks coach retiring after this year, too?" I added.

Nolan nodded in confirmation.

"You could always approach the coaching staff about your interest in the job. The worst that can happen is they turn you away."

Nolan's eyes blazed with new determination. He looked like he wanted to devour me as he pinned me in place with our hands still clasped together. He had nearly a foot on me in height as he towered over me. I took a step back as he took a step toward me. The backs of my thighs hit the edge of the training bed behind me. I fell back into a sitting position as Nolan closed the distance between us.

My eyes flickered to the closed door of the training room, worried that someone would walk in.

"Practice is done. No one is here," Nolan reminded me as his hands came down on the bed on either side of me, taking away any chance I had at escaping. That same desperate feeling I felt in the bathroom of the club blazed through my body—the anticipation, the desire for his hands to be *anywhere* on my body, and the way my body felt like it needed his. It overwhelmed my senses and muddled any of the awareness I had for where we currently were.

Nolan's nose slipped inside the curtain of my hair and traced down the side of my neck, raising goosebumps down my back and arms. His hands remained firmly on the table as his mouth and nose traced a path around my body, barely brushing against my skin.

I had never been one to experience irrational thinking. I'd always had to be the responsible one. The one that took care of my baby sister. The one with a good job to make sure bills were paid in case my father ever went on a drinking bender after a bad fight with my mother. The one that helped my sister through college. I'd never been the one to throw caution to the wind.

But I think I understood why people lost all sense of reason the second that Nolan's lips hovered over mine. My hands buried themselves in his sweatshirt and yanked him closer to me, driven by the need to have as little space between us as possible. The moment before his lips finally touched mine felt like it happened in slow motion. But I didn't mind. The anticipation was just as addictive of a feeling as kissing him was.

Nolan's hands gently held my back as the two of us melted into each other like two halves of a whole finally coming back together again. His lips covered mine and that same sense of comfort I felt before from being in his arms filled me. His teeth grazed my bottom lip. His hands slipped between me and the table as his fingers dug into my ass. Desire for him to mark every inch of me, to claim me as his, surged as his lips latched on to the soft spot under my ear again, as if he knew I'd simply fall into oblivion at his touch.

I yanked at his sweatshirt, suddenly desperate for fewer layers between us. Nolan's lips left my body for only a moment as he ripped the sweatshirt over his head before returning his lips to mine. My breaths came in heavier as his fingertips left my ass, slipped under my sweater, and trailed up the smooth skin of my stomach.

"I want you so bad, Lottie," Nolan breathed into my ear. If I hadn't lost my mind yet, his husky voice tickling my ear took away every responsible brain cell I had. I gripped the bottom of my sweater and pulled it over my head, leaving me sitting before him in only my bra.

"I've never seen anyone more beautiful," Nolan whispered as he pulled away to look at me for a moment. His fingers gripped the sides of my hips and squeezed. "If you'd been alive during the time of the Romans, your beauty would have been immortalized in stone."

I simply wanted to cease to exist in that very moment. My hands buried themselves in his hair as I yanked him back to me.

"Holy shit—" Nolan and I jumped apart at the sound of a third voice in the training room. Derek stood near the doors with wide eyes and his mouth gaping open. I scrambled for my sweater to try and cover myself as I wished for the ability to disappear right into the floor. Nolan stepped in front of me, blocking Derek's view. I pulled my sweater back on and tried to smooth down my hair, so I looked a little more put together and not like I'd just been caught making out with the team's quarterback in the place I worked.

"Dude, can I steal that line about the Romans?" Derek asked, his eyes still wide and unblinking as he continued to watch us. "I had no idea you had those kinds of moves."

"Derek." Nolan tried to stop him in his tracks.

"If I had any idea you were a romantic like that, I would have been coming to you for advice for years."

"Derek."

"By the way, I totally called this." Derek motioned between me and Nolan. "And I will be claiming this relationship at the wedding when I'm the best man."

"Derek! Please leave." Nolan raised his voice, finally getting Derek to stop talking.

Derek's gaze bounced from me to Nolan one more time before he disappeared back out the door to the training room.

"I cannot believe that just happened," I breathed as I covered my face to try and hide my embarrassment. Nolan's hands wrapped around my wrists as he gently tugged my hands away from my face.

"Are you okay?"

I nodded.

"That could have been so much worse than it was," I told him. "Derek was probably the best-case scenario. I can't believe I let myself do that *here*."

Nolan's thumbs rubbed small soothing circles on the backs of my hands. "I'll talk to him. It'll be okay."

"We needed to be more careful than that," I continued, realizing how close I could have been to losing my job if anyone else had walked in. I felt stupid for jumping straight into the deep end the second I was blinded by my feelings. "We can't do that again."

"Derek has been joking that we would eventually end up dating since the moment all of us met. I'm not sure what exactly he saw there in the beginning when the two of us hated each other," Nolan joked, trying to lighten my mood.

"We aren't dating." The words slipped from my mouth like a different kind of reflex.

"I'm not sure what you'd call what we're doing then, Lottie." Nolan dropped my hands and I tried to ignore the cold, empty feeling that replaced the warmth he provided.

"Whatever this is, *this*"—I motioned between the two of us and waved to encompass the training room—"can't happen again."

"That's fair," Nolan agreed. "But my feelings for you aren't going anywhere, Lottie. If you want to wait until after the season, that's fine. But I'm not changing how I treat you. That would be a disservice to what you deserve."

I had always been the girl with her entire life put together—the seven-year plan, the to-do lists, the planner, the career goals. And while I may have planned out my life so much that I'd actually missed out on living it, I had never guessed that truly living life meant risking parts of myself that could be so easily ruined by someone else.

Nolan's eyes were soft as he watched me try and sort through my feelings.

Growing up, I never had the best example of what a healthy romantic relationship looked like. But here was Nolan, doing his best to let me lead whatever was happening between us without letting me stomp out the feelings he had for me. He was working through his own problems that affected him deeply, but still took the time to be considerate of me. For the first time in my life, I felt truly lost and unsure of what I needed to do next.

"I think it would be best if we waited until after the season to do anything official," I started. "If that's what we truly want then. For now, we can just get to know each other."

That muscle jumped in Nolan's jaw. But he still managed to give me a short nod of agreement.

"We have a plane to Wisconsin to catch," I reminded him as I went to grab my carry-on for the game tonight. "And you have a rookie that needs your help."

The airport the team plane took off from was a few miles away and we would be expected there within the next hour. Nolan walked with me to the training room door and held it open for me to walk through first without saying another word.

Now I just needed to figure out how to avoid eye contact with Derek for the rest of the weekend.

Chapter 21

Nolan

"Don't reveal your cards to the defense," I told Caleb during the fourth quarter. He'd managed to keep the Bobcats one score ahead of the Wisconsin Holsteins. He'd thrown a few interceptions within the last fifteen minutes though, as the defense began to realize the crutch that Derek had become for Caleb. His tells had become too obvious. "Have faith in your other receivers. Trust that everyone will do their job and be where you need them to be on their routes. If you continue to rely on Derek, the defense will take that option away from you and leave you scrambling."

Caleb nodded his head as he took a sip of water as we waited for the offense's turn to go back on the field.

"How much quicker do you think I need to be from snap of the ball to release of my throw?" Caleb asked me.

I registered the respect in Caleb's eyes as he waited for my response. The two of us had worked like a seamless team the entire game. I would give Caleb advice and he'd either take it or push back with a different perspective that he'd seen out on the field that I hadn't been able to consider. It was a completely different experience than anything else I'd ever had with football, and it was *exhilarating*. I understood now what Lottie was trying to teach me earlier in the season. Watching Caleb throw touchdowns gave me nearly the same feeling that throwing one of my own did.

"If you trust your receivers, I think that will make up for

the extra time you're spending. You're waiting for the play to develop so you can feel it rather than trusting that your guys will do their jobs so you can do yours." I grabbed the tablet that the team used to review film of the game on the sidelines so I could show Caleb what I was seeing him do. By the time our defense managed to shut down Wisconsin's offense again, Caleb looked surer of himself—boosted by the confidence of my belief in him.

The offense pulled their helmets back on and ran out on the field. I had almost forgotten the disappointment I'd felt from not being able to play in tonight's game. But there were more important things than solely worrying about my own wants and desires.

"You really seem to understand that kid." I glanced over my shoulder to see my head coach now standing next to me. His eyes were on the play card in his hands as he read the next playoff for Caleb to call.

"I relate a lot to him," I told him as we watched Caleb execute the play.

"You have a natural talent for coaching," Coach Randolph noted.

"You really think so?" I asked. If the man who saw enough potential in me to draft a scrawny kid in the first round of the NFL draft saw enough potential in me for coaching, maybe it was time I started taking it seriously.

"I do." The older man gave me one of his rare smiles before returning his attention back to the rookie quarterback and his offense.

"I know that Coach Elliott is retiring at the end of the season." I chose my words carefully. "I wasn't sure if you had anyone in mind to replace him, but I've been thinking about expressing my interest for the job."

Coach Randolph's eyebrows shot up in surprise. I was sure he thought, just like everybody else, that I'd take all the money that I'd made in the league and live a life of luxury doing absolutely nothing. If I was being honest with myself, up until a few months ago I would have thought the same. But after the encouragement from Lottie, who seemed to see the potential I had—just like Coach Randolph had all those years ago—I'd finally begun to feel like I would have a sense of purpose once this crazy ride was all said and done.

"Let's talk on the plane on the way home." Coach Randolph slapped me on the back before he wandered down the sideline, closer to the end zone that Caleb was gearing up to help the team score in.

I felt an immense amount of pride for having the courage to do something for myself that was far out of my comfort zone. I searched the faces of all the Bobcats staff standing along the sideline, looking for one person I wanted to share this moment with.

Lottie stood back near the entrance to the locker room where she normally posted up during the game. She was bundled up in a thick coat, stocking cap, and scarf. The rosiness in her cheeks from the bite of the wind made her look young and full of life. The moment I turned to walk toward her, I saw all my teammates throw their hands in the air around me as they cheered for what I assumed was another touchdown from Caleb.

With each step I took closer to Lottie, I realized that the Nolan Hill that started this season would have been angry and jealous of my teammate for having so much success. Without Lottie, I would have missed out on the unexpected happiness I was experiencing.

"Hi," I greeted once I was close enough. Those beautiful blue eyes crinkled with the smile that broke out on her face.

"Hi!"

I was quickly becoming a shameless man who would do anything to hear the excitement in her voice.

"This has been an awesome game for Caleb."

"It has," I agreed. "I talked with my coach about coaching next season."

I heard her intake of breath and hated that she was

surprised that I had followed through on her idea. I wanted her to know that I didn't want to be someone who wallowed in their misery when they realized their life was changing and there was nothing they could do to stop it. I wanted to be a man of action. Someone she could be proud of.

"Can I cook you dinner tomorrow night to thank you for the idea?" I kept my voice low as some of the athletic training staff wandered around us, refilling water bottles for the team.

I knew that Lottie had set her boundaries for what would happen between us while I was still playing, but I had also made it clear that I wasn't going to stop showing her how I felt about her. It also hadn't gone overlooked that staying with the Bobcats would keep me in Lottie's orbit. If I decided to coach, I was doing that for myself. But I also didn't want to know a future that didn't include Charlotte Thompson. Because a future without her would never be complete.

Lottie nodded after a minute at my request for dinner. "I'll come over to your place tomorrow," I told her.

And as I stared into her eyes and saw those perfect lips pull into one of her beautiful smiles while the crowd roared around us as they celebrated the Bobcats' victory, I felt like I was walking away a different kind of winner.

Cheers erupted on the plane as the guys celebrated another great performance by Caleb. Derek and I joined in from the front as we watched them take videos of some of the linemen trying to hoist Caleb onto their shoulders in the aisle of the plane.

But as soon as we reached cruising altitude, I slipped out of my seat next to Lottie and into the empty one next to my head coach in the first row of the plane.

"Hey, Coach, I was hoping we could continue that conversation about me potentially joining the staff next year."

Coach Randolph nodded his head as he remembered what we talked about earlier. "Sure, sure," he said. "I think you would be a great addition to the staff with the knowledge and wisdom you bring, but I wanted to run one other option by you."

My stomach sank as the first few thoughts of not being good enough began to trickle inside my head.

"I know you haven't been healthy this whole season and I know you intended for this one to be your last, but I've spoken with the owner and the coaching staff about bringing you back for one more year so you can really end it the way you want to."

My mind ran blank as I realized what he was offering me. It felt like everything I had been mentally preparing myself for was short-circuiting inside of my head as I was gifted an opportunity that I would have once considered to come from my dreams—the chance to keep playing and prolong the end for one more year. But I thought about my body and the physical decline I'd experienced these past few seasons and how my career was starting to take a toll on me.

Would I even last another season? It was only November now and I could tell how much slower my body was recovering during the week than it had in previous years. Who was to say next year would be any different? Maybe even worse?

"Now, you don't have to say anything yet. I just want you to think on it. You've done so much for this organization, and we just want to do right by you." Coach Randolph reached over to give my shoulder a squeeze as I sat there still trying to process the curve ball that he had thrown at me.

I didn't even remember walking back to my seat. And when Lottie asked me how the conversation went, I found myself telling her it went well while leaving out the part about playing again next year because I was afraid that I'd only see disappointment on her face instead of the happiness currently there.

My conversation with Lottie about waiting until after the season to date replayed in my head. She had made it clear that for her own professional boundaries she would wait until I wasn't a player anymore because, while her career was just starting and reaching new heights, mine was ending.

Would it be selfish of me to take Coach Randolph's offer only to prolong the inevitable end? Would that ruin any chances I had with Lottie?

I glanced over to catch a glimpse of her with her eyes closed and her head leaned against the window as she tried to get an hour or so of sleep on our short flight home. Her hand rested on the arm rest between us, and I risked the chance of anyone seeing me as I wrapped my pinky around hers for just a moment.

My mind stretched itself into different shapes as it tried to work through every scenario, but my heart clenched when I felt Lottie's pinky squeeze mine before it slipped back into her lap.

Chapter 22

Lottie

"Are you sure you don't need to check on the turkey?" Olivia asked me as she sat at my kitchen island.

It was Thanksgiving afternoon, and the team had a short practice earlier this morning before Coach Randolph had given everyone the remainder of the day to spend with their families. I wasn't sure what had come over me earlier in the week when I had invited all our friends over to my apartment for Thanksgiving dinner because boxed stuffing and a supermarket turkey were the extent of my knowledge—which Olivia was reminding me of with her judgement over my first turkey.

"I'm following the directions," I told her.

"When does everyone get here?" She glanced over at the clock on the wall, which read an hour before I had told people to show up and I had yet to start getting myself ready. My hair was still in a dirty bun, and I still had on the clothes I wore to practice earlier today.

"In about—" The buzzer to my apartment cut me off. Panic clenched at my insides as I began to wonder if I had given someone the wrong time.

"Who is it?" I asked into the intercom.

"Nolan."

I ignored Olivia's laugh as I buzzed him up.

"And the two of you *aren't* dating?" I continued to ignore my sister as she gave me a look that said I was kidding myself.

But before I could reply, Nolan walked through my front door with multiple containers of food.

"Did you make all of this?" I asked as I rushed to help him. My eyes danced over the jeans that accentuated every muscle in his legs that he had paired with a light blue button-down shirt and navy sweater. He was easily the best-looking thing in my apartment, and I struggled to take my eyes off him. I would have stared at him all day if Olivia hadn't cleared her throat to grab my attention and subtly tell me to stop staring at him.

"Of course," he replied, as if it were the simplest of gestures. "I couldn't imagine cooking an entire Thanksgiving meal by myself—especially my first one."

Once Nolan had emptied the containers onto my counter, he stepped back to take in my dirty hair and clothes. "What else needs to be done?"

"The pumpkin pie is cooling on the rack. The turkey is in the oven. The stuffing is on the stove . . ." I paused as I tried to think through everything I had done this morning.

"You know what," Nolan said as he reached out to put both hands on my shoulders. He brought me close, so my attention was forced to focus on him rather than the endless checklist in my head. "I'll handle it. I'm sure Olivia can fill me in. You go get yourself ready before everyone starts showing up. Knowing Adam, he'll be thirty minutes early." If my baby sister wasn't watching the two of us like we were one of her favorite reality dating shows, I would have kissed him right then and there.

"Thank you." I breathed a sigh of relief.

Nolan nodded. "I know today's important." He glanced at the bucket list still pinned to my fridge.

I gave him a smile as my heart warmed. He had remembered my desire for the holidays to be different this year, which meant the world to me. Instead of watching the Thanksgiving Day parade over store-bought pie and turkey with my sister, I wanted us to be surrounded by our friends that had quickly become the family we felt like we never had.

"I think only the salad is left." I watched Olivia show Nolan where I kept my serving bowls while she pulled out the ingredients I had bought yesterday. I hesitated in the doorway to my room as I watched the two work together as they began to chop everything up.

My heart squeezed at the unfamiliar sight. Neither of us had a male figure in our lives that ever took the time to simply spend time with us. I could tell by the set in Olivia's shoulders and the quick glances she cast toward Nolan that she was just as nervous as I was.

By the time I had finished getting ready, I found the two of them chatting on my couch with glasses of wine in their hands like they were suddenly old friends. As if Nolan could sense me entering the room, he turned with his wine glass in hand. He took in my freshly blown out hair, the red sweater I had tucked into a belt at my waist to give myself some shape with the black silk skirt that ended right at the top of my ankle boots.

A part of me wanted to fight against the way Nolan's gaze made me feel like a teenager again with her first crush. A small voice in the back of my head reminded me that men never stayed long in my life. It reminded me that if I swooned at the way his eyes hungrily roamed over my body, I'd be too blind to see the signs of him getting closer and closer to the door. If I let myself put a word to the way I had become excited to see him every day, I'd miss the reality that I was only there to serve a purpose. That I was never going to be the most important thing in someone's life.

"You look beautiful."

Nolan's words brought me back to my living room, aware again of the gorgeous man's attention that I had captured. I glanced over to my sister, only to see her smiling at the two of us as if she were happy to finally see me being treated the way I deserved. When my eyes swung back to meet a pair of brown ones that were quickly becoming a haven for me, I tried to remind myself that I did deserve happiness and not all men were like my father.

I silenced that voice inside of my head—that sounded suspiciously like my father's—telling me I didn't deserve the sincerity in Nolan's gaze and wrapped my arms around his neck to pull him into a hug. The moment his arms encircled my waist, closing me in like my personal sanctuary, the voice finally went quiet. There was a hesitation between the two of us now after the conversation I'd had with him about the boundaries we needed to put in place for the rest of the season that hadn't been there before. I could practically feel how badly Nolan wanted to kiss me in that moment, but instead settled for a hug.

"Thank you," I whispered into his ear.

The buzzer to my apartment went off again and Olivia went to go answer it this time as Nolan offered me the glass of wine sitting on my coffee table that I hadn't noticed he'd poured for me.

"I'm only letting you up if you brought those pumpkin chocolate chip muffins you said you would make," Olivia spoke into my speaker.

"I've got them! Now let me up, it's cold out here," Derek's voice crackled back.

Olivia buzzed Derek in, and my eyebrows shot up as I met my sister's gaze. "And when did you learn that Derek makes pumpkin chocolate chip muffins?"

"After we all went sledding in that snowstorm." Olivia shrugged her shoulders, completely ignoring the curious look I was giving her. "He told me he baked, and I said I wouldn't believe him unless he baked them for me."

Nolan leaned in toward me, so his lips brushed against the outer shell of my ear. "I didn't even know that Derek baked."

The two of us exchanged a knowing look as we watched Olivia open the door for Derek, who had three containers of what looked like bite-sized muffins, and if I wasn't mistaken,

I thought I saw a smudge of flour still on his forehead. Olivia reached up and brushed the white powder off his face and I watched a blush color Derek's cheeks.

"Oh, fuck yeah," I heard Nolan say under his breath. "I finally have something to make fun of that bastard with in the locker room."

The buzzer went off again and Nolan stepped away from my side to let Hawthorn and his family up.

By the time that Jamil, Maggie and Tommy, and Adam and his family arrived, my apartment was filled to the brim with laughter and so much excited energy that I had never really experienced before. I tried my best to commit everything to memory so I could replace all the bad holidays I'd had with today.

Adam's wife, Nora, and Hawthorn's wife, Sarah, joined me in the kitchen to help carve the turkey and get the rest of the food set up for everyone to dish from.

"I don't want to overstep or anything like that"—Sarah spoke softly so only the three of us could hear her—"but I have never seen Nolan look so genuinely happy the way he does when he's with you."

I sucked a breath in when I realized what Sarah was trying to say.

Had we been that obvious or did Nolan talk with her and Hawthorn about us?

"The only person we have seen him with was his ex, Rachel, and those two never looked at each other the way you two do," Nora added as she took the lids off all the dessert containers.

"And please don't be nervous that we know or anything like that," Sarah added quickly because she must have seen the panic all over my face. "Nolan hasn't spoken with us about anything that's happened between you guys. But it's hard to miss the way you look at each other."

"We're not dating or anything." I wasn't sure why I found it necessary to clarify that to these two women that had

Nolan's best interests at heart, but the words slipped from my mouth before I could stop them and then just continued to spill out. "We don't want anything to interfere with his last season or my job while he's still playing."

Nora nodded her head as if that was all quite logical. "All things that are meant to last will always work out in the end." She reached over and placed her hand on mine before she announced to the room that dinner was ready. I stood there in the kitchen for a moment longer, looking down at the hand that she had touched, trying to understand what she saw.

"Coming." I glanced up to see Nolan standing next to me with two plates in his hands. He handed one to me and the two of us went to get in line with everyone else.

For the first time in my life, I got to sit down at a kitchen table in a room full of so much love and not a single argument filled the air.

Derek and Olivia broke the wishbone together and Olivia cackled in his face when her piece came away bigger. Hawthorn took first duty with their kids so Sarah could eat. Adam laced his arm over the back of Nora's chair. Jamil told stories about Thanksgivings with his family of ten back in his hometown in Florida growing up. Maggie and Tommy were snuggled up in each other's arms as they laughed along with everyone else.

It was all just so . . . perfect.

"Lottie and I can clean up," Nolan told everyone once the food was nearly all gone, and another bottle of cranberry wine had been opened. The two of us collected all the plates and brought them to the kitchen together.

"I'll wash, you'll dry?" Nolan asked me as he started filling the sink up with water and soap. I grabbed a couple of dry towels from under the sink and began drying off the dishes he handed to me.

"Thank you for your help today," I told him once we'd settled into an easy rhythm.

"Was it everything you hoped it would be?"

"And more," I told him.

A smile lit up his face when he saw the happiness on mine. "Even Olivia and Derek's fight over the wishbone?"

A laugh bubbled out of me. "Especially that."

"Then I think there's only one thing left to do," he told me as he grabbed a pen off my counter and extended it to me. I gently took the pen from him and uncapped it as I walked over to the list on my fridge.

"Only a few left," Nolan noted as he watched me mark off the one about Thanksgiving.

"A lot of them are thanks to you," I told him.

Nolan studied me for a few moments before he spoke again. "Once I stopped being a complete asshole to you, I realized that I quite like it when you're happy."

This time, I completely ignored that voice in my head telling me that it was all a lie and by tomorrow he'd be bored of me as I reached for him and pulled him toward me until our bodies were flush together. As soon as his arms wrapped around me, I found enough courage to kiss him in a room full of our friends and family simply because it made me happy.

Because I wanted to prove that voice wrong and show it that I was worthy of someone's love, even if it believed otherwise.

Chapter 23

Nolan

Lottie and I spent nearly every moment we could together to try and get my knee healthy enough to play against Denver the Sunday after Thanksgiving. Lottie understood that this team and this game brought me happiness that nothing else I'd experienced in life did and she was doing everything in her power to make sure it wasn't the end for me. Between therapy sessions and discussing the prospect of coaching after the season was over, she had her sights set on what made me happy. There was a part of me that felt guilty for not telling her that the team had offered me another year, but I wanted to make the best decision for myself without anyone else's influence. Especially because I knew that Lottie would always tell me to do what was best for me.

Lottie even showed up to the facility with me early so I could have extra time preparing before the game. She never complained when I asked anything extra of her. In her eyes, her job was to help me be successful and she would do whatever it took for that to happen. Lottie must have sensed the nerves I had about returning to the game without me having to say anything to her and she made sure to stick strictly to our routine to help me mentally prepare.

I felt at home back on the field telling my team the next play in the middle of a huddle. But the two games I had missed had left me on shaky ground during the first half of this game. There was rust on the wheels that I had yet to knock off and after the fifth pass that I threw short of my receiver, I was beginning to worry if I was the right person for my team after Caleb's lights out performances.

"Are you alright?" Derek asked me on yet another third down that looked like we wouldn't reach the first down marker.

"Yeah," I told him with a false bravado that Derek's frown told me he saw right through.

"It's just you and me, bud." With a slap on the back, Derek ran to his starting position for the next play.

I sighed, because while I appreciated what he was trying to do, Derek didn't realize that during every play all I could see was everybody but my intended receivers. I was distracted by the menacing looks on the defenders' faces or the face-painted fans in the stands trying to distract me and doing a marvelous job of it today.

Nobody really talks about the hardest part about coming back after an injury. It isn't doing the movements that you're so used to doing during a game. It's getting past the mental barrier that injury built in the darkness while you were trying to work on getting better. The way that injury secretly tore down every shred of self-confidence you had ever built, making you feel uneasy doing the thing you loved.

No matter how hard I tried to remind myself of all the times I'd succeeded and performed better than everyone else around me, my mind replayed the sharp pain I felt as my body slammed into the ground just a few weeks ago. As if the injury had even poisoned my own mind to work against me.

The crowd in Denver was practically feral as we ran off the field for the half. They had the lead over us, which had been considered unlikely heading into today's game seeing as Denver was having one of their worst seasons to date.

As soon as I crossed the threshold into the locker room, a hand wrapped around my forearm and pulled me toward the training room. I couldn't see Lottie's face under the scarf she had wrapped around her neck. All I could do was focus on the knit ball on her stocking cap bobbing up and down as she walked with purpose away from the rest of the team.

The moment we were alone, she turned on me with a determined look on her face.

"You are still playing as if your knee is going to fail you, Nolan." There was a fierceness in her eyes that called to the competitive parts of me. "It won't."

"It already did once this season," I reminded her.

"Don't argue with me!"

I snapped my mouth shut when I realized how serious she was being.

"Listen to me right now. What did I tell you during that first game? That you are Nolan *fucking* Hill. You've accomplished things other quarterbacks can only dream about. You've put in the work. You've proved that you've made progress. Go out there and let loose."

Lottie was now pacing in front of me. "Have fun for once. Stop worrying about all of this being taken from you or that you aren't good enough. Go out there and give your career the last season it deserves. Give *yourself* a season you deserve. Enjoy it before it's gone. Believe in yourself, Nolan. Because I do. There is no one better fit for this moment right now."

The shine in her eyes matched the ferocity in her voice. That look crawled inside of my heart and laid a claim there as I felt a fresh wave of confidence fill me. It was as if I were looking at myself through her eyes—an athlete who had worked to the top of their career and obliterated all the competition within miles, past or present. I saw the respect she had for the work I put in and I saw the belief she spoke of having in me.

"Come on," she told me, breaking the heavy silence between us. "Let's go to work."

For years I had wondered what it would be like to have someone who put me first and valued every part of me in a way that no one else in the world did. As I walked back out of the tunnel matching the stride of the woman next to me as if the two of us were marching into battle together, I finally understood what that must be like.

Coach Randolph stopped me on the sidelines as the last few seconds of halftime ticked off the clock. "Are you ready?"

"I am." He took in my steely gaze and the determined set of my shoulders before stepping aside, satisfied with what he saw.

I caught Lottie's eye one more time. She flashed me a smile that nearly stole all the air from my lungs and gave me a quick wink. Those blue eyes that shined just for me in that moment were the last thing I focused on before I pulled my helmet on and ran out onto the field with my team.

"Let's show them who's the better team," Derek shouted into the huddle after I relayed the first play of the half.

For the first time all game, I finally felt the possibility of winning this game within my grasp. Lottie's words echoed in my mind as we started our march down the field. She was right, there wasn't anyone better to lead this moment than me, and the moment I started to believe that again was the moment that everything clicked.

People heard athletes talk about getting in the zone in interviews, but few detailed what it took to get there, besides concentration, which was confidence. And when a player loses all confidence in themselves, the only thing that will get them back is someone else believing in them enough to fill the gaps.

My body slipped back into the familiar routines I'd practiced nearly my entire life, fueled by the words from the woman standing on the sidelines with enough belief in her heart to refill mine. Suddenly the noise of the crowd, the intensity of the defense across the line of scrimmage from us, and the expectations I had put on myself for this season all fell away and it was just me and my team playing catch. Everything felt easy.

Moments after I managed to connect with Derek on a longer route that had him free to run into the end zone, a *laugh* exploded out of me. For the first time in years, I felt happy playing the sport I had dedicated so much of my life to and all because I was reminded of what my self-worth was.

As I ran off the field with my teammates as they celebrated Derek's touchdown that tied the game up, I scanned the sidelines. Lottie had positioned herself near the side of the bench where I was sitting this game as if she knew that I would want to see her after completing a drive like that. The two of us smiled at each other.

"I think I have you to thank for that," I told her as I threw my coat over my shoulders to keep me warm while our defense did their job.

Lottie's smile grew wider as she shook her head at me. "I wasn't the one on the field, Hill."

"But your pep talk inspired me, which seems to be becoming a recurring theme." It killed me that all I could do was stand a few feet away from her as my hands itched to pull her into me. It was almost poetic how I thought she would be the last useful person for me and had now become the most important person for my success.

"So, thank you," I told her, hoping she could see how deeply I meant it.

The way the corners of her lips tugged up into the smallest hint of a smile told me that she understood.

"You still have a game to win. Thank me when that happens." Lottie reached out and gently squeezed my hand so quickly that I almost thought I imagined it before she turned and walked away.

"This is our time," Derek shouted over the din of the crowd. "Just you and me, bud."

While it felt daunting to truly open up to Derek or Hawthorn about my struggles with my injuries over the past few years, they always seemed to know that all I ever needed was for them to simply be there. Their belief in me had never wavered. Derek *was* always there for me and as I dropped back into the pocket after the ball was snapped, he did exactly what he always did and found a way to get open and just like that, magic happened.

It happened in slow motion as the ball left my fingertips, each one slowly peeling away as I sent it sailing into the air down the field toward Derek. I could practically see each rotation as the laces spun around and the ball drew nearer to its intended target. There was no air left in the stadium as everyone held their breath, waiting to see if Derek would make the play. Then, all at once, everything moved in real time as Derek's hands wrapped around the ball and secured it in his arms. He dodged a few of Denver's defensemen as he barreled toward the end zone just as the clock dropped under the last thirty seconds of the game.

The noise was the first thing to come back. It sounded at first like my ears were full of cotton as the dull roar grew louder. I ran with the rest of my team to greet Derek in the end zone where he had launched the ball into the stands in celebration.

As my team lifted both Derek and me up into the air, I realized that I didn't need a knockout season to end my career with a bang. All I wanted was to enjoy the moments like this with the people I loved next to me. Because when it was all said and done, I wouldn't be able to recall the statistics or certain plays, but I would remember the joy I felt as I celebrated with my teammates.

"Just you and me, bud!" Derek shouted at me again as our teammates celebrated around us.

Chapter 24

Lottie

After the game in Denver, something changed between me and Nolan. Over the next few weeks, our time together extended beyond practices and games. Suddenly, Nolan was everywhere. After practices he would either invite me over for dinner or show up at mine to cook and it was always just an evening of enjoying each other's company. We hadn't had sex since that first night together at his place, despite several times that I wanted nothing more than to forget the boundaries I had set and just give in to the desire building inside of me. What was most surprising to me was how I didn't seem to mind spending so much time with him and how within a few weeks it felt all too normal.

When the buzzer of my apartment rang the morning after the fourteenth game of the season, I wasn't surprised to see Nolan coming up the stairs with two coffees in his hands. He wore a beanie to fight off the cold winter weather that had started to settle in around the city of Chicago. His sharp cheekbones were hidden behind a layer of stubble that he had started to grow out and my fingers itched to run down the lines of his cheeks to feel it.

"Good morning," I greeted him, happily accepting the coffee he extended out to me. "To what do I owe the pleasure?"

I had given Nolan the morning off after yesterday's win to give his body time to recover. I'd watched a completely different

Nolan Hill play these past few weeks. It looked as if he was free of the burden of pressure he had placed on himself at the start of the season. He looked freer while he was playing, and I even saw him smile and laugh a few times throughout the games. Nolan's change in attitude had unlocked the missing piece of chemistry the team needed, and the Bobcats had marched to thirteen wins and one loss on the season. It was slowly becoming a historic year for the organization, as they now had the best record the program had ever seen.

Normally at this point in the season, the players began to drag—exhausted from how physical professional football games could be on their bodies. But the energy that radiated off Nolan made him look like a man full of excitement rather than someone who had been pushing his body to the limit for the past three and a half months.

"Since you gave me an off day today, I had an idea," Nolan told me as he folded his long frame onto my couch. "I know you wanted to complete your bucket list before the end of the year and there's one thing on it that I kept thinking about. I thought today would be the perfect day to do it."

My mind sorted through the remaining items on my list before I realized which one he was talking about.

"A yes day?" I asked. Nolan nodded, his smile revealing his excitement for his idea. I had been thinking about this since Olivia had put it on my list. Normally a yes day consisted of a day where parents had to say yes to everything a kid asked, but Olivia had wanted this to be a day where everyone else told me to do something that I had to say yes to—with the intention of me doing things that I normally never would have done for myself. Olivia had wanted today to be a day where I was pampered instead of constantly being the person to pamper everyone else.

"I've been working with Olivia and Maggie on it, so it won't just be me telling you to do something for yourself today. I wanted the people that you care about in your life and that know you best to contribute."

Every response I could have had died on my tongue. I wasn't used to someone doing something for me that was so thoughtful. He'd taken the time to include my sister and friend to make sure they were involved in today.

He's just love bombing you. Remember when your father would bring home your favorite candy after he missed out on important events for yet another football game? He knows what you want to hear and what you want him to do and he's using it to his advantage.

I forced that voice out of my mind, refusing to let the man who ruined most of my childhood leech anything else from my life.

"What did you have in mind?" I asked as I sipped on the coffee he'd given me. The taste of vanilla hit my tongue and I realized that Nolan had given me my exact coffee order. He must have noticed it from all those mornings after our runs where I'd make a coffee as he went through his treatment routine.

"I made an appointment for you this morning at the Waldorf Astoria Spa. I got my mother a spa day there last year and she loved it. She suggested it for today."

My heart paused when I realized he'd taken the time to ask his mother about his first idea. Whether or not his mother knew who he was getting a spa day for, a nervous energy swelled in my stomach.

"You don't need to get ready for anything because Olivia made sure I booked a hair appointment while you were there too. She may have said she could count the months since you'd last had a hair appointment by the inches of root that was showing." Nolan coughed when he finished relaying my sister's message, clearly uncomfortable with how the two of us operated in our relationship.

"Of course she said that." I rolled my eyes as I grabbed my coat. "Did you book a massage for yourself while we're there or are you just dropping me off?"

"I was planning on waiting for you. I hadn't booked

anything for myself. Today's supposed to be a day for you, not me." Nolan held the front door open for me as the two of us took the stairs down to his Range Rover waiting on the curb outside.

"Is there any way you can book one? I think you'd really benefit from it . . . And I wouldn't mind having you there with me."

Nolan looked like he wanted to argue again about how today was supposed to be just for me, but he stopped himself when he realized this was something I wanted and not just a sneaky way for me to still worry about taking care of him.

"I'll ask when we get there," he conceded.

The Waldorf Astoria was on the north side of downtown and only a few blocks away from Magnificent Mile, the stretch of Michigan Avenue known as Chicago's premier commercial district. The Waldorf Astoria's architecture was made to replicate the buildings in Paris with its private terraces, dramatic archways, and light-colored stone.

It was easily the most luxurious building I had ever stepped foot in and not somewhere I would have ever taken myself to. A large Christmas tree sat in the middle of the front courtyard, twinkling golden lights flashing against silver and gold ornaments. String lights crisscrossed around the u-shaped space, making the area feel like its own personal Christmas wonderland. The entire lobby was full of smaller Christmas trees and a large roaring fireplace crackled in the corner near a small sitting area. Velvet bows were tied around the old sconces dotted through the lobby and "White Christmas" by Bing Crosby filled the room from an old record player in the sitting area.

People in business professional attire bustled around and I felt out of place in my jeans and sweater. Nolan was dressed similarly next to me, but he'd somehow managed to make his jeans and flannel combination look like it was straight off the runway compared to my dressed-down appearance.

Nolan led me toward a golden elevator, giving a few nods to people that recognized him as we walked through the few people lingering around the lobby. He selected the tenth floor where the spa was and the two of us stood in comfortable silence as the elevator rose.

The spa had the same Parisian architecture that the rest of the building had, except everything was brighter and airier with the hope of providing a relaxing space. A woman dressed all in white greeted us at the front desk.

"I paid for a package for Charlotte Thompson," Nolan told the woman. I watched the woman's eyes roam over Nolan's face and the length of his body before she went to look for the name he'd given her. She hadn't even bothered to notice me standing next to him. My stomach twisted as I watched the woman's eyes flick back to Nolan as if she were hoping his attention would be on her. Part of me wanted to reach out and slip my arm into his, but then I remembered that wasn't necessarily something we'd ever talked about after I had shut down his initial advances.

"I have it here." The woman looked up and finally noticed me standing next to Nolan. Her gaze was full of judgement as she looked me up and down. I tried to keep the heat of embarrassment from flooding my cheeks. "Is that all you needed?"

"I wanted to add a massage for myself while I wait for her," Nolan told the woman, completely oblivious to her interest in him and clear disinterest in me.

The woman clicked on her keyboard for a few moments. "The only thing we would be able to do is switch Charlotte's massage to a couple's massage."

There was a question lingering in the air from the worker as if she were waiting for Nolan to confirm if I was just his sister or if we were together.

"That's fine." It took everything in me to keep my eyebrows from rising in surprise at his answer. The woman pursed her lips before she clicked on her keyboard for a few more moments.

"The two of you can follow me. We can get you in for your massage first." Any interest the woman had in Nolan had disappeared as she led us to a room with two massage beds in the center. Plush white robes were laid out on chairs next to each bed. Steam was being pumped into the room and soft music trickled in from the speakers in the ceiling.

Nolan didn't hesitate before he began to discard his layers while I stood frozen just inside the door. When he realized I wasn't also undressing to slip under the sheet on my massage table, he stopped. "Are you okay?"

On instinct, I nodded my head. But I knew my wide eyes and slack jaw told a different story as I watched Nolan dress down into his underwear. We'd obviously seen each other completely naked before but that had been in the confines of Nolan's apartment where I could have convinced myself that none of it was real and we were living in our own fantasy. Standing in a room with him as the two of us were expected to undress and have an intimate couple's massage together felt very real. Together with how thoughtful Nolan had been with arranging today for me, my feelings were a jumbled mess.

Before Nolan could realize why I was staring at him like it was the first time I'd ever laid eyes on his body, I turned around to face away from him while I stripped down to my bra and underwear. But not before noticing the way my entire body felt drawn to him in a way that I couldn't explain, or maybe didn't *want* to explain.

"You know I've seen you naked before, right?" Nolan asked, sending heat through every inch of my body. I did my best to pretend like I hadn't heard him as I quickly slid under the sheet and lay face down on my table.

"Make sure they work your upper back and neck well, that's where you like to carry your stress," I started to tell him.

Nolan made a noise that cut me off. "You're not on duty today, Lottie. I can take care of myself. Just enjoy the day without having to worry about anyone other than yourself."

I stayed quiet as I realized I didn't know how to worry about just myself. All my life there had always been someone else that was my responsibility to care for—Olivia, my clients, or the players on the team I was working for.

As I closed my eyes once the massage began, I realized that since I wasn't used to having my needs be met, prioritizing myself felt selfish even though it shouldn't. And the man lying next to me right now was forcing me to see how worthy I was of these things.

"This is part two of your day," Nolan told me once he pulled up in front of my favorite Mexican restaurant in downtown Chicago that I rarely ever had the time to go to. "Olivia and Maggie are already inside waiting for you. I'll pick you up afterwards because the last part of your day involves me again."

"You're not eating with us?" I asked, trying to keep the disappointment from my voice.

Nolan shook his head. "It's a girl's lunch. Who would I be to intrude on that?"

The car behind us honked, stopping me from being able to convince him to come in. Nolan gave me the biggest smile, truly happy that he got to do something for me instead of it being the other way around.

"I'll see you soon," he shouted out the window after I shut the door to his car. "Have fun!"

With that, he pulled off the curb and disappeared into the Chicago traffic. I gave Olivia's name to the hostess just inside the door and she escorted me to a table in the back that was already occupied by my two best friends.

"You look like a brand-new person!" Olivia jumped up from the table and wrapped her arms around me. "You've got a certain glow about you now."

"Do we think it has anything to do with a certain quarterback?" Maggie asked as Olivia and I sat down.

I flashed her a look. "Why would you say that?"

"Oh, you know," Maggie replied with faux innocence. "Just that he meticulously planned this entire day and sent detailed texts to both me and your sister about this. Doesn't seem like something that would happen in a casual relationship."

Both Maggie and Olivia were giving me knowing looks as they watched me struggle to come up with a response to tell them otherwise.

"I thought today was supposed to be all about me and what I want, so shouldn't that include answering your interrogation questions?" I asked.

Olivia shook her head slowly. "Not so fast there, Lottie. Today is a yes day where *you* can't say no to anything. So, if we want you to actually have a real conversation about the guy you clearly like, then you kind of have to. It falls under the rules."

I was saved for only a few moments by the waiter asking for our drink orders before it was time to face the music. "I don't know what you want me to say," I started.

"It's a yes or no question, Lottie. Do you like Nolan Hill or not?" Olivia was direct and to the point.

The answer was easy for me. I'd known for a few months that I liked Nolan, that much was obvious. But what I was struggling with was what I was going to do about it. There was just over a month left in the season, but even when the season ended, that didn't address the voice inside of my head telling me I wasn't worthy of him, that I wasn't worthy to be loved, and part of me wondered if maybe it was true. Maybe I was always meant to be there for others but never have someone be there for me. Maybe I really didn't know how to love someone because I'd never had the chance to be taught how growing up.

"I do like him," I told Olivia after I fought through all the thoughts in my head. Even though Maggie and Olivia looked like they were waiting for me to say more, that was as much as I could give them with complete certainty for now.

"That man matches your energy." Olivia's voice was casual, but the intensity of her gaze told me that she thought I better not write this one off like any of the other guys I'd dated, or she'd never let me hear the end of it.

"I've never seen you smile as much as you have since you've sat down," Maggie added. "And I think we can all agree why that is."

I wanted to tell them that I was just happy with where my life was right now, but that wasn't the whole truth. I *was* happy with my life right now, but a lot of that had to do with Nolan. Laughter and smiles always came easy with him. So instead of denying it, I simply let the small smile spread across my face at the thought of him and enjoyed my favorite restaurant with two of my favorite people without letting the fear living in the back of my mind ruin the moment.

Chapter 25

Lottie

"How was lunch?" Nolan asked with that same smile that was there when he dropped me off. It was the kind of smile that turned women's heads and had them wondering how they'd get his attention so that he noticed them. So I actually felt lucky that his attention was just for me as he pulled his car away from the curb and toward the next part of my day that he'd planned.

Maybe Olivia was right, and I should stop getting in the way of myself.

"It was great. Olivia and Maggie mentioned you planned most of today?" I asked slyly, watching red slowly color the tops of Nolan's ears.

"They helped." Nolan's defense was a shrug of his shoulders, as if planning all of this for me was no big deal.

I decided to give him a break as I watched him turn the color of red wine and fidget under my gaze. "Where to next?"

The nervous set of his shoulders deflated at the change in topic. "The grocery store," he told me.

"What?" I asked, wondering if I heard him right.

"We're going to the grocery store." Nolan looked even more excited about this than the spa.

"Why?" His grin grew even wider at the hesitation in my voice.

"Because you never cook for yourself, and I always see

185

takeout menus on your counter whenever I've been at your place. I want to teach you to cook an easy meal that you can manage after a long day."

Nolan was right. Most of the time, I was too tired to cook anything for myself after practice. This gesture almost meant more to me than the massage did. He clearly had a love for cooking, and he wanted to share that with me.

"I thought we could shop together for the ingredients and then go back to your place and cook it in your own kitchen. The next time you think about ordering takeout again when it's just you, you have another option." Nolan parked the car in a spot near the front of the parking lot. The two of us walked together into the store and I was hit once again with how normal it was to be doing this together.

But what stood out even more was how *right* it felt.

Nolan pushed the cart and began listing off the ingredients we would need as the two of us worked our way through the aisles of the store.

"Do you have any Cajun seasoning?" Nolan asked me as we turned into the spice aisle.

I opened my mouth to tell him that I only had the basics when the words died on my tongue. I was sure I was seeing a ghost at the other end of the aisle. It had been almost a decade since I'd last seen him, but I recognized him instantly. His beard was now salt and pepper and I remembered that I used to love watching him shave when I was little before I realized how cruel he truly was. The wrinkles on his forehead and around his eyes had deepened since the last time I saw him. His hair had turned a silvery-white, no longer the color that mine was. He looked much more put together than the disheveled man I remembered from my childhood.

"Actually, I thought I saw a container of Cajun seasoning on an end cap," I told Nolan as I grabbed his arm and pulled him back out of the aisle before my father noticed us.

I had spent years dreaming about the day I might see him again and what that would be like—running into him in a grocery store in the spice aisle was not a scenario I had ever thought would be possible.

Nolan let out a small noise of protest, clearly confused by my erratic behavior, but still followed me out of the aisle. I grabbed the container of seasoning we needed that I had spotted near the self-checkout section and breathed a sigh of relief. I wasn't ready to face the man who had ruined much of my childhood and changed who I was at my very core, especially not while I was with Nolan. The last thing I wanted was for him to see me flounder.

"Is that everything?" I asked him, my eyes darting back toward the spice aisle we'd just left.

"I think so," Nolan replied as he scrolled through his list on his phone.

A moment later, my father exited the spice aisle and began walking our way.

"Okay, great!" I exclaimed. "Let's check out."

Nolan gave me another strange look as I began pushing him toward one of the last open self-checkout registers before my father could reach us.

"Are you okay?"

I pasted a wide smile on my face as we pushed the cart up to the register to start scanning. "I'm great! So excited for this meal, that's all."

My father filed into the first checkout on the other side of the area we were in. I could see him over the shelves separating us. Memories of slammed doors, disappointed nights, and broken promises. I had always thought that the first time I saw him, I'd be brave enough to go up to him and give him a piece of my mind for how he had treated me and Olivia. But here I was, cowering and too afraid to even make eye contact. It had been nearly ten years, but he still had a grasp on my life that I hadn't realized.

"Ready?" Nolan asked once the receipt printed.

I nodded and took over pushing the cart back out to his car, wanting to put as much distance between myself and that man as possible.

Today was supposed to be a day for me, full of things that I loved, and he had no place in it.

"This is my favorite meal," Nolan told me as he stood in my kitchen with my only apron wrapped around his body, "Kiss the Chef" stamped across the front. It was a gift from Olivia last year that she laughed at for hours when I cooked Christmas dinner in it.

Nolan had walked me through the first steps of his buffalo chicken flatbread recipe that he swore by on lazy nights. The two of us worked together, Nolan leading while I completed the tasks that he gave me. He made me prepare most of the meal, so he was confident I knew how to do it.

"Now just sprinkle the cheese on and then drizzle some of the buffalo hot sauce on top of that." Nolan had guided me through the entire recipe with a steady, patient voice that made me feel calm and gave me the space to work without feeling like I was being judged. I could easily see how he would be a fantastic coach in the future.

"You're good at this," I told him.

Nolan opened the oven for me so I could slip the flatbread inside. "Cooking? I think I owe that to my mother. She wanted to make sure that my future wife never felt like that would be solely her job."

I laughed at the thought of a young Nolan working alongside his mother in the kitchen growing up, helping her prepare dinners and sparking his future love for cooking.

"Teaching," I explained.

Nolan lifted a shoulder, as if to say it wasn't a big deal.

"Not many people have that skill, Nolan, and some may be able to do it, but not everyone can do it well."

He grew silent as if he were thinking deeply. I wanted him to realize that he was great at many things besides throwing a football down a field and that he would be successful for many years to come.

"I've never had someone outside of my parents celebrate me in the same way that you do," Nolan told me as he slowly untied the apron he was wearing.

"No one?" I asked, thinking about how none of his past girlfriends had supported him.

Luckily Nolan saw where my train of thought was heading. "My ex-fiancée never actually cared about anything I was interested in if it didn't benefit her in some way."

Nolan's comments from our first run came back to the forefront—his ex was an ex for a reason, and I was sad that he had been with someone who wasn't his biggest supporter.

"Do you remember when I told you that I'd been distracted the week I got hurt two years ago?" I nodded.

"Rachel and I had been fighting that week. She had started to move her stuff out. It took up most of my time that week and I had barely stepped foot in the practice facility outside of practices before that game. The injury was the final straw in our relationship." Nolan had balled the apron up in his hands as he recalled the moments leading up to the day that had weighed the heaviest on his mind this season.

I reached over to squeeze Nolan's arm as I tried to bring his attention away from his own thoughts. I wanted to show him that he was moving forward and clearly in a better place now. "I'm sorry that you had to go through that."

Nolan gave me a sad smile. "Thanks."

"Do you want a glass of wine?" I asked to fill the lingering silence.

"Sure," Nolan agreed.

The silence stretched on as I poured two glasses of wine.

"What are you thinking about?" I asked as I slid his glass over to him.

Nolan traced his finger around the bottom of the glass for a few moments before he finally spoke. "I've had the best day with you."

My wine glass froze just before it reached my lips once I registered his words. The hard brown eyes that I saw the very first time I met him were nowhere to be seen. His eyes shined with a sincerity that had me fighting that voice inside of my head once again trying to sabotage the moment.

"I had the best day and that was all thanks to you." I set my wine glass down on the counter next to me and reached over to squeeze his forearm. Nolan looked down at my hand before raising his gaze back to mine.

"I know you want to wait before we explore whatever is going on between us."

I sucked in a breath and held it as I waited for what he would say next.

"But I would like to talk about what exactly *is* going on, like put a name to it."

The buzzer of the oven rang through my stunned silence and gave me a few more seconds to get my thoughts together. I grabbed a knife to cut the flatbread into pieces for both of us as Nolan went to sit at my kitchen table. His quiet patience felt like a weighted blanket attempting to calm me, but I was aware of its weight at every moment.

"What kind of name are you looking for?" I asked as I set both plates down on the table. Nolan gave me a soft "thank you" as he took it from me. I wished I could be like my sister in that moment and find some way to throw humor into the situation to make it feel a little bit lighter.

But I wasn't lighthearted and wild like my sister, I was responsible and cautious—and I avoided situations of unnecessary risk, much like the conversation that was unfolding currently.

Nolan let out a long sigh as he prepared himself for what he wanted to say next. "I like you, Lottie. And I don't care how many times I have to say it to you for you to believe me. More than any other person I've ever met. I don't know what that means necessarily because you don't want to get

190

involved . . ." Nolan trailed off as I watched his steadiness devolve into distress.

My chest ached as I watched him struggle with putting his feelings out in the open and I wanted to ease some of his worries. I took a deep breath and tried to steady the nervous energy zipping through my body, narrowing my focus.

"I like you, too, Nolan." Nolan's gaze snapped up to meet mine, wide with surprise as if he hadn't expected me to feel the same way despite all that had happened between us thus far. "But we can't deny that our situation is complicated."

Nolan sighed and the look on his face was more defeated than after the Bobcats' only loss this season. His shoulders slumped forward, and he dropped his head into his hands.

"What are you wanting to establish from this?" I asked him. I hadn't expected this conversation to happen today, but I would be lying if I hadn't expected it to happen eventually. But I had gotten swept up in simply enjoying my time with Nolan and hadn't thought about labeling what exactly we were doing—which was very unlike me.

"I want to date you, Lottie," Nolan told me, his face serious. "But I want to respect your wishes, no matter how hard that is for me to do. Because if it were up to me, I'd have you on my arm right now as I proudly told the world that I'm yours. All I want is to be able to tell people that you're my girlfriend, but if we must continue as we are for the remainder of the season, I can live with that."

My breathing grew shallow as I tried to get my brain to function enough to craft a response. Nolan was the first person I'd ever dated where *everything* felt different. It was easy and comforting. He'd quickly become my favorite person to see during the day and the only person I wanted to tell when something good happened. He challenged me to be a better person and gave me a space in his life to make me feel like I belonged there with him.

But the truth was, it wasn't the fear of losing my job that was stopping me. It was the fear of being unlovable, of not being worthy enough for someone as great as Nolan Hill to want to be with me. The fear of losing my job was simply a cover for the more complex feelings I was avoiding.

"I just want to be extremely clear, Lottie," Nolan continued, those beautiful brown eyes boring into mine. "The second this season is over, we are going to be having this conversation again. I understand you want to wait till I'm retired and no longer a player. When that confetti falls from the ceiling of the stadium after we win the Super Bowl, you'll be the person I want to share it with."

Chapter 26

Nolan

The annual Bobcats' Christmas party happened on the Thursday night before our game on Christmas Eve that following Sunday. Every year, the organization rented out the Field Museum for the event and transformed the entire place into a winter wonderland to celebrate the season.

What many fans didn't realize was that the players, coaches, and staff often didn't get to celebrate the holidays the same way that everyone else did. We had practices and games on major holidays and if we did get to celebrate, it was with each other rather than with our families. To bring some semblance of the holiday season, the organization threw a giant party with a five-course meal, music and dancing, and gifts for everyone.

I normally didn't enjoy the party because over the past few years I had shown up alone and had to mingle with the owner and other investors all night rather than having fun with my teammates. These events had never been my style.

But tonight, I didn't mind having to schmooze various investors or the owner's family because I got to watch Lottie glide through the room from afar. She was in a floor-length black dress that hugged every curve of her body that I had memorized at this point. It was as if my mind knew exactly where she was at all times without having to search for her. As I moved around the room talking to different people, I always found her in the crowd like a beacon of light that kept me sane as my face began to hurt from smiling so much.

Lottie laughed with people from the training staff, shook hands with the owner before I had had the chance to talk with him, and then allowed players to introduce her to their families that she hadn't met yet. She was an enigma, radiating beauty and the kind of energy that forced you to notice her.

"I heard that you were given the offer of returning next year for another season," Gary Martinez, the owner of the Bobcats, told me after I'd greeted him with a firm handshake. He was in charge of most of the personnel decisions within the organization, players and staff alike.

"I was," I told him, wary of where this conversation was going and that we were having it in a room full of people that I would rather not overhear it.

Ever since my perspective around the games had changed these past few weeks, the offer that my coach had given me had slipped to the back of my mind. That ugly monster inside of me that worried about if my performance this season would be good enough was finally silenced. All the questions it normally asked were dulled out.

Would I make myself proud enough?

Did I do enough to cement myself up there with the greats that had played in the NFL?

None of those questions had floated around inside of my head these past few weeks and I owed much of the reason for it to Lottie for how she changed my perspective on the game. Her reminder of having fun had helped me to reprioritize what was important to me and allowed me to let loose on the field.

"Have you given it much thought yet?" Gary asked. "We thought it would give you a second chance at a Super Bowl win if this season doesn't end up how we all want it to or even a back-to-back opportunity. Which is something you haven't done just yet."

Gary nudged me like we were old pals and I had to force a hollow laugh out of me to hide the way my body tensed. I would not miss this part of the sport—being the quarterback, the face of the team, and having to perform at social gatherings as much as I had to on the field.

A waiter walked by with a tray of fresh champagne glasses, and I grabbed a new one with the hope of taking a bit of the edge off tonight.

"Back-to-back would be an awesome experience," I agreed, because I truly did believe that. Having the kind of dominance to achieve winning Super Bowls back-to-back would cement the legacy I wanted to leave behind. That voice in the back of my mind whispered to take the offer because that would be even better than how I had originally hoped for my career to end.

My eyes drifted back toward the blonde vision that was now being twirled around the dance floor by Derek. I could hear her whimsical laugh as my best friend dipped her unexpectedly from all the way across the room.

"She's really done wonders for the team this year, hasn't she," Gary said as he followed my gaze to Lottie, completely unaware of the reason why I couldn't take my eyes off her.

"She's been a massive part of my success this season." *For more reasons than just a physical therapy routine.*

Gary nodded his head absentmindedly. "I've noticed a change in you in the second half of the season so far and I've noticed a great deal of difference in the number of snaps that Derek is playing as well. Normally he must sit more than he has this season to give his lower back and legs a break."

Like magic, Lottie's eyes found mine from across the room. Her hair was pulled back into a slicked-back ponytail that showed off her sharp jawline and high cheekbones. She looked breathtaking. Those blue eyes crinkled at the corners as she gave me a smile only meant for me.

"You two seem to work well together. I'm glad our risk in hiring her has paid off," Gary added, still oblivious to the small moment that Lottie and I were sharing.

"Risk?" I asked him once I'd realized what he had said.

Gary took a drink of his scotch, adding to the ruddy color of his face with each sip. He appeared unbothered as he waved a hand as if to brush off the seriousness of my question. "Hiring someone who had never worked in the NFL before, of course. And not to mention she's a woman who's never played the sport before."

My blood ran cold when I heard Lottie being judged on something other than her skills. Lottie had never explicitly mentioned any of the discrimination she'd faced in her career to me, but you could gather just by watching her that part of her work ethic had been built on the opinions from the people that had counted her out simply because she lacked a Y chromosome.

"I think Lottie proved to the entire industry before she even got the job that she was the best at her job for a reason. She even proved her knowledge extends beyond the NFL with how she handled Nash Rousch's injury this season. And I think she's one of the most valuable people in the facility for this organization." Gary was one too many drinks deep into the night to really register my words and I wished I had found him earlier to have this conversation at a time when he'd remember it.

"Yes, yes." Gary nodded his head, already checking out of our conversation. I watched his eyes lock on to Coach Randolph and knew what was coming next. "If you'll excuse me, Nolan."

I didn't stay around long enough for someone else to corner me before I was walking toward Lottie and Derek as their dance ended.

"Can I have this dance?" I was standing a few feet away from her. Her back was facing me as she thanked Derek for their dance. Her blonde ponytail swung around as she spun, and those baby blue eyes met mine once again. The excitement and relief that I felt to be near her was mirrored on her face as she placed her hand into my outstretched one. The band played another soft melody, one of the last of the night before the DJ the team hired to play took over.

"You two have a good time." Derek slipped an arm around both of our shoulders. "But remember, leave a respectable amount of space or I, as the chaperone, will have to do it myself."

With a wink, Derek left the two of us alone. I pulled Lottie's hand in close to my chest as I looped my other one around her waist, cradling her. Lottie's free arm slipped around my shoulders. If we weren't in a room full of people who could look too closely, I would have slipped my arms down the curve of body, but I kept my hands at a respectful height to give off the picture of a quarterback dancing with the physical therapist that has kept the dream of this season alive for him.

"How are you holding up during your first one of these?" I asked her as we swayed around the dance floor.

I almost missed Lottie's response as I got caught up in the silvery eyeshadow she had laid on her eyelids and the deep scarlet she'd painted her lips.

"This is so amazing." Lottie's eyes shone as her gaze drifted around the room. "I almost feel like I'm a little kid again. This is the closest I think I've ever gotten to how the holidays are supposed to feel. I only wish I had brought Olivia as my date tonight."

"Derek would have stolen her from you," I joked. Every time we all got together as a group, those two always seemed to gravitate toward each other as if they were cut from the same happy-go-lucky, scintillating cloth.

"She would have loved to see these decorations," Lottie told me. "I sent her a few videos. We just never really had anything like this. It feels like the magic you see in all those Christmas movies."

I studied the awe on Lottie's face and wondered how she had missed this as a child. Had her parents not given her and Olivia the magic of Christmas like my parents did for me?

"Did you not have this as a kid?" I asked. Lottie had told me about how hard it was for her growing up, but seeing the sadness burrowed so deep inside of her so plainly cracked a fissure in my heart. How could someone not give their kids the joy of the holidays? How could they be so blind and wrapped up in their own problems to neglect their own kids? And how had Lottie turned out so strong despite all she'd gone through?

"I remember when I was younger the holidays felt something like this. But not during the years that I can clearly remember." Lottie's gaze stayed on the decor of the room rather than on me. I wanted to cup her chin and force her to see that I was here to listen and there would never be an ounce of judgement.

"My childhood was difficult. My father was a cruel man. As I grew older, I watched his relationship with my mother turn into hatred and that affected me and Olivia growing up." Lottie paused for just a moment and when she spoke again, her voice was much softer. "Holidays weren't a priority anymore for my mother when her entire life was falling apart."

My grip on her back tightened as I tried to provide her support short of pulling her into my arms in this room full of people so I could keep respecting her wishes.

"Has your mom found some sense of happiness?" I asked.

Lottie gave me a sad smile as the last few notes of the song rang out. "I hope she's found some semblance of peace. She passed away almost two years after Olivia graduated high school. I was just thankful she didn't die while Olivia was still in high school, so she wasn't stuck with our father."

My chest ached when I remembered the first time Lottie told me that she had sacrificed so much of her life that she felt like she had missed out. Now I realized that she had played the role of protector for Olivia and had been forced to grow up sooner than she should have. I wanted to add ten million more items to her bucket list and give her the experiences that she had always deserved.

"I'm not sure if this is crossing a line," I started as a plan began to form in my head. "Can we spend Christmas Day together?"

Surprise flashed across Lottie's face as if the idea had never crossed her mind and I promised myself there would be a time where she never wondered if we would spend holidays together again.

"Do you care if Olivia is there?"

"I want her to be there," I told her.

Because I would be damned if those two women didn't get to experience a Christmas Day full of magic and love.

Chapter 27

Nolan

There wasn't anything more magical during a Christmas Eve game than snow, and for today's game, it was coming down in droves. The grounds crew had spent all morning shoveling as much as they could off the field to make the yard lines visible while other staff pitched in to clear out as much of the snow from the bleachers as they could. Bobcat fans were built differently. For other teams, snow games might mean an emptier stadium than usual. Not for us.

When I first emerged from the tunnel at the start of the game, I would have sworn the stadium was even more packed than a normal game as the snow continued to fall. There was an energy that only a game like today's could bring. Even our mascot had donned a Santa hat for the occasion.

Today's game was a conference game against the Las Vegas Roughriders and with a win we would bring home the conference championship title. From the moment of the first punt return, I could feel the intensity my teammates were playing with. The excitement carried through the first half as we managed to put a decent lead between us and Las Vegas and as we all sat in the locker room buzzing with the energy for Christmas Eve and a potential win, I had the distinct feeling that today—this moment—would be one I would remember for the rest of my life, regardless of a win or not. Seeing the smiles of my teammates and the lighthearted jokes that happened after our coach gave his normal halftime speech cemented itself in my mind as one of my favorite moments.

I was surrounded by all the people that were important to me in life—Hawthorn, Derek, Lottie, and my parents, who were watching from my box in the stadium. I felt immense pride as I sat in the locker room and took in the smiling face of Hawthorn, who was on track to kick the most field goals he'd ever had during a single game, Derek, who was in the middle of telling a defensive lineman about how he'd managed to cross up one of Las Vegas's players on the last drive before the half to score a touchdown, and Lottie, who was standing in the corner wearing a Santa hat, smiling as she took it all in.

Everything happening in my life right now for once felt like it was falling into place.

As the team broke to head back out for the second half, I stopped Lottie just before we exited the tunnel.

"My parents are here today," I told her. "Would you like to meet them?"

Lottie's eyes widened at my question, and I realized the kind of pressure I might have just put on her. I quickly began to backtrack, wanting to avoid making this situation anymore awkward than it already was.

But to my surprise, Lottie shook her head when I started to tell her not to worry about it.

"I've been hoping I would get to meet your mother eventually."

The smile she flashed me nearly sent me to my knees. I'd never experienced having someone who cared so much about me and my success and *wanted* to meet my family. My ex was only ever interested in the optics of attending my game. She was more concerned with posting a picture of herself down on the sidelines before a game or during the game rather than having a conversation with either of my parents.

Maybe Lottie and I had an actual chance.

"Go have some fun," Lottie told me as I continued to stare at her with a smile on my face.

"Right." I nodded my head before pulling my helmet on and finding Derek and the rest of the offense.

For once, I didn't feel the pressure to continue to outperform myself or to constantly give yet another piece of myself to the sport and its fans. As I took the field with my team for the second half, I finally felt at peace.

But the question still lingered, what if I could bring this same feeling into one last season?

"Great game, son!" My father wrapped me in a hug as soon as me and Lottie walked over to where they were waiting in the family room.

"Congratulations," my mother added as I took her in my arms. "What a wonderful accomplishment for your last season—a conference championship."

My smile grew slightly strained, despite what we had to celebrate. "It's coming to an end faster than I had imagined."

My parents shared a sad smile with me as we silently remembered all the memories we had around the sport of football. But before any tears could be shed, I went to introduce Lottie, who was still standing next to me.

"Mom, Dad, this is Dr. Charlotte Thompson. She's our physical therapist this year. Charlotte, this is my father, Harry, and my mother, Francesca." I gestured to Lottie, pulling my parents' attention away from me. "I owe a lot to her this year. She's managed to keep me on the field as much as possible."

My father reached out to shake her hand. "I apologize that you've had to deal with him."

A surprised laugh escaped from Lottie's mouth, and she slammed her lips closed to try and hide it. A wry smile cracked across my father's face and the two of them exploded in a fit of laughter together.

"Thank you for taking care of our son," my mother interjected. "Especially because we all know how difficult he can be sometimes."

"Thanks, guys," I sarcastically added, earning a laugh from all of us.

My mother reached out to pull Lottie into a hug. I watched her stiffen as my mother's arms wrapped around her for a few moments before her eyes drifted closed. I knew I was watching a small piece of Lottie's trauma begin to heal in my mother's arms.

"You're coming over tonight for Christmas still?" My father asked me as my mother began to ask Lottie about the sweater she was wearing.

"Wouldn't miss it," I told him. I watched Lottie gush over my mother's custom Nolan Hill sweatshirt. "I need Mom's Christmas cookie recipes for something I'm planning tomorrow."

"Do you now?" my father asked with a wry smile. He glanced between me and Lottie with a knowing look on his face before reaching over to squeeze my shoulder. "Are you still planning on that New Year's Eve party?"

"If you and Mom are still okay hosting everyone," I told him.

My father nodded his head. "Absolutely. We wanted to have an overflowing house one last time before we don't get the chance again."

"Well, thank you for that." I reached over to shake his hand.

"We're proud of you, son. Don't ever forget that," my father told me as he reached over for my mother. "Come on, honey, let's let these two get out of here. We'll see Nolan tonight."

"But I won't see Lottie," my mother stubbornly told my father as she finished exchanging numbers with Lottie. "Please tell me you'll be coming to the New Year's Eve party we are having?"

Lottie looked helplessly between my mother and me as she tried to figure out what to say back.

"She'll be there," I told my mother, stepping in to save Lottie from having to respond. "I'll see you guys tonight."

My parents waved goodbye to us before they made their way out of the stadium.

"Your parents are sweet," Lottie told me as she watched them leave the family room, a slight sheen to her eyes.

I nodded my head. "I'm extremely lucky to have two parents like them."

"You did wonderful today," she told me. I felt her pinky brush across mine as she reached for me in a room full of people.

"Can I come over tomorrow around eight in the morning?" I asked. "I want to cook you and Olivia breakfast."

"Olivia is sleeping over tonight, so we will be there," Lottie replied.

This time, I reached over to give her hand a quick squeeze. "It'll be a stay in your pajamas all day kind of day."

"Perfect, because I have a plan." The glint in Lottie's eyes had me questioning what exactly was up her sleeve.

"Should I be worried?" I asked.

Lottie shrugged with a wry smile. "I'll see you tomorrow morning," she called over her shoulder. As I watched her leave, I wished I could be waking up next to her on Christmas morning, but this would have to do for now.

The snow had piled up to nearly a foot overnight. Kids across Chicago would be waking up to a true white Christmas. I made my way across the city toward Lottie's apartment, the back of my car full of the ingredients to make chocolate chip pancakes and Christmas cookies later in the day.

My mother had thrust her secret Christmas cookie recipes in my hands as I was leaving last night after she'd beaten me down about my plans for today. She shouted after me that she wanted pictures without asking any further questions about why I was spending Christmas Day with my physical therapist, like the amazing mother she was.

Lottie held the door open for me after she'd buzzed me in. "What's all that for?"

Her hair was braided down her back this morning and she was wearing a plaid pajama set that had a snowman on the breast pocket.

"We're having the Christmas Day of your childhood dreams," I told her as I went to set everything down on the kitchen counter. That was when I noticed Olivia in the same pajamas as Lottie with an extra set in her hands and an excited—maybe even a little bit evil—look on her face. "What are those?"

"It's on my list!" Lottie told me excitedly as she grabbed the extra pair of pajamas from Olivia. "Matching pajamas. I know it's probably cheesy. But I remember my classmates talking about their families getting new matching pajamas every Christmas morning and I thought it was something that should be on the list of things I'm making up for missing."

If any of my teammates ever caught wind that I wore a matching pajama set with the girl I liked and her sister while making Christmas cookies and watching Christmas movies all day, I'd never hear the end of it. But I grabbed the pajamas anyways and went to change into them solely because of the look of excitement on Lottie's face. I would have done anything to keep that look there.

When I emerged from the bathroom, Lottie's fireplace was crackling, and she'd turned on a Christmas playlist while she and Olivia began laying out the ingredients for chocolate chip pancakes.

"Are you taking the lead on this, Chef Nolan?" Olivia turned around as she asked me the question and let out a snort once she saw me.

"That bad?" I asked as I pulled at the stiff material that clung to the muscles in my legs without budging.

"I never thought I'd know what Nolan Hill's butt cheeks looked like and now I'll spend the rest of my life trying to erase that image from my mind," Olivia replied.

Lottie turned at her sister's comment, and her eyes grew

wide when she realized what Olivia meant. Her hand flung up to cover her mouth and the laugh she was trying to hide.

"Just remember," I told her. "This was your idea."

"I may have gotten the wrong size," Lottie realized as she continued to ogle me. Her eyes roamed over every inch of my body and I swelled at the unspoken compliment.

I cleared my throat to grab her attention again. "My eyes are up here."

Red flushed Lottie's cheeks when she realized she'd been caught and grew an even deeper shade once Olivia started laughing at her.

After the two sisters finished talking about how tight my pajamas were, the three of us got to work on our pancakes.

"My mother used to make me snowmen pancakes every Christmas morning," I told them as I strategically placed the chocolate chips to resemble the face of a snowman. Both Lottie and Olivia lit up when they saw the finished products, like two little kids living in the magic that was created for them on a day like today. "Looking back, I think these pancakes might be my favorite memory of Christmas."

"If your pancakes are this good, I can't wait for the Christmas cookies later," Olivia moaned as she took her first bite. Lottie and I exchanged smiles as her sister grabbed another pancake to add to her stack.

"Maybe next year we can all make Christmas cookies with the original chef." The words slipped out of my mouth before I even registered what I was saying. Lottie's fork paused on its way to her mouth when she realized I'd just insinuated we'd be doing this again next year, except *with* my parents.

Even though we'd spoken about how we felt about each other, we were still walking this fine line of if we would eventually be together or not.

"As long as she teaches me all of her recipes," Olivia spoke around a mouthful of pancake. "Because I'm sure her cookies deserve to be eaten more than once a year."

Olivia's obliviousness to the tension between me and Lottie

seemed to take the edge off. Lottie's shoulders relaxed and the two of us continued eating our pancakes in silence.

Once all the plates were empty, I started helping Lottie clean everything up. The two of us worked in sync, cleaning and drying dishes just like during Thanksgiving.

"I got you something," Lottie told me once all the dishes were dried. A tiny bit of relief washed through me as I thought of the little bag I'd hidden under my coat when I first got here. It wasn't much. I hadn't wanted to get Lottie something extravagant due to the nature of our relationship. But I hadn't expected her to get me anything either, although it made presenting my gift to her easier.

Lottie took off for her room and brought back out a wrapped gift in the shape of a rectangle. The size looked familiar and before she could hand it to me, I went to grab my gift for her—a similarly shaped wrapped gift.

Her eyebrows pulled together as she realized I'd gotten her something as well and that it looked like hers. "Did we get each other the same thing?"

I shrugged as the two of us exchanged gifts. "Guess we'll have to find out."

Instead of ripping into my gift right away, I hesitated as I watched the excitement play out on Lottie's face as she opened my gift. The second her fingers touched the glass of the picture frame beneath the wrapping paper her eyes widened before she looked over at the unopened gift in my hands.

"Open yours," she told me as she finished pulling the wrapping paper off the frame.

Slowly, I peeled the wrapping paper back to reveal that Lottie had also given me a picture frame.

The picture I had given Lottie was from Thanksgiving. Everyone that had come for dinner at her house had crowded around her fireplace and smiled for a picture with our arms wrapped around each other. We truly looked the family that we had slowly become over these past few months and judging by the way Lottie's fingers gently touched the glass, I knew that gift was better than anything else I could have given her.

The picture that Lottie had gotten me was one that nearly took my breath away. It was from the game in Denver a few weeks back. Derek and Hawthorn had wrapped their arms around me after the last touchdown that I had thrown to Derek. The smile on my face was pure joy and one of the few times I'd ever seen myself that happy while playing professional football. It was the only picture I now owned that had just the three of us in it, looking the happiest we ever had while doing the thing we all loved. It was also the game where everything seemed to finally click for me this season and I rediscovered my love of the game.

"Thank you," we both said at the same time.

Lottie let out a chuckle while a smile broke across my face. The two of us stared at each other as we clutched photos from one of the most meaningful moments of our lives during these past few months, given to us by someone who recognized its importance.

"Are we going to start baking these cookies?" Olivia called from the kitchen where she was clutching my mother's recipes. "Because these peanut butter blossoms are calling my name."

This time I joined Lottie's laughter as the two of us left our pictures next to each other on her kitchen table and went to begin our Christmas baking. Lottie switched the Christmas music to the *Elf* soundtrack and the sounds of Christmas cheer filled the little apartment.

Olivia left shortly after the cookies had been packed up to be taken home, leaving me and Lottie alone in her apartment to clean up. As the two of us worked side by side, Lottie continued to steal a few glances at me.

"What?" I asked her.

With a sigh, she set down her cleaning rag and looked at me. "Listen, I've been thinking. What if we just did it?"

My eyes widened at her question, which in turn had her backtracking once she realized how that had sounded.

"No, no. That's not what I meant." Now a smile was slowly breaking out across my face as I watched her painfully try to correct the error. After another moment she sighed again before trying to start over. "What if we just gave whatever is happening between us a real shot? The season is almost over and I'm not sure I can take much more of this dance with you anymore. I've grown tired of fighting it."

Lottie looked like she was holding her breath as she waited for me to respond. My heart felt like it had stopped beating in my chest as my mouth fell open out of shock. With each passing moment that I didn't answer, doubt crept over Lottie's face. I could guess exactly what she was thinking.

Maybe I had changed my mind.

Maybe I thought we were only meant to be friends.

I finally unfroze by pushing a stream of air out of my mouth. "Fucking finally."

Within seconds, my hand was cradling the back of her head and my lips covered hers. My heart squeezed when I realized how much I loved kissing her. How she melded to me like a perfect puzzle piece and filled all the missing parts of me.

The two of us moved with familiarity as Lottie's hands shoved me toward her bedroom. "Are you sure you meant that you wanted to date me?" I asked her as I pushed open her bedroom door with my back. My hands caressed her as her lips slanted over mine, matching all the hunger I felt. "Because it really feels like you meant something else."

I could feel Lottie's smirk against my lips, and I loved this spunky version of her. It was a glimpse of the desire that had been building inside of her for this very moment. The moment the backs of my legs hit the edge of her bed, I spun us around, so she landed on the bed first. Surprise flashed in her eyes before it was replaced with something I would describe as hunger. I had to push through the shock consuming me that we had even reached this point so I could show her just how much I'd been waiting for the moment that she would be *mine*.

I trailed a line of kisses from the soft skin just below her belly button up to her mouth where I kissed her hard until she had to pull away, gasping for air.

"You are so beautiful," I told her. She gazed up at me through her lashes, those blue eyes filled with just as much disbelief as I felt. The odds had never felt in our favor to end up in this very position, literally and figuratively.

"Thank you for today," she told me when I pulled back from another kiss. "I'm not even sure I have the words to tell you how much today meant for me and Olivia."

Tears welled at the corners of her eyes, and I reached up to kiss them away. "I loved today just as much as you did. Seeing you two act like little kids was the best Christmas gift I've had in years."

I kissed over her eyelids, then trailed down to her cheeks, then both collarbones with the hope that I would kiss away any doubt that she had that we were right where we needed to be. That this moment was inevitable, and we were always meant to end up in each other's arms.

Lottie slowly pulled at the hem of the pajama shirt I was wearing and pulled it up and over my head. We shared a chuckle when I had to pull away from her to strip off the overly tight bottoms.

Our very first night together had been fueled slightly by alcohol and I wanted tonight to be fueled solely from how much we cared about each other. The moment Lottie slipped out of her pajamas, the air in the room grew thicker and it felt like all that mattered in the world right then was the two of us as our arms wrapped around each other as we consumed each other completely.

This time, we took our time. Our movements were slow as we explored each other's bodies. Completely different from the frantic moments in my apartment after the club. We moved together with the twinkling Christmas lights on the house across from Lottie's apartment shining through her bedroom window.

Skin slid over skin.

Hands threaded in hair.

Moans and whispered breaths of our names filled the room.

Sheets tangled around us.

"Is that all you've got?" Lottie asked me with unkempt hair and swollen lips after she'd already worked me near exhaustion. She was insatiable.

With a growl, I lifted her into my arms and carried her to the shower for round two.

And all I could think about was how the axis I'd operated on my entire life felt righted the second I was able to call Lottie mine.

I lay awake far into the late hours of the evening, my thumb swiping across the delicate skin of Lottie's cheek as she slept on my chest. My heart swelled up to meet where she lay on top of me, wanting her to know that it belonged to her.

Chapter 28

Lottie

"So, when are we going to discuss Christmas?" Olivia asked me as the two of us got ready on my bedroom floor.

The week following Christmas had been full of trying to prepare for the game the day before New Year's Eve. Things between Nolan and me fell into a perfectly comfortable routine as we prepared for him to play potentially his last regular season game. His coaching staff had already expressed interest in giving Caleb the last game of the season for more experience and to give Nolan rest before the playoffs. Today's game was solely for working out any last kinks in plays that they would need for the postseason before Caleb took over with the offense. And when the team came away with a win, we solidified our first-place ranking in the postseason.

Nolan and I went through our normal routine every day. The attraction and sense of comfort I felt for him had only grown after he had given both me and Olivia the Christmas of our dreams. The two of us had crossed every professional boundary on Christmas, with neither of us able to deny the chemistry between us.

Somehow, I'd managed to brush off Olivia's inquiries about what happened between Nolan and me after she'd left, but it had only been a matter of time before she cornered me again and I had no way of avoiding answering. The two of us were getting ready for the New Year's party at Nolan's parents' house, applying our makeup in silence, when Olivia turned to me with raised eyebrows.

"I'm not sure what there is to talk about," I started, even though I knew it was a lost cause to try and deflect again.

"Just the fact that he was thoughtful enough to try and make this Christmas one that you and I would remember. Or that he's invited both of us to a New Year's Eve party at his *parents'* house." Olivia stopped applying her eyeshadow so she could turn and look at me head on.

"We're just seeing where things are going," I told her with a shrug.

Olivia scoffed as if she couldn't believe that was the avenue I was trying to take with her of all people. She turned back around and threw her makeup brush back in her bag.

"Lottie, I love you," my sister started, "but I'm tired of watching you play second fiddle to everyone else around you in your life. When are you going to go after what *you* want instead of always playing it cautious solely because that's what is expected of you?"

"Not everyone can be as unexpected as you are," I snapped back at Olivia, heat filling my cheeks for having to defend myself to her.

"Because you never had the chance to be a little wild. You always had to do what's best for me." Olivia's features softened as she reached for my hands. "But you weren't meant to be the parent in this relationship, Lottie. You have your own life to live. I'm an adult and you don't have to play that role anymore. So maybe it's time you go after what you want in your life. I've already watched you step out of your comfort zone these past few months. I think there are a few items left on your bucket list."

Olivia's message was clear.

My eyes drifted toward the door where I could see the list stuck up on my fridge. Everything was crossed out except for kissing someone on New Year's Eve and finding that spark with someone. Both of those felt like they could be crossed off after tonight if I just summoned up enough courage to do something about it.

"You and I both know that you've found someone special." Olivia gave me one more look before she turned back to the mirror in front of her to finish her hair. "Take a risk tonight, Lottie. Have fun for once."

"Take a risk," I whispered to myself as Olivia and I climbed the stairs of Harry and Francesca's porch.

Harry and Francesca lived in a suburb on the south side of the city. Tall trees lined either side of the road like sentinels welcoming us to the neighborhood as we drove to the address that Nolan had sent me. The sun had set hours ago, and the darkness already wrapped around everything, but Nolan's parents' house shone out like a beacon with golden light spilling from the massive windows on the first floor. The snow that had been steadily coming down all week had finally stopped, leaving everything draped in a blanket of white. Cars already lined the street and filled their driveway when we arrived, and we could see the shadows of people on the other side of the curtains.

"What's going through that beautiful head of yours?" Olivia asked me as we stopped at the front door.

The corners of my lips pulled downwards as I tried to put a name to what was happening. "I'm not sure why I feel nervous. These people are our friends, and nothing has changed."

Olivia reached down to lace her hand in mine. "Well, that's not true, Lottie. You've changed. You aren't the same woman who started this season with the Bobcats. But that doesn't change the fact that the people inside are your family, *our* family."

My sister let me take a few moments to let her words sink in before she reached out to ring the doorbell. That golden light that looked so inviting from the outside spilled out as Francesca stood on the other side of the open door. She wore a light-up New Year's headband and the most welcoming smile.

"Lottie!" In an instant her arms were wrapped around me and just like the last time she hugged me on Christmas Eve, I sank into her arms and allowed their comfort to wrap around me. Every time that I had wanted a hug from someone who cared about me rose closer to the surface.

Memories of my father ignoring me when he got home, more concerned about opening a beer from the fridge or whatever my mother had cooked for dinner. Then memories of my mother, so beaten down by my father's verbal abuse that she could barely care for herself, much less me or Olivia.

"And you must be Lottie's sister!" Francesca exclaimed when she caught sight of Olivia over my shoulder.

My sister shifted awkwardly from one foot to the next as Francesca's warmth was directed at her.

"You must be Francesca," she responded nervously.

Francesca waved my sister off. "Please, call me Fran. Only my mother called me Francesca."

I watched Olivia stiffen as Fran released me and wrapped my sister in her arms. Olivia looked at me with wide eyes, unsure of what to do, before she finally wrapped her arms around Fran and welcomed the kind of hug that she also had been missing most of her childhood.

"I know you two are about to liven this party up," Fran exclaimed as she looped her arms through each of ours and pulled us inside.

If Fran herself was dressed for the occasion, her house was decorated for the party of the year. Gold and white balloons covered every inch of the ceiling with the tails of the balloons hanging down like confetti. Disco balls that were cut in half held bottles of champagne in various locations. Plates of food covered nearly every available surface. New Year's Eve glasses sat on an entry table for guests to grab.

"Lottie? Olivia?" The three of us were stopped in our tracks by Derek, who had a pair of New Year's Eve glasses sitting slightly askew on his face and a silver boa wrapped around his neck. A half-drunk glass of champagne dangled from his fingers as he pulled me into a hug and then my sister, whose cheeks turned a suspicious shade of red when she pulled away.

"Having a good time?" I asked Derek, eyeing the drink in his hand. There was no way that was his first of the night.

"Well, you see," Derek started, swaying slightly. "Nolan bribed me into coming over early to help with the set up and Fran put me on balloon duty. After about the hundredth balloon, I needed something to quench my thirst."

Olivia slipped away from Fran and wrapped an arm around Derek's back. "Direct me to the liquor, kind sir."

Derek's eyes lit up behind his New Year's Eve glasses. "Right this way, m'lady."

Fran and I exchanged a smile as we watched the pair weave their way into the party. Soft music played from built-in speakers throughout the house and mingled with the sound of many different conversations happening throughout the space. Lots of the team were scattered around inside of Fran's home, and I even spotted Adam Steel and his wife.

"Do you guys do this every year?" I asked, taken aback by the sheer amount of people that Nolan's parents were hosting.

"Oh goodness, no." Fran laughed at the idea. "We've done it a couple of times over the years. Nolan's apartment isn't nearly as big as our home, and he likes being able to have his team all in one place to celebrate the holidays. It's like his way of giving back to them. We just wanted to do this one last time before we don't have the chance again."

Fran paused in the entryway to her kitchen where I finally spotted Nolan conversing with his father. He was wearing a black sweater with a pair of dark jeans and brown boots that matched the color of his eyes. His brown hair was styled, and his face was freshly shaven. But it was the easy smile that was the best accessory he was wearing. Nearly all the tension I'd seen in the set of his shoulders from the beginning of the season was gone and, in its place stood a man who was enjoying where he was at in life while surrounded by the people he loved.

"I will never get over having all this energy under our roof." Fran patted my arm. "Now, no matter how much I love your company, I know I am not the person you truly want to spend your time with tonight."

With a wink, Fran drifted back into the party, leaving me in the kitchen staring at the side profile of the man I'd been so conflicted over these past few months. But as I stood in a room full of people that had helped knowingly or unknowingly to heal a piece of the little girl within me, I found a spark of courage. I wanted my life to be one where I lived for the moments like tonight, surrounded by friends and family. Not full of worry about how the things that I wanted would affect my career or that I was undeserving of them.

Harry noticed me first. "Lottie! You made it."

My eyes were locked on Nolan though, as I watched, in what felt like slow motion, as he turned around to see me. His entire face lit up as soon as he saw me, his eyes crinkled at the corners as he smiled. Like a glimpse of the future, I saw Nolan with deeper-set wrinkles around his eyes, grey peppering the edges of his hair, and a salt and pepper beard that framed his sharp jawline. Those same eyes but years older still looked at me the same way they were right now.

"Happy New Year, Lottie," he greeted. He reached out his arms like he wanted to pull me into a hug, before thinking better of it and dropping them back to his sides.

Take a risk.

Before I could lose the courage I'd found, I slipped my arms around his waist and tucked myself into his body. Nolan stiffened against me but only for a second before his arms wrapped around my body and pulled me in tighter.

"You look breathtaking," Nolan bent down to whisper into my ear.

When I pulled back out of his arms, I noticed that his

father was nowhere to be found and it was only the two of us, tucked away in our own corner of the kitchen.

"This place looks amazing," I told Nolan as I took in yet another room filled with balloons, disco balls, and more food than I could fathom.

"My mom and I had a fun time getting all of this ready," Nolan told me as he admired all his hard work.

Take a risk.

But before I could open my mouth, Nolan slanted his mouth over mine, silencing my thoughts as he pulled me into his arms. I didn't even register in the moment that his parents were watching us with wide smiles from the doorway of the kitchen before they left to give us some privacy. All I could focus on was the feel of his lips and the overwhelming sense of happiness I felt whenever I was in his arms.

"Wait." I managed to pull away with bruised lips and heavy eyelids. Nolan was practically a mirror image, like he'd already drunk a few bottles of champagne. "I have a question."

Nolan nodded, urging me to go on.

"Will you be my kiss at midnight?" I asked.

His laugh filled my ears like music before he nodded his head. "It would be the greatest honor I'd have all year."

I glanced around the empty kitchen to ensure no one was close enough to hear me as I stood on tiptoes to whisper in Nolan's ear. He bowed his head to meet me halfway and I was immediately enveloped in his cologne—vanilla and cashmere. "Maybe we can sneak away before the night really gets going?"

Nolan's eyes flashed with surprise as if he hadn't imagined I would ever suggest sneaking off to somewhere private in his parents' house full of our friends and family. To be honest, a few months ago I wouldn't be able to believe it either, but Nolan Hill made me feel so emotionally and physically safe with him that I finally felt comfortable enough to reach for a few wild ideas.

Take a risk.

"I know just the place," Nolan told me, his surprise morphing into a smile that fit a co-conspirator.

He wrapped his hand around mine and together we weaved through the crowd of people, greeting those that saw us before climbing the stairs. The noise faded away as soon as we reached the top where a hallway stretched out with various doors on either side. A runner softened our footsteps as we crept into a room that Nolan opened. It looked to have been recently updated, but clearly still held signs of who used to occupy it based on the trophies that decorated the shelving on the walls and the framed posters of old NFL quarterbacks from when we were young.

"Was this your bedroom when you were a kid?" I asked as my hand trailed across the top of the dresser, just in front of three framed pictures of Nolan as a kid with braces and the same wide smile that I loved.

"It was." Nolan stood near the bed, watching me with unfiltered emotion on his face. It nearly took my breath away to see the way he was drinking me in. His eyes were full of so much emotion that I had to remind myself not to run out the door, to be brave. Because I deserved this moment. I deserved to be loved. I deserved *him*.

"And that was yours?" I asked, pointing to the teddy bear on the chair in the corner, heat crawling up my neck as his gaze stayed on me without wavering. Nolan knew what I was pointing to with just a quick glance before his eyes were back on me.

"That is Theo the Bear," he told me with a hint of that brilliant smile pulling at the corners of his lips. With each word, he took a step toward me until he was only a step away.

His arms reached out to wrap around my waist and pull me into his chest. "Everything in this room is mine," he told me with a squeeze of his arms. "Especially you."

It was becoming more and more noticeable how the moment I was in Nolan's arms, my body turned into jelly.

Nolan made it incredibly difficult to keep second-guessing if I was worthy enough for him by the way he held me to his body like I was the most precious thing he'd ever had in his hands or the way his breath hitched at the first sweep of our mouths.

Nolan's hands slid down my back, sending tingles in their wake, before he lifted me into his arms and turned to walk us toward his childhood bed. There was this underlying need for devouring each other as the desire in our kisses intensified with each passing moment. Our hands mirrored the desire in our kisses as we both tried to remove as many layers of clothing that were between us as quickly as we could.

The two of us felt like either side of a string that had always belonged to the other half, just waiting until we eventually met in the middle.

Skin slid against skin, finally free of the clothes keeping us from one another. Nolan hovered over me, his muscular body on full display as he looked down at me like he was ready to worship at my altar. I reached out to let my hands trail over his shoulders, feeling the way his muscles tensed at my touch. They dipped around to his back where I let my fingernails dig into his shoulder blades, driven purely by the need building inside of me.

Nolan's hips bucked toward me at the bite of my nails.

"You are so beautiful," he whispered, his words meant for only me inside our little oasis as a party raged on downstairs. His eyes held an emotion I was too scared to name in the moment, too afraid that I might be wrong, and it would pop the bubble that we'd created.

His hands slid underneath my back and my legs wrapped around his waist, letting him know exactly what my body desperately wanted right now.

"Condom?" I whispered into the dark as our bodies first pressed together, eliciting a sigh of pleasure from me and groan from him. Nolan pulled away and his absence was immediately felt as he went to dig for his wallet in the pocket of his pants. I breathed a sigh of relief because if we had to go searching around his room for a dusty old condom from his high school days I might have died on the spot.

"You have taken up residence in nearly every free square foot of my mind," Nolan told me as he settled back over the top of me. He kissed down my body, setting fireworks off inside of me with every pass of his lips against my skin. One of his hands reached up to trace the outline of my lips and I sucked a finger into my mouth the moment he parted my lips. A growl of approval sounded from somewhere down by my legs as he began to work me over. I reached over to grab a pillow, knowing I would need to muffle my cries at the rate that Nolan was going. My hands tangled in the thick locks of his hair and when I breathed his name out, he looked up at me with a devilish smile.

That smile should have been a warning for what was to come. The confident trail of kisses he placed across my body left me trembling even before Nolan slid into me. I tried to follow his lead by going slow and enjoying the moment, but the desire building inside of me had me taking the lead in a way that left us both gasping. It felt chaotic and wild to let myself go like that, but I felt safe in Nolan's arms the entire time. Never forgetting that he was there worshipping every inch of me.

The moment the two of us found release, the balloon of pleasure building in the room finally popped. The only sound was our deep breaths as we gulped down any air that we could. Nolan's muscular chest heaved in and out as he tried to catch his breath, while I lay under him, feeling like I was having an out-of-body experience.

Nolan lowered his forehead down to mine. "Holy shit. Fuck," he breathed.

"Yeah, we already did that," I got out between breaths, which drew giggles from us both.

The sound finally returned to my ears as Nolan stood up from the bed and extended his hand to me.

"Do you think anyone has noticed that we're gone?" I asked as he handed me my clothes.

"I doubt it," he replied as he reached up to pat down the stray hairs on my head that would have given sex-hair vibes the second we walked downstairs.

I glanced at the bed to see that we'd knocked nearly every pillow off, and the bedspread was askew. "We should fix that."

"Definitely," Nolan agreed.

Once the room looked like we had never been there, the two of us walked back down the stairs to rejoin the rest of the party.

"Hey, lovebirds," we heard Derek call out from the living room as our feet hit the first floor. "It's trivia time. Get in here and stop making out in the kitchen."

The two of us shared a sheepish look as we realized we might not have been as discreet as we thought we were when we snuck upstairs.

"I think they noticed," Nolan leaned over to whisper in my ear.

With my hand in his, we joined the rest of our friends and family in his parents' living room for a game of trivia as we waited for the remaining minutes of this year to tick away and welcome the new year that was already looking much more promising than the last.

Chapter 29

Nolan

The playoffs were already the best part of the season. There was an elevated energy about those few weeks that everyone brought—the fans, the players, the rest of the organization—and I felt like I was floating on cloud nine not only because we'd secured the first seed, but also because I'd gotten to wake up almost every morning after New Year's to Lottie's beautiful face while she slept next to me in bed.

Every morning I got to roll over in bed and watch her sleep, so peaceful and unburdened from any of the responsibilities that she carried throughout the day. I noticed I was beginning to see Lottie grow less guarded as the days passed and, in turn, I felt the same happening in myself.

The normal pressure that came with the postseason wasn't there this year. There was only a mixture of excitement and acceptance—excitement for the weeks to come and acceptance that the biggest and most important chapter of my life was coming to an end within these next few weeks. But most importantly, excitement for the first time in years for what was next.

"Do you want a coffee?" Lottie asked from my kitchen where she was getting ready to head to the training facility.

I finished tying my shoes before walking out of the bedroom to greet her. Somehow, this early in the morning, Lottie looked like she was ready to walk a red carpet. Her hair was pulled back into a sleek ponytail, her face was clean and glowing, and she somehow made her workout clothes look like high fashion. I wanted to thank my lucky stars that somehow the universe had decided I could finally convince Lottie I was worthy of her time after working so hard to be patient enough to let her come to that decision on her own.

"I'd love coffee," I said as I came up behind her as she reached up into the cabinet where I had my travel mugs. She stretched up onto her tiptoes, the hem of her sweatshirt rising to show off a strip of skin on her stomach. I gently slipped one hand along the exposed skin as I reached above her to grab the travel mugs she was trying to reach.

"Thank you." She gave me a smile over the side of her shoulder that had me wishing the two of us could ditch our responsibilities for the day and stay in bed.

"You are very welcome," I told her as I dipped my nose into the slope of her neck and shoulder before placing a gentle kiss just under her ear.

Lottie turned around in the small space she had between the edge of the counter and my body. She draped her arms over my shoulders and her fingers threaded themselves in the hair at the nape of my neck. She pulled on the back of my neck until her lips fit perfectly into mine. I had been a ship lost at sea until I realized that Lottie was my shining light in the distance, bringing me home.

In one quick movement, I lifted her onto the counter. She hooked her legs around my waist and pulled me nearly flush to her body. My hand caressed her cheek down to the swoop of her shoulder and the curve of her waist until she decided to playfully bite at my lip.

Game on.

"I think we have a few minutes until we need to leave," I mumbled against her lips.

Lottie playfully swatted at my chest to try and put some separation between the two of us again. "Nolan, we have to get your run in."

"Running is just cardio, and I have a better idea for how we can get some cardio in."

Lottie barked out a laugh at my poor attempt to convince her to stay home and steal just a few more moments for the two of us.

"Nolan, we can't—" Lottie tried to get out between kisses.

I pulled back again and gave her my best devilish smile. "And who says we can't?"

"Me!" Lottie gasped when I slid my hands underneath her ass and lifted her off the counter. "I say we can't."

I placed a kiss on her lips with each step I carried her back toward the bedroom. By the second kiss, Lottie was no longer protesting skipping our morning run in lieu of something a little more . . . fun.

The second we passed over the threshold of my bedroom, the rest of the world faded away. It was only me and Lottie and there was nowhere else in the world that I wanted to be.

Now that she and I had finally decided to give us a shot, I wanted to savor every moment we had together. So even though we did have to be at the training facility within the next hour or so, I was about to take advantage of every single second that she was willing to give me.

The sweatshirt Lottie was wearing was the first article of clothing to be discarded. Shortly after mine followed. A trail of clothing followed us to the bed as our hands scrambled over each other, yanking at each piece of clothing after the next. Lottie's thighs hit the bed and she fell back onto it, breaking our kiss.

Her ponytail fanned out around her head like a golden crown and her lips were swollen from where I'd nipped and pulled on them. She looked like a goddess that myths would be written about. I paused for just a moment as I stood above her. If it were possible to keep a mental image forever, this moment with Charlotte Thompson would be the one I'd want to have.

All the worries I had over the legacy I wanted to leave

behind slipped to the back of my mind as I realized Lottie was the only person I cared about to know me wholly and truly.

"What are you waiting for?" Lottie asked me.

"Nothing anymore now that I have you," I told her as I sank down on top of her.

The two of us together was like a dance that I had never had to learn. I knew exactly how she would move before she did. Our bodies moved in sync as her fingertips dug into the skin on my lower back to pull me closer to her.

I had never understood what it meant to make love to someone until Lottie held me in her arms with fervent intention. Only then did I understand what it meant to share something so intimate with another person.

Lottie trailed kisses across my collarbones. "We should probably get dressed," she told me.

"Just a few more minutes," I replied as I curled myself into her side and relished the feeling of her fingers running through my hair. My favorite place in the world was quickly becoming my head on Lottie's chest—the only place I felt all the stress I carried with me slowly disappear.

"Okay," Lottie whispered as her fingers continued to comb through my hair. "Just a few more minutes."

"You look like you've got a new pep in your step," Derek observed as he sidled up next to me in the hallway on our way to the practice field.

"It's playoff week. Of course I'm excited." I cast him a sideways look.

Derek's eyes narrowed as he looked me over from head to toe. "I'm not sure that's all this is. You look put together— freshly shaven, fresh haircut"—Derek leaned in closer—"and is that perfume I smell?"

The glint in his eyes told me everything. Derek was more observant than everyone gave him credit for, and he might as well run his own NFL gossip account for the way he was gathering dirt on me.

My friend gave me a pat on the back as we emerged out onto the practice field and the cold January air. There were a few flakes of snow falling from the sky, but we would still be expected to practice since Gateway Stadium was exposed to the outside.

"Tell Lottie that I know your wardrobe and I could tell the sweatshirt she's wearing today is yours," Derek leaned in close to tell me before he ran off toward the other tight ends.

My mouth dropped open as I watched him run away from me, but not before making a mental note to never leave Derek unattended in my home again.

"How are we doing, buddy?" Hawthorn asked as he sidled up next to me. Most practices Hawthorn never did more than a few kicks, but he was fully dressed for today to work with the slippery conditions from the snow.

I could tell by the look in Hawthorn's eyes what he was getting at. "Just taking it all in," I told him. "You don't have too many of these left either."

Hawthorn shrugged. "Maybe a few more. But hell, if we happen to win it all this year, I think I may just leave it all behind and go out with you. The kids are getting older and I don't want to miss out on any more of their firsts than I have. Plus, it's time that Sarah got a chance to take on something she wants to for once instead of sitting in the backseat like she has all these years."

"You two have managed to make it work," I told him. It was amazing watching the sacrifice and love that those two showed each other year after year.

"We have," Hawthorn agreed. "But only because we understand when it's time to stop choosing ourselves and start choosing the other person. It's a give and take. We both know we each need our moments to focus on our wants and goals, but often that comes at the other person sacrificing theirs. It's time that I choose Sarah's wants and goals."

The two of us stood next to each other quietly for a few minutes as we watched the rest of the team start their warmups. "It's been an honor watching and learning from you and Sarah over the years. And it's been an honor to be able to call you a teammate and a lifelong friend."

Hawthorn stuck a hand out for me to shake before he pulled me into a hug. "The feeling is mutual. I'm excited to watch what's next for you, but I know you're in good hands."

I followed Hawthorn's gaze to where Lottie stood on the sidelines.

"You would make a fantastic coach, Nolan, and I think the two of you may just be the backbone of this team next year."

Warmth flooded my body at his compliment. "Thanks, man. That means a lot."

"Now, let's go get this shit done. It's too damn cold out here," Hawthorn told me as he pulled his helmet on.

I chuckled.

He'd never kick the stereotype of kickers being soft.

Chapter 30

Nolan

The parking lot outside of Gateway Stadium was even more full than usual as I pulled in and began to drive past everyone braving the snowy conditions to tailgate outside. Many of the fans recognized my Range Rover and cheers broke out as I crawled by them.

People were in winter overalls and stocking caps to keep the cold away, but you'd never guess they were tailgating in these conditions from the smiles on their faces. Bobcat flags were raised high on flagpoles throughout the parking lot. Some people even had custom flags that read "The GOAT" with a picture of me on it. Most of these fans wouldn't have tickets to the game, but simply being here and watching the game from televisions they set up in the parking lot was enough for them.

I may be biased, but I truly believed the Bobcats' fanbase was the best in the entire NFL, and they would be something I would miss playing for. I only hoped that Coach Randolph and the rest of the organization had considered my offer to take over for Coach Elliott after he retired so I could remain a piece of this place.

Workers were ambling around the parking garage the players and staff used underneath the stadium. But there was one person I noticed immediately that had me hesitating to get out of my car.

"Nolan!" Gary Martinez, the Bobcats' owner, greeted me as soon as I closed the driver side door.

"Mr. Martinez," I replied cautiously, feeling like I was wandering into a conversation that I wasn't prepared for.

"How are you feeling for today's game?"

"Ready to get the Bobcat Nation a win." The reply slipped out of my mouth like the rehearsed answer of a politician rather than something I'd say.

"Good, good." Gary nodded his head as if he wouldn't have cared if I'd told him I was about to throw the game because he was clearly on a mission for something else entirely. "Listen, I wanted to add something else to our offer to you for coming back next year."

My stomach sank when I realized where this conversation was going. I could honestly say I hadn't given the offer much thought these past few weeks. I'd been perfectly content with my decision to be done after this season and move into coaching. But a selfish piece of myself anxiously awaited his offer.

"We think we can give you about ten million more dollars to your contract for just next year if you come back."

I had to fight to keep my jaw from hitting the floor.

"Oh, sir. I'm not sure—"

Gary cut me off, waving his hands around. "Please don't answer me right now. Really think on it."

Before I could say anything else, Gary slipped away into the crowd of fans that lined the hallway leading toward the locker room.

I dressed into my warmup clothes in a complete fog as I thought about Gary's offer. I never thought I could be swayed by money, but for some reason all my previous conviction over my decision was slowly slipping away.

Lottie was preparing the training room for me and Derek when I walked in, my mind still heavy with Gary's offer.

"Hey!" Her brilliant smile was the only thing that managed to pull me out of my own head.

I hadn't seen her yet today. She had made the executive decision the night before that we should sleep at our own places solely because we still weren't getting much sleep when we stayed with each other, and she didn't want to be the reason that I wasn't prepared for today's game.

Lottie pulled a heating pack out for me and met me at one of the training beds. "How are you feeling?"

"Rested and ready for today," I told her because that was how I had felt up until thirty minutes ago. I had mentally prepared myself on the ride over to the stadium and had felt ready to take on the Dallas Hogs, a lower-ranking team in this year's playoffs. But teams like that were typically the ones that snuck up on you after you wrote them off as a win before the game was even played.

"Anything feeling sore or that you want to put extra attention on?" Lottie asked me, slipping right into her physical therapy mind. "I want to go through all of the exercises for your knee still, but if there's anything else, we can also do that."

I tried to stay present as I worked through the exercises with Lottie, but all I could think about was how long she'd held out on pursuing anything with me to keep things professional.

How would she feel if I decided to play another year?

Should I tell her now?

Would she understand?

"I'm so sorry if you are trying to get in the zone," Lottie said, bringing me back out of my thoughts. "I just want you to do these last few exercises to wake up your stabilizer muscles and then you can head out to the field to get some throws in."

Lottie kept her distance because she thought I was trying to focus for the game. She had no idea about the mental interrogation I was giving myself.

The line of questioning switched from any concern I had about how Lottie would take it if I decided to return for one last year to if I was *actually* ready to give this up the second I stepped out of the tunnel and onto the field.

The stadium was nearly already full, and the place erupted in cheers as I walked out—a hero's welcome.

Am I really ready for this to end?

"How are you feeling?" I turned to see Caleb standing next to me, his eyes wide with awe as he took in our stadium like it was the first time.

"I'm good. How are you doing with all of this?" I asked him, gesturing to the increase in media and the higher energy levels.

"It feels like I'm riding some sort of high," he told me with his eyes still scanning the stadium. "I'm sure this is old news to you having done this so many times."

I shook my head. "It never gets old."

A little boy near us was screaming my name and waving a foam football and a marker. I walked over to him to sign what he was holding before returning to Caleb.

"They love you," he observed. "I just hope I can fill the big shoes you're leaving behind."

Guilt clawed at my throat, reminding me that I was clinging to something for selfish reasons and ignoring the signs that it was time to go. "You will. You have so much talent."

"You've done so much for me. I wish I had a few more years to learn from you," Caleb continued, conflicting my emotions even further.

I reached over to grasp his shoulder. "Maybe you will. We will just have to see."

I watched the confusion cross his face before I turned to leave him, only to come face to face with Harper Nelson, one of the ESPN reporters.

"Hi, Nolan!" Harper's megawatt television smile nearly blinded me. "Do you have a second for a few questions? I won't take up too much of your time, I know you're trying to get ready for the game."

Normally, I avoided reporters before the game and most of the time reporters understood that. But I respected the hustle that Harper Nelson had. She worked harder than nearly all her peers and she was half the age of most of them.

"Sure," I told her.

Harper looked surprised that I agreed for only a split second before she snapped back into her professional demeanor and flipped her notes app open on her phone.

"You were vocal at the end of last season that this would be your last. But with a season plagued with injury, I'm sure you would agree that this hasn't been the ideal final season for someone like Nolan Hill." Harper looked up at me expectantly, awaiting my answer.

"I would agree that this season hasn't quite met the hopes that I originally had for it," I told her.

Harper powered on with her next question. She didn't dance around players' responses because with every conversation she was on a mission to achieve the one goal she set out with at the start: to find a good story. "Is it true you are considering coming back next year? Reports from the Bobcats are that you may be coming back for one more year."

And there it is.

Had Gary tipped her off?

Anger flared through me that my choice to make that public had been taken from me. I knew this was all business, but for me, this was my life.

I now had two choices. I could either tell her that I had no plans of coming back next year to play and use that as an opportunity to put the coaching staff on the spot with my offer to take over the quarterbacks coaching position, or I could tell her that I had started to consider what that might look like if I came back for another season. Both would have consequences I'd have to live with. The question was which one I truly wanted.

"I've had conversations about coming back next year and I'm exploring all avenues of what makes sense for me and my career," I finally told her.

Judging by the way Harper's eyebrows shot up, she wasn't

expecting an answer like that from me. I hadn't indicated at all this entire season with any of the press that I'd been thinking of rescinding my idea of retiring.

"Thank you." I excused myself while she was still shocked from my response before I could potentially stumble into any other situations.

As I walked back to the locker room to change into my uniform, I knew phones across the country would be notified with my response to Harper Nelson's question in minutes. Analysts would dissect my response and play out every angle. Fans would either support or put down the idea of me coming back. Gary Martinez would get excited that I might just be considering his offer.

But what no one truly understood was how hard this season had been for me. Not many people had to face the end of their careers so early in their life and be forced to pivot into something else. The average person celebrated the end of their career with retirement—a true retirement where they went on an extended vacation or played too many rounds of golf. I didn't have that luxury, because while I was paid a lot for my time in the NFL, I still wanted an income for when I wanted to start a family or take care of my parents when they inevitably needed the help.

That comment would be scrutinized by many across the nation because it was easy for others to add their opinion on someone else's life simply because it took the focus off their own. I didn't feel I deserved to be judged or crucified over struggling with a decision only a few thousand people ever had to make.

Even still, I knew I'd be facing a reckoning once this game was over.

The locker room had emptied a while ago as I continued to sit in my cubby, replaying the win in my head and the reality that I was heading toward my third NFC Championship game of my career—one step away from the Super Bowl.

No one had brought up my comment to Harper during the game, but I noticed the way the coaches snuck glances at me as if I were a jackpot that they were a dice roll away from winning in Las Vegas.

"Are you really considering playing again next year?" a soft voice asked me from the entry of the locker room.

Lottie stood in the doorway, looking much smaller than her full height, as if she weren't sure if she should be here or not. My heart sank when I noticed the hurt that she was trying her hardest to keep from showing on her face.

I crossed the room in three quick strides until I was only a foot from her, close enough to notice the tear stains on her cheeks.

Who the hell made her cry?

The thought that someone had done something to hurt her bad enough for her to cry made my chest become unbearably tight. I reached for her, wanting to pull her into a hug as words seemed to escape me. I wanted to do whatever I could to try and comfort her, but she stepped out of my grasp.

"Are you really considering playing again next year?"

For just a moment, I wanted to punch Gary Martinez for taking any opportunity of discussing this with her and leaking that to the press to force my hand. I sighed when I realized the two of us were about to walk onto a battlefield together, except we might be on opposite sides.

"The coaching staff and Gary Martinez approached me a few weeks ago about playing again next year. It was when I'd asked about coming back to coach."

There was an almost inaudible gasp from Lottie at my confession.

"Weeks ago?" This time, Lottie didn't bother hiding the hurt on her face. "Why hadn't you talked to me about it?"

I had flashbacks of my previous relationship and how all Rachel cared about was how my career affected her. She loved the benefits but hated how my attention was often pulled away from her. As Lottie stood before me, anger radiating off her for not informing her on a decision that I had made for my own career, I feared something similar happening.

"But only because we understand when it's time to stop choosing ourselves and start choosing the other person. It's a give and take." Hawthorn's advice from practice earlier in the week rang through my head like a warning, but I chose to ignore it. If Lottie wasn't going to think rationally, neither was I.

"Well, you hadn't decided yet if I was worth the risk, so I didn't feel like I needed to tell you. I wanted to make the decision for myself," I told her, a sour feeling filling my stomach as I realized we were gearing up for a knock-down-drag-out fight.

"I made it clear to you that I wouldn't date you if you continued to play! It's unprofessional and against my contract to date a player," Lottie exclaimed, throwing her hands up.

"Is that really what the problem is, Lottie? Because you seemed to decide against your own rules that we should give us a shot. You and I both know that there are easy solutions to that problem. I think you know there's something else happening here," I told her, hating how every sentence I threw at her felt like it was hurting me just as much as it was hurting her.

Lottie shrank away from me as if I'd physically hit her with my words. But now that I knew I'd hit the mark, I wasn't stopping. "What really bothers you about me coming back for another season?"

Her lower lip trembled as she looked at me like I was someone she didn't recognize anymore. But then I watched her steel herself as she prepared to answer me.

"I watched my father continue to choose football and his career over his family and I refuse to let history repeat itself. His choices made my mother a shell of herself and forced me to grow up much quicker than I needed to. I don't want to see myself constantly put on the back burner so you can cling on to the last bits of your career." The hurt in Lottie's eyes slowly turned into a determined fire as she tried to repair the armor I had tried my best to damage.

"I thought you said you'd support me in whatever I wanted to do," I reminded her. I had no idea why I was still trying to add gasoline to the fire, but the words slipped out of my mouth on their own.

"Of course I will," Lottie replied, exasperated. "I will always support you. I want you to make the decision that's best for you. But if your decision is not what's best for me, I can still support you while also choosing myself. I still believe you'll be a fantastic coach, Nolan. And I'm excited for when you realize what I see in you. But I think it's for the best if we stop seeing each other until you figure out what you want to do with your life."

I never expected fighting with someone you truly love to hurt so badly. It was like fighting without any armor. And it was as Lottie suggested that we stop seeing each other that I finally realized that I did truly love her. But it was clear we both had things we needed to address. To love each other, first we needed to learn to love ourselves better.

"This conversation is not going the way I had wanted it to." I scrubbed a hand over my face as I let out a sigh.

I began pacing.

"I've never admitted this out loud to anyone before, but I've been terrified for the end to come because I'm afraid that once I'm on the other side of this, I'll realize that was the best life had to offer for me. I'm afraid that there's nothing else that I'm truly good at or that will bring me the same joy I feel when I play."

Lottie studied me, her head slightly cocked as she watched me lay out all the pieces of myself that I normally hid from everyone else.

"I'm aware that taking this offer might be selfish. I would be taking away an opportunity from Caleb and potentially ruining the team's future if Caleb gets traded. What's even worse is that I hadn't even really considered the offer when they gave it to me—not until they offered me even more money than my current contract. I would have liked to think I was the kind of person that couldn't be bought, but that was the only thing that had me second-guessing if I should do it. Maybe it's not about the money. Maybe this offering stroked my ego that they wanted me that badly."

Every few sentences I stole a glance at Lottie, fearful that she'd be looking at me with disgust. To my surprise, her eyebrows were pulled together and she looked like she wanted to reach out to let me know she was there. It was the only thing that gave me the courage to keep going.

"I know in my heart that I must make the best decision for myself. The problem is that I don't know what that is yet. What I do know is that you have managed to melt the frost on my heart that grew over these last few years. You've managed to make me into a better man—one that might be capable of treating you right . . ." I paused. "Might even be capable of truly loving you right."

Lottie froze.

"I want to kiss every scar that time has left on you, Lottie. That your father has left on you. I want to give you the life that you've always deserved. I truly believe that."

A gasp sounded through the room as Lottie flopped down into the chair at her desk. She wrapped her arms around herself and rubbed her hands up and down as she wrestled with how to respond. A single tear broke free and trailed down her cheek as she stared down at her empty desk.

"I want to move forward with you, but I don't think I can," she finally choked out. "Maybe we are meant to be in the future, but I can't risk letting myself get hurt. Not again. Not right now."

"I dare you to let me treat you right," I fought back. "I promise you it'll be worth it. I know it. Let me prove it to you."

I never thought I'd ever beg for anyone, but there was a first time for everything.

Lottie shook her head. "I can't."

I sighed. A part of me had always known this was how this conversation would end as soon as I started it. Nothing had changed for either of us, so I was only rehashing the same things expecting a different result. Albert Einstein had a word for that.

"I don't think you can either," I told her. "Not until you can forgive the man who broke your heart first. Because I don't think it was ever healed."

The moment I turned to leave, I realized I had never really felt real pain until then. Not even with all my injuries. The kind of pain that physical therapy couldn't fix was far worse because there was nothing but time that could heal it.

Chapter 31

Lottie

I woke up to an empty tub of ice cream from the night before still lying next to me in bed. The spoon I'd used stuck to my nightstand. It had been five days since Nolan had ripped my heart out. I had given him the day off on Monday, partly because he needed the rest for his body and partly because I wanted to avoid seeing him. At practice, I had reverted back to my avoidance tactics with his therapy. I'd left a sheet of exercises for him to do on his normal training bed and only stopped to ask him how he was feeling. Even that question had felt like the hardest sentence I'd ever had to say to someone.

Nolan looked as worse for wear as I did with unkempt hair and rumpled clothes. He seemed pained to watch me return to such professionalism with him, but I knew it hurt me more.

The rest of the week was much of the same: trying to avoid any unnecessary communication with him and sticking only to the interactions required for his performance.

Today's practice was in the afternoon, and I was dreading it. It was the practice that Nolan and I normally spent the entire time together as we tried to get his body ready for the game, which was on a Saturday this week.

I'd been miserable this entire week. It was the first time in my life that I hadn't felt excited to go to work. The moment that I decided to give Nolan a chance, I gave him a piece of my heart, which now felt broken. I didn't know exactly how I felt about him—all I knew was that I really loved being around him and I'd started to consider him one of the more important people in my life. That chance I'd taken on him turned out to hurt me more than anything.

"I come bearing gifts," my sister's voice rang out in my apartment. She walked into my bedroom with two large coffees in her hands.

"Oh, yes," I breathed, reaching out to grab it from her.

Olivia eyed the spoon and empty ice cream tub with a raised eyebrow. "Not a good week, huh?"

"It could be better," I admitted as I took my first sips of caffeine for the day.

My sister pulled the covers back on the other side of my bed and slid in next to me. "Want to talk about it?"

It felt like all the times that I had done the same to her while she was in middle school, feeling terrible after being bullied at school. Except now the roles were reversed and I was the one needing the advice and comfort this time.

"Does it have anything to do with that interview Nolan did with Harper Nelson?" Olivia asked.

Quiet stretched out between us as I figured out how I wanted to navigate this conversation with her. Because neither of us had truly discussed the trauma we had courtesy of our father.

"When he told me he was considering coming back for another year, I felt like I was twelve years old again, doing everything I could to get our dad's attention, but still always playing second fiddle to what he wanted," I told her.

Olivia sat quietly for a moment before she responded. "Does Nolan know about Dad?"

I cringed every time Olivia called our father "Dad". I'd stopped calling him that the moment he forced me to play the role as parent for him. But I'd made sure to protect Olivia the best I could so that she never had to see all the ugliness our father truly had.

"Pieces of the story." I remembered seeing our father in the grocery store those weeks before with Nolan on my yes day. "I saw him the other day."

"Who?"

"Our father," I told her. I watched her freeze, and her eyes widen, like the reaction I had when I saw him that day.

"When?" Olivia asked. Her voice had dropped down to a whisper. Neither she nor I had seen him since her high school graduation where he'd left halfway through.

"At a grocery store on my yes day."

Hurt flickered through Olivia's eyes for a split second when she realized how many weeks ago this was.

"I didn't talk to him. I bolted out of the aisle I saw him in and dragged Nolan with me before he could see us."

"I never realized how badly our childhood had affected you or how much you'd done to make sure I didn't have to take the brunt of it like you did." My sister reached her free hand down to squeeze mine. "I know where he lives."

"Our father?" I asked her, completely shocked. The disbelief was like a heavy weight pulling me under. I'd tried so hard to protect my little sister from the wrath of our father, to keep her from his clutches, yet she'd still sought him out behind my back.

Olivia nodded, her body stiffening like she was preparing for a blow. "He sent me a card after my high school graduation apologizing for not having been able to stay the whole time. I've kept tabs on him since then. He's still at the address he listed on the envelope."

"And you didn't think to tell me?" I asked her, ignoring the way she flinched at the bite in my words. How could she think I *wouldn't* be angry to hear that she'd known his whereabouts all this time without bothering to tell me until now.

I clutched at my chest as my breathing grew shallow, the betrayal like a knife slipping between my ribs.

"You made it clear you wanted nothing to do with him

for years!" My sister fought back. "But that's what *you* wanted. I can make my own decisions."

"And you decided that you wanted to have a way to contact that man if you ever wanted to?" I asked incredulously. "After everything he did?"

"You got to leave sooner than I did. You got to sever that relationship while I didn't. I've reconciled his actions in my mind. But it doesn't seem like you have."

The fire in Olivia's eyes made me pause. She'd never stood up to me like this on any other topic before. It made me wonder if I'd been too quick to anger. Only viewing our father through my experience while abandoning any grace toward Olivia and the many more years she'd had with him.

I sighed. "I'm sorry. I shouldn't have gotten angry."

Olivia reached an arm over my shoulder. "It's okay. Your relationship with Dad is much different than mine. You can be mad at him while I'm not. I've already come to terms with his actions and forgiven him. Maybe it's your turn to do the same."

I squeezed my sister's hand again, wanting to convey to her how badly I'd hoped to shield her from the pain I had to endure, but I realized that I'd only made it worse for myself in the process.

The two of us sat in silence, both of us reliving our own moments with our father.

"Have you tried to think about Nolan's situation from his point of view?" Olivia asked as the two of us sipped on our coffee.

"Of course I have," I told her. "I told him I'd always support him, but I can't put myself in a position to go through what our father put me through again."

Olivia frowned at me. "You don't give Nolan enough credit. He's not our dad. He has to make the best decision for himself. He's facing a scary time in his life, moving into the unknown. But I know he's nothing like our father because I've watched him constantly treat you better than anybody else possibly could. Don't forget that man threw us a Christmas."

"Of course, I know what he's having to do is difficult," I tried to defend myself.

"It's only one more year at the most, Lottie. Even if he decided that *was* what he wanted to do, he deserves to be given a chance and not be compared to someone who never would have done half of the things for you that Nolan has."

I hated how logical my little sister sounded because for one moment she was the adult teaching me instead of the other way around.

"Since when did you grow up?" I asked her, wondering when Olivia had changed from the little girl that had been my baby sister into the beautiful woman she was today.

"I'm just following in your footsteps," she told me with a smile.

"How are you doing?" I asked her, realizing these past few months had been mostly focused on me and I really had no idea what was going on in my sister's life.

"I've been thinking about branching out into something different with my career. I love my job with the Cougars, but it hasn't been as fulfilling as it once was. I'm not sure what it is I want to do yet. I'm waiting for a sign." Olivia gave me a smile, a hint of sadness dulling its usual shine. "And being single has just been harder than normal recently. Being around everyone."

My sister had never shown any desire for finding a serious partner outside of her normal dates that she went on simply for entertainment. My eyes prickled with tears when I realized this might be the moment that Olivia shed the last bits of her youth and she would no longer be the little sister I needed to care for.

"You'll find somebody that is so enthralled with you—even all of your craziness." I grabbed Olivia's cup of coffee and set both hers and mine on my nightstand before I pulled her into my side. "And if you want to try new things in your career,

I'll be the first person to tell you to take the risk. Whatever you want to do, I'm here to support you."

Olivia wrapped her arms around my waist and buried her head in my hair like she used to do as a little kid. No matter what happened—who we fell in love with, who broke our hearts, or whether our hearts would ever be whole again after suffering a thousand cuts from our father—we would always have each other.

"You deserve love, Liv," I told her, my lips pressed against her forehead.

"You should listen to your own advice," Olivia replied softly. "I'm not sure what you have to do—if you have some sort of soul searching you need to do first, or healing. But I can feel it in my heart that you and Nolan aren't over."

Olivia lifted her head so she could look me square in the eyes. "You deserve love too, Lottie," she said more fiercely.

"Thanks, Liv." I squeezed one more time before I let her go.

Despite the pang of hurt that felt like it might pull my heart in two after learning my father had been this close, but still hadn't bothered to reach out to us, now that I'd seen him again after all these years, I wondered if I was only setting myself up for more disappointment at even considering going to see him. But maybe I needed to go through disappointment once more to close this chapter and move on.

"Are you going to stop trying to avoid Nolan at practice today? Because I know you have already thought about it and I think you should." Olivia gave me a knowing look.

I wanted to disappear into my mattress, embarrassed by Olivia needing to call me out for my antics.

"We'll see," I mumbled with my hands covering my face.

"I expect an update tonight."

I winced as Olivia jabbed a finger toward me. "Don't you have something to do today?" I asked her, suddenly ready to be done with the lecture.

"It's the off-season for me. I have nothing but free time on my hands. All I care about right now is if the Bobcats win the Super Bowl because I'm forcing Nolan to take both of us to Disney with him if you two manage to make up."

My heart sank at the thought of Nolan achieving everything he wanted to when he set out on this season and then not being able to celebrate fully with him.

"Will you be alright?" Olivia asked me as she rolled out of my bed.

I don't know.

But I nodded anyways with the hope that eventually my heart would stop aching. Maybe I had been foolish to think someone like me deserved to be happy and was capable of being in a relationship because the truth was, I wasn't sure if I actually knew how.

Chapter 32

Nolan

Dark circles had appeared under my eyes by the end of the week. I had barely slept a handful of hours after the first playoff game and my conversation with Lottie. She had done her best throughout the week to minimize the number of times we needed to be around each other, and I did my best to respect that decision.

My conversation with Hawthorn kept replaying over and over in my head. Before Lottie, a relationship was not at the top of my priority list. But after I got to know her, I'd realized what I had been missing in my life. All the accolades and championship rings wouldn't compare to Charlotte Thompson. But I'd let my selfish desires fueled by fear cloud my judgement and rule my decision making.

Lottie was right, I had to make the decision that was best for me, and she would follow accordingly with what was best for her. No matter how badly that hurt. If I didn't walk away from this decision completely satisfied with it, I would always wonder about what could have been.

With tomorrow's game quickly approaching, I wanted to talk with her one more time with the hope that we'd be able to smooth things over for the remaining games of the season.

My intention was to tell her that I still wanted to be friends and that I thought we worked better as such if only to make this easier on us both. But as soon as I walked into the training room and caught sight of her as she got ready for practice,

I realized being just friends with Charlotte Thompson for good would be nearly impossible.

Just seeing her made my palms begin to sweat and I ached to reach for her. My breath caught in my throat as I closed the last bit of distance between us. All my carefully crafted thoughts went right out the window the second she turned around and we made eye contact.

Her eyes were as red as the circles under my eyes were dark. I hated myself for making her this sad. While our time apart had been near agony, it helped me realize where I wanted my life to go next. I wanted a partner and a family that I could put my focus into. The idea of postponing starting that next chapter of my life had my stomach sinking while the potential of that new chapter starting in a few short weeks felt exciting.

We continued to stare at each other for a few more seconds—both of us realizing that we were about to speak for the first time in nearly five days. It was the longest we'd gone without talking since we met.

"Hi," I told her.

"How are you feeling?" Lottie asked, jumping right into physical therapist mode.

I missed the Lottie I used to have that would smile when she first saw me and joke about anything under the sun. Even when we weren't sure what was happening between us.

"Concerning my body, I feel ready to win a conference championship tomorrow. Regarding everything else, I think we really need to talk," I told her.

Lottie took a deep breath in and held it for a few seconds before she slowly blew it out between her lips. Finally, her eyes met mine and she gave me a small nod. "Okay," she agreed.

"I'm sorry that I've created this divide between us, and it's been the longest week without you in it." I watched her face soften as she listened to me and gave me the space to get my feelings off my chest. "I play my best and *am* my best when I have you in my life. All I'm hoping for is that we can work together like old times to finish out this season. I owe so much of my success to you, and I want you to enjoy it as well."

Lottie folded and unfolded an extra towel in her hands before she finally spoke. "I appreciate that very much and I've missed having our normal weekly conversations, too."

When she gave me the smallest hint of a smile, my stomach started doing somersaults. If I had it my way, Lottie and I would still be together, but I had to respect her wishes. I had to give her the space to work through her own problems, just like I had to work through mine. Even if I was slowly realizing that what I truly wanted next year was to remain in this facility giving knowledge to the next generation of players as a coach while starting my own family I could be proud of just like Adam and Hawthorn.

A comfortable silence filled the room after we finished clearing the air between us to the best of our ability for right now. The realization of where I'd come to for my decision on next year bounced around in my head while Lottie helped me to get my body ready for the game. So much so, that by the time that she wrapped up her treatment, all I could think about was how I truly was ready to be done at the end of this season. No matter if we won or lost.

I walked back out of the training room, headed for the locker room, when my eye caught my very first Super Bowl trophy—proudly displayed in the hallway most traveled in the practice facility.

Next to the trophy was a framed picture of the team from that Super Bowl win. Hawthorn and I were clutched in an embrace, happiness all over our faces as confetti fell around us and the rest of the team. Derek hadn't yet been drafted that year. We had been considered the underdogs and had managed to take down a giant of a dynasty with a last-minute drive down the field where we got Hawthorn close enough to put one through the goal posts. I remember the immense amount of energy that burst from my chest the moment I saw that football sail through the middle of those two yellow poles. Everything I'd worked for since I was a kid was suddenly realized. I had been sure in that moment that nothing would ever top it.

"I remember being at home with my family during that game," Caleb said. He was standing a few feet behind me, dressed in his practice gear. His eyes were locked on the picture in front of us. "I had on your jersey. You were my idol."

Caleb's eyes met mine and that look, mixed with everything that just happened between me and Lottie, nearly made me shed a few tears. My throat tightened and I had to fight to speak around it.

"I was that kid once, watching the Super Bowl game with my favorite quarterback's jersey on. It's surreal when the script flips and that time is coming for you."

The rookie glanced back at the Super Bowl trophy for one more look before he gave me a nod. "I can't wait for that feeling in a few weeks. It'll be one of my favorite moments— sharing a Super Bowl win with you. Eventually I hope I can quarterback my team to one of those myself."

Caleb gave me a smile, completely unaware that I was falling apart. "I'll see you at practice."

The choice between coming back next year as a player or a coach was supposed to be easy. The conflict I felt had started as soon as I welcomed the idea of playing one more season. Making that decision shouldn't come with this much turmoil or guilt.

Caleb left me standing there in the hallway, feeling like the biggest asshole in the league. I didn't continue to the locker room after him, instead I turned on my heel and walked toward the coaches' offices.

When I walked in, I nearly ran right into Coach Randolph. "Woah!"

"Sorry, Coach," I told him, reaching out to steady him.

He laughed. "That's alright, Nolan. What can I help you with? I'm assuming you're not in this part of the building for just a walk."

I took one deep breath before I let myself get straight to the point. "I'm not coming back next year. There's no guarantee I'll be healthy all season next year either. I've had a great season this year and I want this one to be my last."

Coach Randolph's face sunk with disappointment.

"And I want to be the quarterbacks' coach next year. I know I can help Caleb get to championship caliber. That kid has worked his ass off this year and to let me take next season from him when he could win a conference championship for this team on his own would be a travesty. I need to retire. I'm ready to be done. It's time to face it."

He stuck his hand out toward me, and I stared down at it for a few seconds before I grasped it.

"It's been a pleasure, Nolan. There won't be another player like you. But I think I'm more excited to coach with you. I'll let Gary know and we will work up a contract."

A tentative smile slowly spread across my face before it broke out into a full-blown grin. "Thank you," I told him.

"I'll see you at practice. We have a conference championship to win." He gave me one more pat on the back before he moved past me toward the practice field.

Coach Hill had a nice ring to it.

Chapter 33

Lottie

I couldn't stop thinking about what Nolan had said during our conversation in my office. We'd managed to be a little less awkward with each other during practice that day and then during the conference championship game. We'd slipped back into our familiar partnership that we formed early in the season. But even as the team celebrated their win and the fans went wild, all I could think about was whether he was right or not.

Did I need to forgive my father to move on with my life?

Was he holding me back?

I hated that I couldn't even fully celebrate that we were going to the Super Bowl because of that man. He never deserved another inch of space in my life, yet here he was still taking up residence in places I didn't want him to be. He'd invaded my head during the few recovery days the team was given after the conference championship game. There were two weeks between the conference championship game and the Super Bowl.

This year's Super Bowl was to be played in Los Angeles and we would fly out to start practices there this coming Sunday—three days. I knew that I had to take care of this feeling building inside of me now or I'd miss my chance.

My sister picked up on the third ring. "You're interrupting my rewatch of *Vampire Diaries*. What do you want?"

"Oh, hi. Nice to hear from you, Lottie. I love you, too," I mocked, fighting the urge to roll my eyes at her.

"Yes, hi. I love you. What do you need?" Olivia asked again.

"Can you send me our father's address?" Silence met me on the other side. For a moment, I thought the call might have dropped.

Finally, she replied, "Are you sure?"

"I have something I need to do," I told her.

Olivia sighed. "If you're sure."

"I am," I told her. After thinking about it nonstop, I realized that if I wanted to try to move forward with Nolan—if that was still even a possibility—I needed to speak with him. I needed to see him. I hoped that once I finally told him how badly he hurt me, the scars on my heart would start to heal.

The notification for my text messages sounded. "Thank you," I told her.

"Lottie?"

"Yeah?"

There was a long pause on the other end of the line. "I've just been thinking. Dad didn't make you unlovable and Nolan proves that. Just remember that for me, okay?"

I stayed silent as I mulled over her words. Part of me wondered if she was right. Because I was starting to believe it.

"Talk to you soon?" I could hear everything she wasn't saying in that sentence.

"I'll call you later."

Once I hung the phone up, I tapped into my text messages and stared at the address that was on my screen. Now I knew where he lived. I'd taken the first step and I needed to see this through.

It was comical that all these years he only lived on the other side of my town. I could have run into him a hundred times, but I'd only ever managed to once. The odds had always been stacked against me, but somehow, I'd managed to beat them all for quite some time.

Before I could talk myself out of it, I pulled on all my layers to fight off the cold. The snow had finally let up this week. As I drove across town, my fingers gripped the steering wheel tightly, the color slowly leeching out of them. I had to count my breathing as I inched closer to the address plugged into my GPS system because I was afraid that the second I stopped focusing on it, I would hyperventilate and crash before I even got there.

The building I pulled up to was run-down, but there were signs of warmth within it. Some of the balconies were still decorated with Christmas lights. Front doors had welcome signs and nice entry mats. I spotted the number of the apartment I was looking for and all that work I'd done to count my breathing slipped away from me as the air in my lungs caught in my throat.

What will I say?
Why did I do this?
Do I want to do this?

A million questions raced through my head as I tried to regain the courage that had gotten me here in the first place. Once my mind was quiet, only one thought remained.

I wish I could tell Nolan I was doing this.

I hated that I couldn't pick up the phone and text him about this because he was right. I needed to do this for myself just like he needed to figure out what he wanted for himself. Maybe then—and only then—would either of us be whole enough for the other, if there was anything left between us when that happened.

The apartment didn't have a buzzer like mine, only an old-school knocker on the front of it. I reached out, my hand shaking, to hit the knocker against the door. There was a scuffle on the other side, as someone hurried to answer.

For just a moment before the door opened, everything froze in time. I remembered the last time I saw my father at Olivia's graduation. How he'd been checking his phone the entire time for updates on his favorite NFL team as the new draftees checked into the team. When he read about his favorite player being cut, he grew so angry that he had to leave the ceremony before Olivia even walked the stage. I didn't even bother asking him where he was going because I knew he'd end up at a bar somewhere in the city, drinking his sorrows away. My mother had sat next to me, her back stiff as she weathered the curious glances of the parents around us. They had just finalized their divorce and that outing was the first time they'd seen each other since the proceedings.

The door opened and there in front of me stood a man I barely recognized, the same man from the grocery store. It had been almost a decade since I'd last seen him, but he looked like he had aged a lifetime. His hair was a shock of white and there were deep lines around his lips from smoking.

We both stared for a few moments. Both of us realizing that we were standing in front of each other.

My father was the first to speak. "Charlotte?"

I flinched when I heard my full name. I felt like I was ten years old again, being chastised for having not thought to make dinner while he had stayed later than he was supposed to at work when it was my mother's night to work late.

When I didn't say anything right away, he spoke again, "Is it really you?"

"Can I come in?" I asked him.

My father's eyes grew big with surprise before he hurried to open the door wider for me. I shuffled in uncomfortably just inside the threshold and watched him rush to tidy up his home. I wasn't sure what I had expected my father's place to look like, but a matching sofa set, with a nice rug and actual decor, was nowhere on the list.

"Do you want to sit?" He gestured to one of the couches as he hovered, waiting to see what I would do so he could follow my lead.

This was not the man I remembered. Suddenly, my rehearsed plan didn't apply to this situation. I thought it would be easy to get everything off my chest. To tell him how he had ruined so much of my life. But I hadn't expected to see the man I'd watched come home angry after a bad loss and take it out on his family to be wearing a pair of jeans with a nice pullover sweater and loafers.

"Uh, sure," I told him as I sat on the edge of one of the couches. My father followed suit and sat down in an armchair that looked like it was his usual spot.

"How have you been?"

I stared at him and wondered how he could sit here and act like a changed man as if he hadn't caused so much harm to me and Olivia.

How could he act so casual?

I struggled to remain the confident woman I'd grown into. As I sat in front of this man, I wanted to shrink myself. But I was no longer that same little girl.

"I came here today to try and fix some part of myself that you ruined all those years ago, but I guess I'm just having a hard time right now. I hadn't expected you to look like . . ." I trailed off.

"Healthy and with no anger issues anymore?" My father supplied.

I nodded.

"After you and your sister cut me out, for good reason I might add, it was a wakeup call. I realized how badly I'd messed my life up and how far it had all gotten. I knew I needed help, so I went to a program." He reached for a framed certificate displaying his achievement. My mouth dropped open.

The man I grew up with never would have admitted he had done something wrong. He had always been too proud to do something like that. Nor would he have taken necessary steps to make himself better.

"I'm sure that might come as a shock," he continued, as if seeing my father look like a respectable human being should be far more normal than it was. "I'd always meant to reach out sooner, but I hadn't felt ready. I've been working with my therapist, and we've been developing a plan for me to talk with you and your sister—"

All the pain I had to endure as a little girl played out in my head as my father tried to right his wrongs with just one conversation. But the hurt ran too deep, and the apology became too much.

"Please stop," I told him as I held up a hand.

The rest of his sentence died on his tongue as he watched me struggle to get my thoughts together.

"I came here because I need you to know how badly you hurt me," I started. "You forced me to be an adult far before I was ever meant to be. You were supposed to be the one to show me what it meant to love someone; except I watched you degrade my mother into less than a human being."

My father's skin paled as the words started coming out of me faster and faster.

"I've never dated anyone seriously because *you* made me feel like I wasn't worthy to be loved. I'm a raging workaholic because I needed to feel like I was good at something. You made me feel worthless, so I've always searched for my worth in everything I do. I hate you for that."

At this point, I was practically heaving the words out as my body edged me closer to sobs. The first tears slipped down my face as I repeated the words, "I hate you."

Heavy silence filled the room. Even though I wouldn't be leaving this conversation with forgiveness, I would be leaving here having let go of the past and the baggage I carried with me.

"Rightfully deserved," my father replied softly. "All of it. I deserve all of it."

He reached for a half-drunk glass of water on the end table next to him before he spoke again. Sweat had broken out on his forehead.

"I'm sorry that I failed you as a father and forced you to be something that you weren't ready for. You deserve to have someone who's going to treat you like you matter every single day. Not just when it's convenient for them. I only hope eventually you and Olivia will give me a second chance. Whenever that is, I will be forever grateful for it."

Part of me had expected to feel the holes in my heart mend while I was here with him, but instead I only felt like every piece of myself had been thrown to the wind and I was scrambling to put it all together again. I had known that hurt for so long that it had become part of my identity.

Why does this feel like letting a piece of myself go?

But the only way to fully move on from this and allow myself the grace to move forward without his presence looming in my life was to relinquish the hold he had on me forever. The work he'd done to improve his life was evident simply in the tidiness of his home, the lack of alcohol bottles on top of the kitchen cabinets that I could see in the back of his apartment, and his genuine desire to start fresh with me.

I must have taken too long to fill the silence because my father eventually filled it for me. "I've followed your career," he told me. "You should be proud of what you've accomplished, and I take no credit for that. You did all of that on your own. I know you'll find someone who celebrates all those qualities in you because you were never one to settle. If you wanted something, you always found a way to get it."

Too many feelings were swirling around inside of me as I sat there and let them run rampant. I stood suddenly and my father followed suit. I was overwhelmed and his home felt suffocating. I desperately wanted to leave, but there was a piece of my mind willing me to stay and see this through.

"I need you to know how proud I am of you, Charlotte. How sorry I am for how I treated you. I'm sorry I didn't love you the way I should have, but I'm hoping I can make up for it."

"I hope you realize how difficult coming here today was for me and while I'm not sure I'm ready to move on as if nothing happened, I do see how much you've tried to work on yourself." I scanned the pictures on his walls of me and Olivia when we were younger. They were framed and hung to be displayed proudly. "Maybe the first place to start is if you could call me Lottie. I've never really liked Charlotte. It always makes me feel like I'm getting in trouble."

My father's eyes widened at my small peace offering. I was insinuating that there would be another time where he could call me by Lottie and that we'd see each other again. "I can do that, Lottie."

I gave him a short nod before I slowly started walking toward the door. But just before my hand landed on the doorknob, I noticed a framed photo on the wall next to the door. It was a picture of me and Nolan this season, celebrating a win after he'd come back from his injury. It felt wrong that he had a picture of the two of us in his house. He was the man who broke my heart and Nolan was the one that loved me despite my brokenness.

"I know you were working mostly with Nolan Hill this season. I've been trying to keep up on the team, if only to stay up to date on you." My father looked at me sheepishly. "I gave up watching football after everything that happened. The program told me to treat it like an addiction. I only follow along in articles the day after the games."

"Thank you for letting me stop by," I told him. I hesitated once more. "I am happy for you and what you've done with your life."

"Of course," he hurried to reply. "That means a lot, by the way, to hear you say that you can see that I'm making an effort to change."

I took one last look at the picture on the wall before I walked out of my father's house with a new realization. He was right. If I wanted something, I'd find a way to get it. Because the man who broke my heart was never going to be the one to heal it in the first place.

That was all up to me.

Chapter 34

Nolan

Leading up to today's game, I had managed to compart-mentalize my life. All my issues with Lottie had been put in a crate and shoved to the back of my mind so I could focus for my team. That didn't mean I didn't wake up in the mornings and reach for the empty side of my bed, wishing she was there.

This is it.

Today's the day.

You'll put that jersey on one last time and then you'll take it off for the very last time.

I studied myself in the mirror of my hotel room. I had picked out my favorite suit for today's game. When I got up this morning, I didn't change a single thing of my normal routine. I ordered room service—two eggs over-easy with three strips of turkey bacon and orange juice. I showered and took my time getting ready, trying to treat today like it was any other game day.

My phone rang, pulling my attention away from my reflection.

"Nolan," my mother's voice came across the line. "How are you doing?"

I stuck the phone in between my ear and shoulder as I placed my bag by the door for when it was time to head down to the team bus.

"I'm doing okay, Ma," I told her. "Are you guys heading to the stadium soon?"

"We are. Hey, I don't want to take up too much of your time before the game. I know how you need it to prepare. Your dad and I just wanted to tell you that we love you and that we're proud of you."

My heart squeezed. My parents had been on this crazy ride just as much as I had. They were the ones that took me to every practice or game growing up. They were the ones that made sure my uniform was perfectly white after I got grass stains all over it. They were the ones that helped me through college so I could chase my dreams. Now they were watching me reach for one last dream today before this was gone. Today wasn't just for me. It was for them, too.

"Thanks, Ma. I love you guys, too. Thanks for everything all these years," I told her. My hand squeezed my phone tightly as I fought to keep the tears from falling. It was too early to cry yet today.

I grabbed my bag as soon as I hung up the call with my mother. The elevator was empty as I took it down to the lobby. As soon as I stepped out, I saw every television turned to the pregame broadcast. Analysts were talking about each team's odds for winning today.

"Nolan Hill may just be playing his very last game today. He's not just playing against San Diego today; he's playing against time as he tries to soak up every moment the day has to offer."

"Are you ready, champ?" Derek came up from behind me.

"Are you?" I asked.

Derek let out a chuckle as he wrapped his arm around my neck. "When am I ever *not* ready, Nolan?"

I reached up to ruffle Derek's perfectly styled hair, earning a punch to my gut in return.

"You and me, buddy?" Derek asked as we walked out to the buses.

"You and me."

That's all I wanted today's game to be. Me and all my friends playing one last game together.

"Heat pack?" Lottie asked me when I walked into the training room.

There was a lightness about her that I hadn't seen in weeks. We'd stayed friendly this entire week during practices here in Los Angeles. But I hadn't given her much attention because I needed this week for myself. If I wasn't playing again next year, I was going to soak up every ounce of these last few moments before they were gone.

And it seemed like she understood that.

"Please," I told her.

The normal charades of the Super Bowl were dulled inside the training room, but we could still hear the bass from the song the DJ played out on the field. The NFL hoped for today's event to be the biggest sporting event of the year, so no expense was spared. Between the entertainment they brought for before the game and the halftime show or the tailgating events they hosted for high-paying individuals, the entire thing was a spectacle.

But in this room, it was just the two of us. Like it had been the entire season. Exactly how I wanted it to be.

"Are you ready to have fun today?" Lottie asked me. She didn't ask if I was ready for the game like so many others. She didn't ask me if I was nervous. She only asked me if I was ready to have fun.

I remembered all the pep talks that she had given me throughout the season, but the one that stuck out the most to me was her reminder to have fun because I owed myself and all the work I'd put in that much.

Any nerves I had left floated away with her question.

"Are you?" The smile she gave back to me had me thanking the heavens that I got to walk into today's game with that image on my mind.

"First Super Bowl game I've gotten to be a part of. Can't

say I'm not excited." Lottie's calm demeanor was slowly brushing off on me the longer I sat in here with her.

"I don't think it'll be your last," I told her.

Lottie laughed. "And it might not be yours either."

I don't think she intended her words to be a dig, but they stung, nonetheless. Her mouth dropped open when she saw the hurt on my face. I missed her and I wanted to clear the air between us. I wanted her to know that I'd made my decision, and I made it for myself. "I don't know about that."

The last thing I saw as I walked out of the training room was Lottie's slack jaw as she watched me leave—wondering if I had just told her I really was retiring after this year.

"One more game?" Hawthorn asked me as we all filed into the tunnel to run out onto the field.

"One more game," I agreed.

The cue from the NFL producers came shortly after. We burst out of the tunnel and into the deafening noise of the stadium. The coin toss went in our favor as we chose to receive the kick.

Clear your mind.

All the noise slowly faded away as I stepped out onto the field. It was just me and the game I loved.

Breathe. Throw.

The ball sailed from my hand toward my receiver, and I relished in how comforting I found this moment—being in charge with the game at my fingertips. I had the power to win it all or lose it all with the football in my hands.

Clear your mind.

But as I marched down the field with my team toward the end zone, I felt for the first time a sense of readiness. I'd slowly come around to this chapter closing during all that time I'd spent fighting the end.

Breathe. Throw.

I'd heard plenty of athletes talk about how you knew when you were done, and as I threw my first touchdown of my last Super Bowl, I knew. I watched Adam and Hawthorn shifting their priorities toward their family and I wanted to do the same.

The linemen lifted Derek into the air as they celebrated our first touchdown and when my best friend pointed down at me, screaming at the top of his lungs as he celebrated, I joined him.

People talked about how there were many great loves in one's life. For me, football would always be one of them. There would be a place carved out for it in my heart for the rest of my life. It was the place that allowed me to express my truest self. It was the freest I'd ever felt, but it was also a place that had made me feel the most exhausted as I had to constantly strive to be better than what I had just accomplished. Now all I wanted in life was to be appreciated for me and not have to evolve into something else yet again.

Clear your mind.

Lottie stood away from the team as I ran off the field and the defense went to take our place. The excitement I was feeling was mirrored on her face—despite it all, she was still cheering for my success and my dreams.

The defense managed to get a stop and we were back on the field. I relayed the play to my team. But as we lined up, another revelation dawned on me.

Breathe. Throw.

My eyes shifted toward Lottie standing on the sidelines as I ran to group the team back up for the next huddle. I would be here next year, as would she, but I knew that if I didn't do something about the gaping hole between us we would eventually consider each other only colleagues.

And that would be the most disappointing thing of all to come out of this season.

Clear your mind.

Another touchdown. This one ran up the middle and into the end zone. We were hitting our stride as a team and stretching the gap between us and San Diego. It was a completely different game compared to the first time we played them during the first game of the season. I had been shaky and not confident in my performance. The team was underprepared. Since then, I'd turned into a different person and we'd come together as a team.

This season had been far from perfect. I'd started the entire thing with an attitude unfit for a leader. I assumed that Lottie couldn't have possibly helped me with this season. Little did I know that she would be *exactly* what I needed. Not just to help me complete the season of my dreams, but to fit a gap in my life that I never knew needed to be filled.

Now I only needed to do something about it before it slipped away from me forever.

Chapter 35

Lottie

I watched from the sidelines as Nolan led his team toward a sure victory. He dominated the game, turning nearly every possession into a touchdown. It was like watching a great warrior completing his heroic arc right before your eyes. Tears pricked at my eyes as I watched him succeed—happy he was accomplishing his dreams, but also sad because with every touchdown it felt like he was drifting farther away from me. Eventually I would have to let him go completely as we approached a crossroads that would take us in opposite directions. The tears were salty on my lips as I took in the bittersweet scene.

He'd taught me what it meant to live life without worrying if I'd done enough—*been* enough—as we both navigated what life would look like once we stopped trying to live up to imaginary expectations. He had shown me what it looked like for someone to care about the things I wanted. The most heart-wrenching part was that in a perfect world, he would be in my life.

Olivia had been right. Our father hadn't made me unlovable, and Nolan proved that by loving me through all my insecurities and baggage.

The clock ticked down on the fourth quarter, eating away the last few minutes of this season. All the Bobcat fans in the stadium and the staff were collectively holding their breath as we watched the defense attempt to stop

San Diego one last time and cement their win in history.

Nolan stood just down the sideline from me and I watched him instead as he took everything in. His chest moved steadily up and down as he scanned the fans in the stands. He smiled when he spotted his name handwritten on signs in the crowd. He looked content as he sat on the bench watching the seconds tick off the clock. I glanced up toward Nolan's box to see Maggie and Tommy, Adam and his wife, Olivia, and Jamil surrounded by Nolan's family, already celebrating with champagne bottles. It didn't take much to imagine what it sounded like in that tiny room.

Seeing their excitement for Nolan's and this team's success made me want to be a part of it. Not standing off to the side, silently cheering him on. I wanted to relish in his success *with* him. If what he told me earlier was true and this was his last game, then I had to do something about it.

Without even thinking, I walked over to him. "Are you ready to be a three-time Super Bowl champion?"

"Feels unbelievable," he replied as I sat down in the empty space next to him.

"It's well deserved." I reached over to give his hand a squeeze. Nolan turned his hand over so he could hold mine.

Together we watched the defense get the final stop against San Diego to solidify the Chicago Bobcats' win. Everything happened in slow motion as we leapt to our feet. The noise in the stadium rose to a ground-shaking level that had my own ears ringing as I watched Nolan and his team rush the field to celebrate.

Navy and red confetti fell from the rafters. Media crowded around the players as they tried to snap pictures. I lost sight of Nolan, Derek, and Hawthorn in the madness. Reporters had surrounded them to get postgame statements. Bodies ran into mine as they tried to fight their way onto the field. I was sent hurtling forward. My hands reached out to brace for impact as the ground drew closer.

"Hey!" An arm wrapped around my waist, saving me from being trampled. "Are you okay?"

I looked up to see Nolan peering down at me, concern etched on his face. He was now wearing a Super Bowl Championship hat and a piece of confetti stuck to his cheek.

"Thanks to you," I chuckled as I reached up to peel the confetti off.

Nolan's hands stayed on my waist as his eyes danced across my face.

"What is it?" I asked.

"I miss you."

I miss you.

My heart squeezed so tightly in my chest at his words that I was afraid it might burst.

"I'm sorry for not talking with you about the offer I was given. I know we weren't anything official yet, but we were making plans. And that offer affected those plans." It was hard to hear him as the roar of the fans grew louder. The Lombardi trophy was being brought out, so I leaned closer until we were almost wrapped in an embrace with his eyes intensely boring into mine.

"Lottie, you are the best thing that's happened to me this season. I think it's complete fate that you were brought into my life at the same time I was moving on from playing."

My eyebrows pulled together as I wondered if I had heard him correctly. "Are you saying this really is your last season?"

Guilt filled me. Was he ending his career earlier than he wanted for me? Because that was the last thing I wanted, which was exactly why I had let him go.

"The coaching staff and owner, Gary Martinez, agreed to my offer of taking over the quarterbacks next year. I realized over these past couple of weeks that my time is done, and I was only clinging on to the idea of playing another year because I was afraid. Afraid of the unknown and the future." Nolan looked up at the confetti falling from the sky. "I'm ready to be done. There's nothing further for me to do with the game. When I was asked to coach, that path felt easy to choose, exciting even. But just the thought of returning next year to play had me drowning in anxiety. That was when I realized that playing wasn't the easy decision. It wasn't the *right* decision for me, regardless of the people in my life and how that would affect them."

My breathing grew shallow as I realized what he was saying. Now I understood why he had looked so content the entire game. He was walking away from football finally happy with his career.

"That's amazing, Nolan," I told him, and I truly meant it. "You've got what you wanted."

"Not even close," he told me. "The entire game I couldn't stop thinking about you. I thought that if I just won one more Super Bowl, I'd finally be happy. But then I realized that would never be the case because I'm my happiest when I'm with you and it killed me to think I could be celebrating this win without you. Lottie, I love you and I will always choose you, because while what I do will always be important to me, who I share it with is infinitely more important."

My heart felt like it was in my throat as I listened to him. *You are worthy*, I reminded myself to quell the irrational fear rising within me.

"I work hard for what I want and what I want is to be with you. I intend to work hard at being worthy of your love every day."

I remained perfectly still as Nolan looked for any sign that I felt the same, his head tilted slightly. He looked worried I was about to break his heart. Even though I was sure that would never be possible.

"Do you mean it?" My voice hitched and I swallowed to keep it from breaking.

"I swear it," he replied fiercely. His hands reached up to cup my cheeks and as confetti still rained down around us, he brought his lips to mine in a tender kiss. The gruff Nolan I met all those months ago was nowhere to be seen. He had

269

been replaced by a man who was happy and wonderful and exactly the Nolan I always knew he would be. He was released from the shackles of his own expectations.

I pulled away from his kiss and rested my forehead against his. "I love you, too. And there's nothing to forgive you for. You needed to do this for you."

"I think maybe we can finally cross off that last item on your bucket list," he told me. The corners of my mouth lifted. "And I think it may be time to make a new one."

Nolan lifted me off the ground and I squealed like a kid as he spun me around.

"Coach Hill has a nice ring to it," I told him once he set me back down.

"That's what I thought!" Nolan exclaimed as he pulled me in for one more hug. I finally realized what the peaceful feeling was whenever I was with him—home.

"Does this mean you get to go to Disney?" I whispered into his ear, remembering what Olivia had said.

Nolan laughed. "It does. Are you saying you want to go?"

"Me and Olivia." I pressed my lips together to try and keep the smile off my face. "Add it to the list?"

He just shook his head. "The two of you are going to be the death of me, aren't you? Alright, add it to the list."

"Hey! The trophy ceremony is starting." Derek ran up to us, a Super Bowl champion hat sitting precariously on his head.

"Lead the way, champ," Nolan told him.

Derek glanced between the two of us before his grin grew wider. "Hawthorn owes me fifty bucks!"

"For what?" I asked.

"I told him you'd get back together before Nolan even touched the Lombardi trophy."

Nolan sighed like a disappointed father as he looked at his friend.

"Come on," Nolan told Derek as he tried to set off toward the makeshift stage that the NFL had made.

Derek hesitated. "Are you coming, Lottie?"

"Oh, no. It's just for you guys," I told him. I was perfectly happy to watch from the crowd. This was their time.

"You're just as much a part of this team as any of us. Come on. I want a family picture." Derek threw one arm over my shoulder and his other over Nolan's as he steered us toward the trophy.

I caught Nolan's eye as he peered down at me over Derek's head.

"I love you," he mouthed as the three of us climbed the stairs of the stage.

I watched Derek and Nolan join the rest of the captains as they accepted the Lombardi trophy. They lifted it above their heads as the crowd cheered, celebrating their favorite team's win, because for them they were just as much a part of this journey as the players were.

"Lottie?" Nolan called back to me. "Come here for a picture."

I slid in between Nolan and Derek as cameras flashed in front of us. I knew this photo would be framed and hung right next to the one Nolan had given me for Christmas.

"Are you okay?" I asked Nolan as we separated from the rest of the group.

"I am now," he told me, the Lombardi trophy gripped in one hand while his other was in mine.

Epilogue

Three Years Later

Nolan

"How are you feeling, Caleb?" I asked my starting quarterback.

We were sitting in the locker room before the game waiting out the last few minutes of peace before we walked out into the stadium where Caleb's first Super Bowl as a starting quarterback and my first Super Bowl as the offensive coordinator for the Chicago Bobcats awaited us.

"Nervous," Caleb admitted.

The young quarterback had success thus far in his three-year career. Under my guidance, he had two conference championships and was showing the league why he had been the first pick overall in the NFL draft almost four and a half years ago. But every year he had come up short of his first Super Bowl ring.

Not this year. I was determined to get him through the finish line this year.

"That's a good thing," I told him as I wrapped my arm around his back. "It means you care."

"How'd you handle all of the attention that's on a game like this?" Caleb asked me as he stared down at the Bobcats logo on the helmet in his hands. I could see him trying to work through the nerves so he would be able to lead his team when he stepped out on that field. "There are so many people counting on us to win."

"You are the most prepared person in this league for this moment. You must believe that."

Those words were reminiscent of a similar speech given to me by the one person who believed in me the most. I hoped they did the same trick for Caleb.

I gave him one more pat on the back before I vacated the locker room to give him space.

Standing out in the hallway was one of the most beautiful people I had ever seen laying into Derek Allen about how he couldn't skip getting his back and legs stretched out before a game just because it was the Super Bowl. She was in the middle of telling him that he had just turned thirty and he needed to take care of his body better. Derek caught my eye and gave me a look that said, *help me*.

I just shook my head at him. He was on his own on this one.

"Lottie, you've always been scary—but now that you're building a tiny human inside of you, you've grown exponentially more terrifying," Derek told the love of my life.

"This baby has been hanging on to my rib cage all day, so if you don't want to see any more of my wrath, you will walk your ass back into my training room and let me stretch you out. I am not losing because you have tight hamstrings. The coaches will murder me and then I'll haunt you for the rest of eternity."

Derek threw his hands up in surrender as he followed Lottie back into the training room.

"I'll see you out there," I called after both.

The tunnel slowly started to fill up with Bobcat players and the anticipation became palpable in the air. Caleb was at the head of the pack and was soon joined by Derek after Lottie was satisfied that he was limber enough for the game. On one of the NFL producer's cues, the team ran out of the tunnel and into the stadium that held some of the most die-hard fans in the league.

Judging by the wide smile that spread across Caleb's face as he took it all in, I knew he was made for this moment. A hand slipped around my waist and a body fit perfectly into my side. I glanced down to see Lottie staring up at me.

"You'll do great, Coach." She gave me a tight squeeze before she pulled away.

"I need good luck from the little one." I reached for her again and managed to wrangle her back into my arms. My hands slipped down to her round belly where our baby was taking his time to meet us. I turned her around so her back was pressed into my stomach and reached under the base of her belly before pulling up. Lottie let out a sigh of relief as her head fell back against my chest. I could feel my son kick against my wife's stomach as if he knew I was the one supporting him right now and he wanted to wish me good luck, too.

"I love when you do that," Lottie breathed as she rejoiced in a moment of reprieve.

"Don't forget we get to check off another item on your bucket list if we win," I whispered into her ear. "We get to go to Disney again and I made sure to request Mickey beignets since they were out last time."

Her laugh rumbled out of her and vibrated against my chest. "I'm going to need a wheelchair to get around that place if that happens."

"I'll have one reserved for you."

"Because a Mickey beignet is what matters most for winning this game," Lottie replied sarcastically.

"It matters to you, so it matters to me and it's on your list so it's a non-negotiable," I told her.

Lottie placed her hands over mine and gently helped me lower her belly back down before she turned around to give me a kiss.

Charlotte Thompson was my entire world. She was one of the biggest reasons that my life had turned out the way it had. She'd not only helped me rediscover what it meant to play football and have fun while doing it, but she helped me find my second calling in life.

Her hand slipped into mine once she dropped back down from her tiptoes. She gave me one last squeeze before she slipped away down the sideline to check on her players.

The national anthem and opening ceremonies flew by in a blur and before I knew it, we were neck deep in the middle of the second quarter of the game. It was a close game, with Caleb only leading the Bobcats over the Arizona Roadrunners by a touchdown. Arizona had the ball during the last couple of minutes before halftime and were practically walking the ball down the field. All of us watched from our sideline as the Arizona quarterback sent the ball into the back of the end zone for a touchdown just as the final few seconds clicked off the clock, announcing that it was halftime.

I watched the wind go out of my team's sails as they watched the ball go through the goal posts. The team shuffled into the locker room as if we were down by three scores rather than tied at the half and I found myself struggling to find the right words to try and lift them up.

My eyes found Lottie's because I knew that if all else failed, she would always be the one to have my back when it was against the wall.

Lottie

I could hear the head coach trying to encourage the team but judging by the silence after his speech was done, it hadn't quite hit the mark.

Derek lay on the training table in front of me as I worked on his lower back to try and loosen the muscles that had started to plague him more in recent years.

"If we win, we're all going to Disney, right?" Derek asked me, his voice muffled by the pillow his face was in.

"That's what Nolan says," I told him. "But you all need to kick this thing into overdrive and pull out a win. You guys have been dilly-dallying on offense."

Derek's normally boisterous laugh turned into a coughing fit as he nearly suffocated himself with the pillow.

"Nolan always says you could be an honorary coach on the staff."

"Stop trying to compliment me right now, Derek." I pushed harder into his muscles and felt him tense under me. "You're getting double-teamed right now, but when has that ever stopped you before?"

Derek stayed quiet as he thought about what I had said. I had watched him break out of double coverage all year. Why was tonight suddenly different?

"You're resourceful on the field. You find ways to get open for your quarterback. Be the leader you are and energize the offense. Now I have an offensive coordinator and quarterback to go fire up."

"Lottie?" Derek called after me as I started to head toward the locker room.

"Yes?"

"You're going to be a fantastic mom."

I smiled down at the bump that had grown significantly in the past few weeks. Our baby boy was due in only a few short weeks. Nolan had wanted me to get off my feet sooner before my due date, but there wasn't a chance in this world that I was missing tonight's game.

"Thanks, Derek." I gave him a small smile. "Now go win a fucking game."

I marched across the hallway and gave the coaches trickling out a smile before I slipped by them. I spotted Nolan talking with Caleb in the corner as the two looked over the play call sheet. Neither of them noticed me approaching until I was nearly on top of them.

"How's Derek?" Nolan asked me.

"He's fine, but that's not why I'm here." I pointed a finger at my husband. "You are Nolan *fucking* Hill. You've won three Super Bowls. You know what it takes to get through this next half. Don't forget it."

I let out a long breath before my gaze swung over to Caleb, who was staring at me with wide eyes. "And you are Caleb *fucking* Willis. You're a two-time conference champion. You're a front runner for the MVP award this year. Don't forget it."

The two men stared at me with equal looks of shock.

"Now go win this damn game because you *know* I hate losing."

With that, I turned on my heel and waddled back out of the locker room as fast as a nearly nine-month pregnant woman could.

The last time I had to give that pep talk ran through my mind as I watched the team come back out onto the field after halftime. I smiled as I remembered the woman I was at that time. I'd achieved everything I'd wanted with my career, but I had been dying to experience life. Now here I was three years later with nearly thirty countries under my belt and countless other experiences to remember there was more to life than just climbing a ladder.

Both Caleb and Derek started the second half with newfound excitement and managed to rally the rest of the team behind them. I knew I had done my job when the Bobcats scored on their first possession. All they needed was a bit of encouragement.

And when the confetti fell in the colors of navy and red at the end of the game, all that mattered to me was the look of pure joy on Nolan's face as he watched Caleb and the rest of the team hoist the Super Bowl trophy over their heads.

I mentally crossed an item off my newest bucket list— *watch the love of my life achieve greatness doing the thing he loves most.* There wasn't an accolade in the world that I would trade this very moment for. Not even when Nolan scooped me up in his arms drenched in sweat and in desperate need of a shower.

We had found each other at a time in our lives when we were both trying to figure out what was next without realizing that we would be each other's answer. We learned that the best way to love the other was not to change them, but rather to help each other reveal the greatest versions of ourselves. Souls never meet by accident, and it seemed that we were always meant to show the other what it meant to truly live.

Acknowledgements

First and foremost, I must thank every single reader that has supported this series. I could never have been prepared for the people that I would meet and the support I would receive. This dream I've had since I was little has come true because of you. It is such a privilege to write stories that get to move others, provide an escape from the real world, and bring us all together under a common love of reading. I am so grateful you decided to take a chance on a new author and stick with me through this book. All I've ever wanted from this process is to make a reader feel something—happiness, sadness, and every emotion in between.

This process has been one of the most difficult journeys I've been on yet. Writing a book is hard. Writing a series is really hard. I've never questioned myself so much in my life. The confidence I've built up for myself throughout my life has felt useless with this process. I've redefined it, strengthened it, and learned that I can still do hard things. But that wouldn't be the case without the people that have supported me along the way.

Thank you to my agent, Saskia Leach, for continuing to champion this book and this series through this entire process. You've continued to guide these dreams of mine into something that is starting to look more like a career every day. I'm wildly proud to have you as my agent and to be a part of the Kate Nash Literary Agency family.

To the teams at 8th Note Press and Embla Books, I am always blown away every time I get to collaborate with such inspiring individuals. Your ability to make this dream of mine come to life never ceases to amaze me. I am so thankful for each and every individual that has had a hand in making the Chicago Heartbreakers series a reality. There have been so many people that have worked tirelessly on editing, copywriting, the cover, the audiobook, and without all of you, none of this would have happened.

Thank you to my family and friends for supporting me endlessly—between buying extra copies and telling all their friends about it, I have been so appreciative. To my best friend, Sydney, for telling every stranger that appears to be a romance reader that they should read my book. I know why you are so successful at your job.

And Dawson—thank you for your solid support of me through this process. I'm grateful I have someone in my life that encourages me to face hard things head on and be brave enough to try new things.

About the Author

Ally Wiegand currently resides in Texas. *Going for Two* is her second novel in the Chicago Heartbreakers series. She loves her family, fall, and writing love stories that make your heart squeeze. Ally has dreamed of being a writer since she was a girl. She is a coffee addict, a classic car lover, and a cat mom to two furballs. Her dream is to make readers happy, make them sad – but, most importantly, to feel something.

To keep up with Ally and learn more about the Chicago Heartbreakers series, visit her online at www.allywiegand.com

About Embla Books

Embla Books is a digital-first publisher of standout commercial adult fiction. Passionate about storytelling, the team at Embla publish books that will make you 'laugh, love, look over your shoulder and lose sleep'. Launched by Bonnier Books UK in 2021, the imprint is named after the first woman from the creation myth in Norse mythology, who was carved by the gods from a tree trunk found on the seashore – an image of the kind of creative work and crafting that writers do, and a symbol of how stories shape our lives.

Find out about some of our other books and stay in touch:

X, Facebook, Instagram: @emblabooks
Newsletter: https://bit.ly/emblanewsletter